"You want one photograph for yourself?"

Millicent asked as she looked into Matt's eyes.

"Yes. I do. If it's not too much trouble."

"It's no trouble at all."

Matt felt as surprised as Millicent looked at his request. The words had just popped out of his mouth, but he didn't want to take them back. He wanted a photo of them together. But why? And how would having a photo of the two of them help him distance himself from her? And did he even want to do that now?

He picked up another photograph. This one Julia had taken when they'd all gone to Central Park one day. Again, this one was of him and Millicent, and it appeared they were sparring a bit. They were grinning at each other, but Millicent's eyebrow was raised as if challenging something he'd said. He'd seen that expression on her quite often in the past year and, if truth be told, he'd enjoyed bringing it about.

Janet Lee Barton loves researching and writing heartwarming romances about faith, family, friends and love. She's written both historical and contemporary novels, and loves writing for Love Inspired Historical. She and her husband live in Oklahoma and have recently downsized to a condo, which they love. When Janet isn't writing or reading, she loves to cook for family, work in her small garden, travel and sew. You can visit Janet at janetleebarton.com.

Books by Janet Lee Barton

Love Inspired Historical

Boardinghouse Betrothals

Somewhere to Call Home
A Place of Refuge
A Home for Her Heart
A Daughter's Return
The Mistletoe Kiss

JANET LEE BARTON

The Mistletoe Kiss

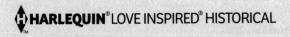

HARLEQUIN® LOVE INSPIRED® HISTORICAL

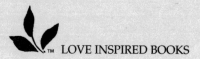

PLEASE RECYCLE • THIS PRODUCT IS RECYCLABLE •

Recycling programs for this product may not exist in your area.

™ LOVE INSPIRED BOOKS

ISBN-13: 978-0-373-28337-8

The Mistletoe Kiss

Copyright © 2015 by Janet Lee Barton

www.Harlequin.com

Printed in U.S.A.

Trust in the Lord with all thine heart;
And lean not unto thine own understanding.
In all thy ways acknowledge him,
And he shall direct thy paths.
—*Proverbs* 3:5–6

Chapter One

New York City, Heaton House, September 1897

Mathew Sterling entered the parlor at Heaton House surprised to find only the other male boarders gathered there, having just parted ways after the baseball game to get ready for dinner on time.

"Are we early?" he asked, looking at the clock on the mantel.

"No, we aren't, but dinner is going to be late. Mrs. Heaton said the ladies should be arriving soon and we'd sit down to eat shortly after they get home," Joseph Clark said.

"Where are they?" Matt asked. It wasn't like any of them to be late to a meal unless they were working. "Did they go shopping?"

"Perhaps, but Mrs. Heaton didn't say," Stephen Adams explained. "Just that we'd eat when they got back. I hope it's soon. I'm hungry. I know I had those Cracker Jacks at the game but they don't hold one forever."

"No they don't," Matt said. He'd enjoyed his day

off going to the Giants game with Stephen and Joe. But the weather had been so nice, they'd walked back from the Polo Grounds where the game had been played, and all that walking mixed with the cool crisp air made him even hungrier than normal.

They heard the front door open and the three lady boarders entered—Matt knew because he'd come to recognize Millicent's tinkling laugh anywhere. They seemed to be quite excited about something, from all the chattering going on between them.

Then suddenly everything went quiet and Julia Olsen, the boarder who'd been there the longest, peeked into the parlor. "We know we've kept you waiting for dinner. I'll go tell Mrs. Heaton we're here now."

"Sorry we're late." Millicent Faircloud hurried into the parlor. She looked very pretty, her cheeks flushed and her deep blue eyes sparkling. It was evident she'd enjoyed the outing.

"We're glad you're finally here. We're starving," Stephen said.

"I don't see any packages—you didn't go shopping?" Matt smiled, thinking they'd gone to the Ladies' Mile for the day. Shopping was one of their favorite things to do.

"No," Emily Jordan answered. She was one of the newest boarders at Heaton House, along with Stephen and Joe. The three of them had moved in at the same time a few months earlier.

"Where'd you go, then?" Joe asked.

"We went to a suffrage meeting," Emily offered. "First time I've even been to one. It was wonderful!"

"You went to one of those meetings?" Joe asked.

"They can be dangerous, Emily!" Stephen said.

"It was in broad daylight, gentlemen. Nothing happened," Emily said. "I quite enjoyed it. Don't you think women should have the right to vote?"

"Vote!" Joe exclaimed. "I—"

"How would you feel if we had that right and you didn't?" Emily asked.

Her questions left both Stephen and Joe speechless for the moment and Matt turned to see Millicent shaking her head at Emily. "So you've brought Emily 'round to your way of thinking now, Millie?"

"I don't control anyone's thoughts, Mathew. If I did, I'd have changed yours by now." Millicent came back at him. "Emily found out Julia and I were going to a meeting and wanted to know what they were all about, so we invited her to come with us."

"Oh, I see and—"

"Dinner is served," Mrs. Heaton said from the foyer. "Come along, all. I'm sure you must be starving by now."

They all moved toward the dining room and Matt fell into step beside Millicent. "I don't know why you—"

"Shush, Matt. No more talk about the meeting," Millicent whispered. "We'll never agree about them and we don't want to upset Mrs. Heaton with our arguing. You know she doesn't like any of that at her dinner table."

Matt let out a huge sigh and gave a short nod of agreement. He loved their landlady. She was a mother figure to them all and no one liked seeing her upset. Besides, Millie, as he thought of her, was right, he couldn't see them ever agreeing on the women's movement. From what he'd heard about it, it wasn't all about getting the right to vote; they encouraged women—even married ones—to be more independent. And how much more independent could Millie get—wanting to open up her own business? And why did it matter to him anyway?

Before he could offer Millicent his arm, Stephen beat him to it and Matt's chest tightened as he watched her put her hand on his arm. He turned to Julia and offered her his, escorted her into the dining room, pulled out her chair and scooted it in closer to the table. He then took his own seat next to Millicent.

When Mrs. Heaton asked him to say the blessing, he had to take a minute to put all thoughts of Millie's desire for independence and those suffrage meetings out of his mind.

"Dear Lord, we thank You for this day and Your many blessings. We thank You for this meal we are about to partake of, and for Mrs. Heaton, who always takes such good care of us. May we keep that all in mind as we enjoy the meal she planned for us. In Jesus's name we pray, amen."

Millicent breathed a sigh of relief at Matt's prayer. She hoped his words would serve to remind everyone that some conversations didn't belong at the dinner table.

To keep peace, and from past experience, the women had decided it best not to mention the meetings or anything about the movement around the men, if possible. But she and Julia evidently forgot to inform Emily when she moved in. It wasn't that they didn't want the men to understand; they very much did. But one couldn't force a man's comprehension. Millicent sighed inwardly. It seemed impossible that the men living at Heaton House would ever grasp why the women were all so interested in the movement—especially Mathew Sterling. She'd discovered since they both moved into the boardinghouse within days of one another the year before that he was one of the most stubborn men she'd ever met.

As Mrs. Heaton's maids, Gretchen and Maida, began to serve the meal, Millicent tried to put her and Matt's differences out of her mind and concentrate on the wonderful dishes being passed around.

"How was the ball game?" their landlady asked, guiding the conversation to a safe subject. Mrs. Heaton seemed to have a way of quieting any disturbance between her boarders almost before it began.

"It was great," Matt said. "Our Giants won by one point in the last play of the game."

"They did a bang-up job!" Stephen added.

"Oh, Millicent, I forgot to tell you—Elizabeth telephoned and asked me to remind you about having Sunday night supper with them tomorrow," Mrs. Heaton said.

"Oh, I haven't forgotten." Millicent smiled at her landlady. "I'm looking forward to it. She said they want to talk to me about something but didn't say what."

"Maybe they want you to take more photos of one of the apartments in the tenements," Julia suggested.

"They might. It's been a while since I took any for them." She'd been blessed when Elizabeth and John, one of the couples who used to live at Heaton House before they married, asked her to take photographs for some articles they were doing. It'd brought her some much-needed business and continued to do so now. But it still wasn't enough that she felt she could open her shop yet.

Matt handed her a basket of rolls and smiled at her, as if asking, *Are we okay now?* She sighed, raised an eyebrow and smiled back, trying to let him know that if he didn't bring up the topic of the meeting again, neither would she.

But as she took the basket from him and their fingers brushed, what she wished for most was to quiet her suddenly racing pulse. Why did this man have the ability to do that to her? He was very nice looking—with his almost black hair, sky-blue eyes and smile that showed even, white teeth. But he also could make her more frustrated than anyone else. She'd felt that way ever since the first night she'd moved in, when he'd made clear he disapproved of any woman wanting to open her own business.

He'd brought Robert Baxter to mind, the man she'd almost become engaged to. That was, until she'd seen his true side and realized all he wanted was someone to take care of *his* needs. From that time on, she'd decided she'd be better off making a living for herself than giving her heart to a man with no interest in her ideas and opinions. A man who thought his word was law. She was so glad she'd seen through Robert and never accepted his proposal.

Matt's attitude and that reminder seemed to have set the tone for their relationship from the first—in spite of any fleeting attraction she felt for him. And over time, when the topics they disagreed on weren't brought up, they managed to get along for the sake of Mrs. Heaton and the other boarders.

Millicent hoped that would continue—but perhaps it was better to be reminded of her resolve to *not* fall in love, in order to keep on guard when Matt did something to make her heart flutter.

As dinner came to an end, Millicent found she wasn't in the mood to spend time in the parlor with everyone. She didn't want to take the chance of another argument. "I think I'm going on up tonight. I'm kind of tired. 'Night, all," she said as she headed out the door. But Matt stopped her with a hand on her arm before she got to the staircase.

"May I speak with you a moment, Millicent?"

"What about? I don't—"

"Don't worry. It's not about the meeting."

"Oh? What is it, then?"

"John went to the game with us this afternoon and asked me to come to Sunday night supper at their place, too. Said he might need my help on something."

"I wonder what they want to talk to us about."

"I don't know, but I suppose we'll find out tomorrow. I thought I'd offer to escort you over. Seems silly not to go together and there's no need in having Joe or Stephen escort you when we're both invited."

Her heart gave a little flip. She didn't think they'd ever gone anywhere, just the two of them. But someone would have to escort her anyway—it was one of Mrs. Heaton's hard-and-fast rules. The female boarders must go in a group or have an escort if they went out at night.

At first Millicent thought her rule a bit old-fashioned—it was nearing the turn of the century after all.

But then she'd found out Mrs. Heaton's daughter had gone missing and that was the reason she'd started the boardinghouse to begin with—so young women would have a safe homelike place to live. Thankfully, Mrs. Heaton and her daughter had been reunited, but the edict remained in place. She must have an escort.

"Oh, I… Yes, you're right. Thank you for your offer."

"You're welcome. John said six-thirty, so I'll meet you in the parlor at six, if that time works for you?"

"That will be fine. Good night."

"'Night, Millicent."

Millicent turned and hurried upstairs. What could John and Elizabeth possibly want to talk to the two of them about?

The next evening Millicent came downstairs and entered the parlor to find most of the boarders gathered waiting to be called to supper. Apparently, Matt hadn't come up from the men's quarters yet, and she felt quite proud of herself for being ready before him.

She'd chosen a brown skirt with pleated ruffles on each side, a green-and-brown bodice trimmed in green ribbon and a short green jacket to complete the outfit.

"Millicent, you're all dressed up. Are you going out?" Emily asked.

"Yes, I am. Remember, I'm going to the Talbots' tonight."

"Oh, that's right. We'll miss your company," Stephen said. "Do you need an escort?"

"No she doesn't," Matt answered from behind her, something in his tone sending her heart pounding.

"I'm escorting Millicent tonight, as I've been invited to dinner, too."

He looked quite striking in a brown suit, cream shirt and brown-and-cream tie. Matt worked as a fore-man on a high-rise building that once finished would be the tallest in the city. Normally he hurried home in his work clothes to change into nicer pants and a clean shirt. That attire always seemed to emphasize the broadness of his shoulders—but in his Sunday suit, they seemed wider still, and Millicent fought down the fluttery feeling his presence quite often brought her.

"You ready to go, Millie?"

She'd let him know the first time he ever shortened her name that she wanted to be called Millicent only. But it hadn't stopped him. In fact, she was certain he did it just to get a reaction out of her.

"I've been ready and waiting for several minutes."

He grinned, as if he knew she was irritated with him, but he didn't apologize, only crooked his arm and said, "Then let's get going. We don't want to be late, do we?"

She fought to keep from showing her vexation. That was exactly what he wanted her to do, and she wouldn't give him the satisfaction—not here in front of the new boarders. She took his arm and gave him a smile. "Of course not. Let's be on our way."

But as soon as they were out of sight from any of the boardinghouse windows, she disengaged her hand and looked straight ahead as they made their way to the trolley stop.

"Did I say something to upset you, Millie?"

"Why, no, *Matty*, whatever would make you think that?"

He threw back his head and laughed, causing her to expel a breath of frustration. But his laughter was contagious and Millicent giggled in spite of herself— frustrating her to no end. They had the oddest relationship ever. One minute he had her laughing with him, the next he said something that tempted her to wallop him over the head with her parasol—or anything else within range. They reached their stop a few minutes early and she hoped they could make it through the evening without him irritating her to that point.

Their trolley arrived and Matt motioned Millicent on first, then followed her up the aisle, taking a seat beside her once she'd slid over by the window. She pretended to be looking at the scenery outside while trying to relax before they arrived at the Talbots'. It did no good to let Matt get under her skin—doing so only served to frustrate her further.

It was a beautiful September evening. Not too cool yet, with only a light breeze, making her glad she had a jacket on. If she didn't already know she and Matt were totally wrong for each other, she'd be thrilled with the opportunity to spend this time with him without the others around.

"How is the quest to open your business going?" Matt asked.

His question surprised her. Matt rarely showed any interest in her profession, and she wasn't going to pass up the chance to talk about it. She loved being a photographer.

"Actually, quite well. After taking wedding photographs of Luke and Kathleen, John and Elizabeth, and Ben and Rebecca, word is getting around, and I have several weddings booked this month. I'm thankful my business is growing. I'm hoping to find the right place for a studio before long."

"That's good news, I suppose. You do take very good pictures."

What was going on with him? He'd never complimented her about her photographs or anything else she did. "Why, thank you, Matt. It's something I love to do. I'd be taking photographs even if I never got paid for it."

"Really?"

"Yes, I would. But since I do need to support myself, I might as well be in charge instead of working at a position I don't like."

He gave a little nod. "I suppose I can understand that. It'd be awful to have to work at a job I hated."

"Are you saying we might have something in common after all, Matt?"

Matt laughed. "Oddly enough, I think we might."

Their trolley came to a stop and they hurried out into the aisle, Matt blocking the people from behind until Millicent made it out in front of him.

He crooked his arm once more and raised an eyebrow as if challenging her to take it. The way she'd felt when they first got on the streetcar would have her ignoring the polite custom, but there was no need to start their visit with friends on bad terms. She took his arm and they headed down the residential street to the Talbots'.

John opened the door wide for them to enter. "Come in, you two. We've been watching for you."

"I hope we aren't late," Matt said. "If so, it's entirely my fault."

"No, you aren't late," Elizabeth said from behind her husband. "You're right on time. It's wonderful to see you both."

She led them into the parlor and Millicent noticed the brass bowl the boarders all had chipped in to buy their friends for their housewarming party. It held a nice fern and sat in the bay window. "Your home is as cozy as Heaton House, Elizabeth."

"Thank you," Elizabeth said. "I must say I admire how Mrs. Heaton makes it feel like a true home for all who live there. Much of my decorating skills, such that they are, came from seeing how she arranged things and the little touches she added. Let me just go dish things up and we'll be ready to eat very soon. Come keep me company, Millicent. John, you and Matt can take your seats now if you wish."

The ladies soon returned and began placing dishes in the dining room.

"We took the table's leaves out to make it a bit smaller, so that it has a more intimate feel when we're dining with only a few guests. Most nights John and I take our meals in the kitchen, so it feels like a real event when we eat in here," Elizabeth said as she took her seat at the end of the table nearest the kitchen. John seated his wife while Matt pulled out a chair for Millicent before taking the one across from her.

John said the blessing and began serving the roast chicken his wife had prepared. Once they were all served, Matt turned to John. "Now tell us, what it is you want to discuss with Milli—cent and me?"

Millicent was surprised at his effort not to call her

Millie. Lately he'd begun to use it even more, and she appreciated his restraint at the moment.

"As you know there's been a couple of near-fatal accidents to others working on your building in the last few months."

Millicent's stomach clenched. Matt never mentioned anything about those accidents—at least not in her presence.

"I do. And there were several less serious ones last week. Thankfully, no one was badly hurt, although it could have been disastrous if their harnesses hadn't held them. Are you doing an article about the accidents for the *Tribune*?"

Because of the articles he and Elizabeth worked on, him for the *New York Tribune* and her for the popular ladies magazine the *Delineator*, describing the appalling conditions of the tenements, John had recently become one of the paper's top reporters. He shook his head. "Not an investigative piece so much as informative one. Many people aren't aware of how dangerous it is to build those sky-touching buildings you love to work on. I'm hoping my boss will get your supervisor's permission for me to do a series of articles on the building. He wants me to write about how these high-rises are built and the danger in working on them. It'd be great publicity."

"So what is it you're thinking of doing?"

"I'd like to be able to go floor to floor and interview the workers, see for myself how dangerous it is and—"

"Elizabeth, aren't you worried about that?" Millicent found herself interrupting.

"About John going up so high? Not really. I feel

if they get behind the article, they'll keep him away from the really dangerous areas."

"I'm sure we would," Matt said. "But what do you need me to do? I'm not the boss. I can't give you permission."

"I know. But should he bring it up to you, should he want to know what you and the men under you think about it, I'd like you to give me a good word."

"You'll have it."

John nodded. "I appreciate it."

"But how does any of this have anything to do with me?" Millicent asked. "Or is there something different you want to talk to me about?"

"Not really different," Elizabeth said. "You take such wonderful photographs—you tell her, John."

"My editor at the paper asked if we could talk you into being the official photographer for the articles. Elizabeth is going to do a different take for her articles for the *Delineator*—more of a human-interest piece on what the families of these men think about the work they do. Our articles about the tenements were received so well, our editors love the idea of doing the different kinds of views of the Park Row Building and we're really excited about it."

"What kind of photographs will you be wanting me to take?"

"You'd need to take the ones you feel would best illustrate the stories we want to write."

"What do you think, Millicent?" John asked. "We know you don't like heights, but you are the best photographer we know and we didn't even have to bring your name up. You've been asked to come in with us. Will you do it?"

Millicent let out a deep breath. There was no doubt in her mind this could be the opportunity she'd been waiting for. But why did the chance of a lifetime have to involve her going to the top of what would be the tallest building in the city—the very thing that paralyzed her with fear?

"Even if you get permission to go up, John, I'm not sure my supervisor would ever agree to letting Elizabeth and Millicent up where the men are working. And with Millicent's aversion to heights—"

"Oh, surely when he knows she's the one the *Tribune* trusts to do the job—"

Matt shrugged.

"We won't know until he's asked. I'll make my decision then," Millicent said decisively. "At least I have time to think it over."

"The color drained out of your face at the thought of it now." Matt glanced over at John. "There's no need to put her through—"

"It's Millicent's decision to make, don't you think, Matt?" John asked.

"Of course it is." Matt shrugged again. "It may be a moot point anyway. I just don't see how having a woman on the job is going to happen."

Not if he had any say about it, Millicent was sure of that. And that attitude irritated her. *If* the opportunity to do this photo shoot came about, she'd pray and ask the Lord to ease her fear, at least long enough to get the job done. One thing she knew for sure. She certainly wasn't going to let Matt's opinion keep her from trying.

Chapter Two

By the time Millicent and Matt left Elizabeth and John's, she had a raging headache. After their friends told them they'd be in touch once John's editor gave them the go-ahead on the articles, they'd played a few games of charades after dinner. But Millicent could think of little else than what she would do if Matt's supervisor said yes. Now on the trolley back home, she rubbed her temple and closed her eyes.

"You know," Matt began, "you don't have to say yes to this, Millicent. I realize it's a good opportunity, but I also know how emphatic you've been about your fear of heights. If you don't want to—"

"Matt, John's articles are probably going to make the front page, and the exposure of my photos could bring in enough business that I could finally open my shop."

"What if you agree and then find you can't...do it? What will that do for your reputation?"

"Thanks for your vote of confidence in me."

"Now, Millie, you know I—"

"I'm hoping no one but you and the Talbots will

know that I fear heights. I'm pretty sure John wouldn't splash that information all across the front page."

"No. Of course he wouldn't. But—" Matt shook his head and sighed. "The decision is yours."

"I'm not pretending this will be an easy choice. I'll need to think things over and pray about it. And I don't know if I will accept the offer or not. That's so high up."

"You might not want to look down."

"But isn't the view the best part?"

"It is for me, seeing the city laid out below, but it might not be for you. You'd probably get dizzy."

Was he trying to talk her out of even contemplating taking the job? Millicent felt a little queasy just thinking about looking down at the streets below, but she certainly wasn't going to let Matt know. "I'm sure it's a sight to see."

"It is."

Their trolley stopped and Millicent was thankful for the break in conversation as they got off and hurried to Heaton House. The night air was cooling quickly and she was glad to be inside once more. The boarders were in the parlor with Julia playing the piano as she often did. But she stopped playing as Millicent and Matt joined them, and one of the maids brought in tea for everyone.

"You must be a mind reader, Maida," Matt said.

"No, sir, I just heard the front door open and knew that at this time of night, you and Miss Millicent must be getting home."

"How nice of you, Maida." Millicent took a cup from her and took a sip. She loved living at Heaton House. It'd become home in a short time. And even having boarders come and go hadn't changed that feeling. For one thing, they still saw all those who'd moved out fairly often, and though there'd been a period of time when Mrs. Heaton's table felt a bit empty, she'd managed to fill it back up with new people in no time.

As Millicent looked over at Matt, she found his piercing blue gaze on her, and her pulse began to race as it had the first time she saw him. He was very handsome, that lock of dark hair falling over his forehead and with well-cut lips that seemed to want to smile at her, but didn't. What was he thinking? Probably how to keep her from bothering him and his workmen.

She smiled at him, daring him to smile back, but not prepared when he did. Her heart seemed to dip into her stomach—a reaction she didn't even want to think about. For while there was much to like about Mathew Sterling, his views were so opposite from hers on so many levels and—

"Millicent?"

She heard Julia call her name and broke her gaze. "I'm sorry. Did you say something, Julia?"

"I asked how dinner with Elizabeth and John went."

"Very well. She's a very good cook."

Julia and Elizabeth were boarders at Heaton House together for several years until Elizabeth and John married. "They wanted to speak to Matt and me about a chance they might have to do some articles on the building he's working on. They want me to take photos."

"Oh, I did wonder why they asked just the two of you," Julia said.

Millicent was glad she'd told her why they'd been invited and that Julia's feelings hadn't been hurt. "I'm not sure Matt's boss will be agreeable to it, but they wanted us to know about the possibility."

"Would you have to go up high to take your photos?" Julia lowered her voice.

"Yes. But the *Tribune* editor asked for me specifically and I don't think I can refuse this kind of exposure."

"Oh, that is an opportunity, isn't it?"

Millicent nodded. "One I don't want to turn down. Nor do I want to accept and not be able to carry through. I'll be praying for the Lord to guide me in this decision."

"I'll pray, too," Julia said.

"So will I," Emily added.

"Please do, for I truly am not sure what to do." She could only hope the Lord would let her know sooner rather than later.

The next afternoon at quitting time, Matt stretched and gazed out at the view. The taller this building became, the more of the city and surrounding area he could see. He loved looking out to the ocean and the ships that moved in and docked, or eased out into the Atlantic. He turned and picked out Macy's, where Emily worked, and the huge Siegel-Cooper company on Sixth Avenue where Stephen was employed. He knew right where to look to see the top of Heaton House in Gramercy Park. He loved looking up at the sky and feeling closer to the Lord somehow.

But much as he enjoyed working up here, he couldn't help remember the fear he'd seen in Millicent's eyes and the trepidation he'd heard in her voice. But she was also one of the most independent, stubborn women he'd ever met, and he wouldn't be surprised at all if she took the offer—if it came about.

"Hey, boss." Burl Callaway, the man Matt counted on to train the newer men on the job, came up to him. "Looks like we've almost caught up where we ought to be after Jim and Ned got hurt. Have you heard how they're doing?"

"I checked in on them Sunday afternoon and they should be back next week," Matt said.

"That's good to know."

"Yeah, it is. How's that new guy…Ed…doing?"

"He's a hard worker, just needs to learn a few more things."

Matt nodded. The kid was young, but they needed the help. "Just make sure he puts his tools where they're supposed to go. And we need to tie down the tarp over there," Matt motioned to a tarp flapping in the breeze.

"I'll see to it."

Matt watched as Jack Dennison and Tom O'Riley, two of his best workers, finished making sure the area they'd been working in was cleaned up and in order before waving good-night.

Matt waved goodbye to some of his other men as they called it a day, and then made sure everything was secured for the night. As foreman, it was his responsibility and he didn't take it lightly. Once he was satisfied nothing was amiss, he looked out over the city one more time before calling it a day and heading to the freight elevator that would take him down to street level. He was taking off his work belt to hang in the locker room when he heard footsteps. He turned to see his supervisor approaching.

"Sterling! You're just the man I want to see."

"Oh? What's up, Mr. Johnson?"

"Well, the boss man just told me he's agreed to give some reporters and a photographer free access to the building to do a series of articles. Says you might know them."

"Afraid I do. I was hoping he'd say no."

Johnson chuckled. "I'm glad to hear you think like I do. But we aren't the ones who make the decisions. He is and we've got to 'help in any way we can.'"

"Yes, sir."

"I suppose if you know them, you also know one of the reporters and the photographer are women?"

"I do." He wasn't going to tell the man about Millicent being petrified of heights, although he wondered if he should.

"Well, it's going to be up to you to see that none of them get hurt."

Matt let out a long sigh. "I can't say that thrills me, but I'll do my best to keep them out of harm's way." Especially Millicent—he knew John would be watching out for his wife.

"I know you will. Not sure when they'll begin, but I'll let you know soon as I know. Or, since you're friends with them, you can let me know if you find out anything first." The slap on the back Matt received did nothing to calm the frustration he felt over their boss actually agreeing to the crazy idea. No one needed inexperienced people on a building site like this.

But he didn't have a say, so he just nodded. "Will do."

"I know I can count on you, Sterling. See you tomorrow." With that Johnson gave a wave and walked away.

Matt wondered if Millicent had heard the news

yet. It truly was a golden opportunity for her and he could understand why she felt she must accept it. But it wouldn't be easy on her. He shrugged. It wasn't going to be easy on him, either.

He was attracted to Millicent—more than he was comfortable with and way more than he should be. And she'd looked so pretty the night before, dressed in a blue-and-white summery outfit that made her eyes appear even bluer and her blond hair lighter.

Even when they disagreed on something—and that was often—he felt more alive around Millie than any other woman he knew. Distancing himself seemed to be the only way to counteract it. And trying to do that was difficult enough living in the same place. How could he manage putting distance between them when it'd be his job to watch over her while she took those photographs?

Matt headed to his trolley stop while silently praying, *Dear Lord, I don't know what Your plan is, but if possible, I'd sure appreciate it if You'd nudge Millie to turn down this offer from the* Tribune *and give her another opportunity to make a name for herself. Please forgive me if I'm being selfish, but only You know what I'm dealing with here. If it's Your will that she take the offer, I accept it, but oh, Lord, I sure hope it's not.*

Somehow he wasn't surprised to see John standing at the trolley stop when he got there—they sometimes rode home together, on their way to their respective homes. His friend grinned from ear to ear, alerting Matt to the fact that John must have heard the news.

"We got the assignment," he said.

He couldn't help but be happy for John even as

he dreaded the weeks to come. "I just heard. Congratulations."

"Thank you, Matt. This means a lot to me and Elizabeth."

"I know it does. Has Millicent been told?"

John shook his head. "No. I telephoned Elizabeth, though, and she's going to get in touch with her."

Matt nodded.

"I thought we could meet tomorrow evening at the ice cream shop to do some planning on when would be best for your crew for us to come to Park Row."

"Good idea. I'll check with Millicent when I get to Heaton House. She might need more time to make a decision."

"We do need an answer by tomorrow evening."

"I'm sure she'll have one for you by then." She didn't have any choice.

Millicent checked on the last photos she'd developed that morning. It wasn't a paying job, wasn't actually a job at all, but something personal. All the boarders, Mrs. Heaton's family and the former boarder couples had gone on a picnic to Central Park a couple of weekends earlier, where she'd taken snapshot after snapshot.

She smiled now as she took them down from the drying line strung up in a storage closet on the third floor that Mrs. Heaton let her use for a darkroom. At one time, Mrs. Heaton's son Michael had allowed her to use a storeroom in his office building. But being able to do her developing at Heaton House made things much easier—at least until she could afford to open her own shop one day. What a dream come true that would be—to have a studio where she could take photos and develop them all in one place. But was she willing to face her fears to make things happen faster?

She'd gone out earlier in the day to look at the Park Row Building John and Elizabeth wanted her to photograph. Her heart had begun to race as she'd looked up shielding her eyes against the sun to see how high the structure climbed into the sky. The actual floors only went a little over halfway up the steel frame, but still, the floored part stood taller than any of the surrounding buildings. When finished, the Park Row would be the tallest in the city. She'd shuddered and swallowed hard, willing her heart to slow down at the very thought of being up so high.

Thinking about it made her queasy now. "Dear Lord, please give me guidance in what to do if John and Elizabeth get the assignment," she whispered. "I would so like to do this and I think I'd enjoy looking out on the city from that vantage point. Matt's stories have always made me want to see what he does from up there. I'd really like to get past this fear I don't understand. Maybe this offer is just what I need to get over it. Lord, I'd appreciate your help in letting me know what to do. In Jesus's name, amen."

Millicent turned out the light and closed the door before heading down to her room. While Christmas was still several months away, she'd decided to make Mrs. Heaton a photograph album of the group outings and the photos she'd taken of them at Heaton House.

Letting herself into her room, she laid the photos on the desk that looked out onto Mrs. Heaton's small garden and then hurried to the bathroom to freshen up for dinner. She'd work on the album when she came back up later that night.

The aroma wafting up the staircase made her tummy rumble and she realized how hungry she was. The telephone rang just as she reached the bottom of the stairs and she hurried to answer it. "Heaton House."

"Millicent?"

"Yes. You sound excited, Elizabeth, have you heard something?"

"We did. We have the assignment and we're wondering if you're going to take the photos for us. Have you decided if you'll be our photographer?"

Millicent's stomach did a dive while apprehension warred with excitement. "I wasn't expecting to have to make up my mind quite this soon. I—"

"I understand. And I'm sorry, but we really need your answer by tomorrow, please."

"All right, I'll have one for you by then."

"Thank you, dear friend. Have a good evening."

Millicent hung up the receiver and prayed once again, *Dear Lord, please help me to know what to do.* Then she joined the others in the front parlor to wait for Mrs. Heaton to call them to dinner.

Julia and Joe, along with Stephen and Emily, were there, and just as she wondered if Matt was going to be late, he rushed in. His damp hair told her he'd probably just got home and she hoped there'd been no more accidents at his work.

"You running late again, Matt?" Joe asked.

"A little. But I made it before—"

"Dinner is ready," Mrs. Heaton said from just outside the dining room, interrupting what he'd been about to say.

They all headed across the foyer and Matt seated their landlady and then held Millicent's chair out for her before taking his seat beside her. Joe and Stephen performed the same courtesy for Julia and Emily.

Mrs. Heaton asked Matt to say the prayer, and then Gretchen and Maida began to serve the meal of roast beef, scalloped potatoes, green beans and rolls. Meals at Heaton House were always something to look forward to, along with the table conversation.

Their landlady always asked how each of their days went, which helped get conversation started and led to easy rapport among them all. Millicent remembered how welcomed she'd felt from the very first night at Heaton House. It'd meant so much to her that she'd tried to emulate Mrs. Heaton's example when the new boarders came in. But tonight her attention wasn't on the conversations going on around her. All she could think of was the decision she needed to make.

Once they'd finished their desert of coconut cake, they all headed toward the parlor once more, and Millicent and Matt both turned to one another.

"May I speak to you for a moment?" Matt asked.

"Of course. I wanted to tell you Elizabeth telephoned—"

"And she told you the news? My boss told me this afternoon and then I ran into John at the trolley stop. Have you made up your mind?"

"Not yet. I was hoping to have more time to make a decision. I told Elizabeth I'd let her know tomorrow. I'm sure they really want an answer now, but—"

"I understand. John wants to meet with us tomorrow evening to make plans."

"I suppose I'd better do some serious thinking and praying."

"Might be a good idea. And just so you know, I've been assigned to keep you safe while you take your photographs."

"Oh…well, that does make me feel better, I suppose." She managed a smile.

"You don't have to take the offer, Millie."

"I know."

They walked toward the foyer. "I'm sure there'll be another one of these days."

"Perhaps. I assume you want me to say no."

"It might make my job easier." He grinned but then turned serious and surprised her when he said, "Actually, Millie, I want you to do whatever you believe the Lord is leading you to do."

He sounded so sincere Millicent felt bad for presuming she knew what he was thinking. "Please say a prayer I get some direction soon."

"I will."

Millicent nodded. "Thank you. I think I'm going on up. Good night." She headed upstairs. Oh how she wished she and Matt weren't so different, that he didn't disapprove of her starting her own business. Especially now she'd seen a side of him he'd never shown her before—his strong belief in letting the Lord guide them.

As always, the next day passed fairly fast for Matt. There was always much to do and he loved seeing the progress being made. When they broke for lunch, he told his crew about the upcoming photo shoots and wasn't surprised by their reaction.

"What? Is the boss crazy? He's letting women up here?" Burl asked.

"He is. I don't like it much, either, but we don't have a say in the matter. We just have to watch out for them, and a few of you men need to watch your language, too. You know who you are." Some of his men talked as if they'd been raised out on a ship somewhere and he certainly didn't want them offending Elizabeth or Millicent.

"Yes, sir," several men murmured.

"I don't like it, though," Henry said. "I know all too well how easy it is to lose one's footing up here."

He was one of the men who'd had a near accident earlier in the week. "I know you do, Henry. I'll try to keep them away from the edge. I don't think it will be too much of a problem." With Millicent's fear of heights, he wasn't very worried. But he wasn't about to tell his men about that fear—they were already skittish about having women on the job as it was.

The rest of the afternoon, they mumbled and grumbled about the upcoming week, but he knew they were just getting their frustration out. Better they do so now rather than later.

Matt wished he could relieve his stress as easily, but it was *his* friends who were going to be disrupting their work, and he didn't know who he could complain to, except the Lord. But He already knew how torn Matt was with wanting to help them and not wanting them in his workplace.

When the work whistle blew letting them know it was time to quit for the day, Matt waved goodbye to his crew and after checking the jobs they'd all done to see where they'd begin the next morning, he took off, too.

The men's grousing had set them back a bit on getting the day's work done and by the time Matt arrived home, it was almost dinnertime. He hurried downstairs to wash up and made it back up just in time to hear Mrs. Heaton announce that dinner was ready.

He was burning with curiosity to hear Millicent's decision. Would she decide against taking the offer or would she face her fear?

At the dinner table, he pulled out her chair and heard her whisper to him, "Elizabeth and John want to meet us at the soda shop around eight so we can talk about a schedule of some kind. Will that work for you?"

"You've decided to take the offer, then?"

"I have. I telephoned Elizabeth this afternoon."

Matt nodded. "Eight will be fine with me, then. I'll meet you in the foyer around seven forty."

"I'll be ready."

Matt wondered if she really were ready for this assignment. But he knew she wouldn't want any advice from him. She was aware he knew heights frightened her and that he'd been assigned to keep her safe. Her decision was out of his hands and all he could do now was pray that he could keep her out of harm's way.

After dinner, Millicent hurried upstairs to neaten her hair and get a lightweight jacket for the walk to the soda shop where she and Matt would meet Elizabeth and John. As the clock in the foyer chimed the time, she rushed downstairs to find Matt standing in the entry to the big parlor talking to the other boarders while he waited for her. Something about his profile, the way that lock of his hair fell across his brow, made her pulse skitter through her veins.

"Are you ready, Matt?"

He turned with a smile. "I am. Just waiting on you."

"Let's go, then."

Once they were on the sidewalk outside, she said, "I hope we won't disrupt your workday too much."

He shrugged. "You all won't be there every day. We'll catch up if you do."

"That's true. I'm not sure what the scheduling will be or how you and the Talbots want to go about it all. I suppose it's a good thing they want this meeting."

"I'm sure we can figure it all out."

Millicent enjoyed the walk with a star-laden sky overhead and lights appearing in the windows of the homes they passed. They turned the corner and walked down to the next, to get to the soda shop the Heaton House group often frequented in warm weather. They didn't visit it much when the days and nights became much cooler. Somehow ice cream didn't sound quite as good when it was cold.

Their timing was good. John and Elizabeth were approaching from the other direction and they all reached the shop at the same time.

Their friends' excitement was evident on their faces and Millicent prayed once more that the Lord would give her courage to do the job she'd agreed to do. She didn't want to disappoint them and she badly wanted to conquer the fear that threatened to paralyze her. And if she were honest with herself, she wanted to show Matt that she could.

They all entered the shop and Matt looked down

at her. "Do you want a sundae or a shake? Or maybe a cone?"

"A chocolate cone, I think." Millicent began to dig in her reticule for some change.

Matt stilled her digging hand with his. "This is my treat."

"No, it's mine," John said. "After all, you two are agreeing to this because you're our friends. Come on, Matt. Elizabeth, I know what you want. Why don't you and Millicent grab that table there by the window before more customers arrive?"

"All right, dear."

Seeing the look Elizabeth gave her husband, Millicent felt a small stab of envy. She wanted the kind of relationship they had, but she didn't think it was in her reach. She'd come to believe that all men were against women being independent and owning their own business.

She sighed and followed Elizabeth across the room and took a seat at the small round table overlooking the street. They watched as the young man behind the counter made their cones and handed them to the men, one at a time.

"John is so happy you've agreed to help us, Millicent," Elizabeth said. "He's thrilled about these articles and so am I. We do love bringing attention to the needs in the tenements and won't stop doing that, but we're glad for the chance to do something different."

"I understand." And she did. She'd been along with them to take photos several times. "Reporting about the conditions so many live in must get depressing at times and this will be a nice change for the two of you. I'm excited about it, too."

"I'm glad to hear you are," John said as he and Matt approached with a cone in each hand.

Matt handed Millicent hers and took a seat beside her while John sat down next to his wife. Millicent took a lick and closed her eyes. She loved chocolate ice cream.

"Well, I thought we should talk about a schedule of some kind, so we all can plan. Matt has said late morning or early afternoon might be best, as the weather will be getting pretty cool going into fall. He's used to working up high in changing climates, but we are not. So I think the decision should be left to you women to make."

Millicent and Elizabeth exchanged glances. Both of them were morning people.

"We'd like mornings," Elizabeth said.

"Sounds good. How about nine?" Matt asked. "That will give us time to get some work done and know what needs to be taken care of for the rest of the day. Hopefully, I can keep the men working instead of ogling you two lovely ladies."

Millicent felt her face heat at his compliment. "Nine is fine for me. What about you, Elizabeth?"

"Yes. That time is good."

"We'll start there. As it gets cooler, we can change the time if we need to. I do feel the need to warn you—I've talked to my men, but there are a few whose language is not appropriate for a lady's ears. Should you hear anything like that, please let me know and I'll take care of it."

It was decided they would begin on Friday afternoon.

"We can be as flexible as you need us to be, Matt. My editor will be happy with an article each week if possible, but if not, then hopefully one every other one."

"That should work well for us. First time up, we'll show you what's been done until now and that might be your longest day. After that, you'll be able to move floor to floor with us."

Millicent's stomach fluttered. But was it with excitement or apprehension? She wasn't sure. She glanced at Matt and found his gaze on her. He smiled.

She answered with one of her own, hoping he couldn't see how very nervous she felt about it all. When he winked at her, she almost dropped her cone. Oh, that man!

Chapter Three

The rest of the week Millicent waffled between being excited about the assignment, and fear that she'd lost her mind in agreeing to take it and wanting to find a way to get out of it. She tossed and turned at night until she finally gave it all over to the Lord, asking for peace about her decision. She'd accepted the job and she didn't want to let anyone down.

Thankful to keep busy with several requests to take family photographs over the next few days, if Millicent wondered why Matt didn't mention anything at all about the assignment, she told herself it was because he dreaded having people disturbing his workday as much as she dreaded being there.

She'd worked on the album for Mrs. Heaton after coming up from downstairs each night, and Julia and Emily joined her. Emily had to work the coming Saturday, but Millicent and Julia made plans to go to another suffrage meeting that day and decided to make a quick trip to the Ladies' Mile afterward, so this time when the men asked they could honestly say they'd gone. No need to listen once again to their negative opinion of their attending another meeting.

Still, busy as she'd kept herself, Friday came way too quickly for Millicent. John and Elizabeth picked her up in a hack to have room for her professional equipment, and Millicent felt more nervous than she'd ever been as they met Matt at the bottom of the Park Row Building.

"Come on, let's go," Matt said as he led them into the elevator. "I'm glad John helped you get your equipment. I suppose I thought you'd use your Kodak."

"I wasn't sure what I'd need," Millicent said as the elevator began to move. Her stomach did a little flip before settling back in its place and she took a deep breath. She could do this. The Lord was with her and He would get her through.

"I thought I'd stop at each floor so that you'll be able to see the progress on each one."

Millicent grasped the rail a little tighter.

"You all right?" Elizabeth asked, looking at her closely. "You're a little pale."

No way was Millicent going to admit to being scared—not with Matt there. "I'll be fine."

The elevator lurched before coming to a shuddering stop and Millicent's stomach did a deep dive, while her heartbeat thundered in her ears.

But when the door opened and she saw a mostly enclosed floor, with window openings instead of open space, she began to relax.

"I think I'll need my tripod and camera for the inside shots," Millicent said. Matt helped her set it up while Elizabeth and John explored a bit. After she took a few shots, they went up to the next floor and on to the next. Each floor was in varying degrees of construction. Some had offices already enclosed, and others were only framed. They didn't tarry too long on any landing—only long enough for her to get a few photos of the differences on each. If it weren't for that jerky elevator, Millicent could say it wasn't near as bad as she'd thought it would be—until they got to the higher floors, which were mostly open expanses.

"This one is the last one we've got floored," Matt said as the elevator doors opened. "It's where my men and I are working."

He went out first to help her and Elizabeth out. Millicent breathed deeply and briefly closed her eyes while his attention was on her friend, trying to fight her way through the fear of being up so high. She opened them again as Matt said, "There's no ceiling yet, but the floor is solid. Just watch out for equipment and don't go near where the men are unless I give you permission."

He took hold of Millicent's arm and turned to John, who held his wife close. "Follow me."

As they walked, she caught her breath. Even from the middle of the wide expanse, Millicent saw out to the ocean. "Oh…" she breathed. "It is beautiful up here, Matt."

"It is, isn't it? Once you get a little closer, you'll be able to see more. But you don't want to look straight down your first time up. But don't worry. I'm not about to let you get that close to the edge today."

While the view was everything Matt ever claimed it to be, Millicent began to tremble at the very thought of being near the edge—even though a solid metal rail surrounded it all, she could imagine leaning out too far and—

Matt grasped her arm and turned to John and Elizabeth, bringing her back from where her thoughts were carrying her. "In fact, I don't want any of you getting near the edge until I believe you'll be safe and my men can do their jobs without gawking at Millicent and Elizabeth. You'd think they'd never seen a pretty woman before."

He turned around and strode closer to his workmen. "You men get back to work or I'll send you home and you'll be a day short in your pay!"

The men quickly quit staring and returned to doing what they were hired to do, while Matt shook his head and hurried back to Millicent's side. "I knew it'd be like this."

"I'm sorry for the disruption, Matt," John said. "At least we'll only be here for a while one day a week. Hopefully, they'll get used to us before long."

"Oh, they'll get used to you or they'll go home," Matt said. "Come on. You should be able to see the Statue of Liberty from over here." Matt led her and Elizabeth farther out onto the floor while John followed with the rest of Millicent's equipment.

He stopped about ten feet from the edge and pointed to the left. "There she is. Can you see her?"

"I can," Elizabeth said.

"She's lovely," Millicent replied. She took her camera from John and set it on its stand in a position to get the best shot at that time of day, and took several photographs of the statue.

In the meantime, she heard Matt point out a man he called Burl to John and Elizabeth, and tell them that they could go ahead and interview him first, and then when the other workmen took their break, they could speak to them while he stayed with Millicent.

She turned her camera a bit and got shots of ships at sea, and then she turned back to Matt a bit too fast and became quite dizzy. As Millicent tried to focus, seeing all the open sky behind him, a wave of nausea washed over her. She swallowed hard and forced a smile.

"You're white as a sheet, Millicent." He moved to her side and gripped her arm as if he thought she might collapse. "Do you need to sit down?"

"No! I'm fine. I—" *Dear Lord, please give me strength. I don't want to embarrass Matt in front of all of his men.* And she didn't want to embarrass herself in front of *him*.

"You aren't fine. You look like you're going to… be sick."

She fought back the notion that he was right and stood straight up. Right now, all she wanted to do was run for the hills—if she could find any. And she wasn't going to give Matt the satisfaction of thinking he was right all along. She gritted her teeth and whispered, "I am *not* going to be sick, Matt. I *can* do this."

"Millicent, as much as I understand how you want to prove something to yourself, this isn't the place for a woman, especially one who's nearly paralyzed with fear being up this high," Matt said in an exaggerated whisper. "You didn't have to agree to this… I tried to—"

She looked him in the eye. "Mathew Sterling, I am *not* going to quit. I'd like to take some photos of

Central Park from up here. Can you help me get my equipment to where the best view would be?"

He stared at her for several moments, then let out a deep breath and shook his head. "You are without a doubt the most stubborn woman I've ever met!" He picked up her tripod and camera and took off in the opposite direction. "Come on, follow me."

Millicent made a face at his back and followed. *Dear Lord, please help me to do this.*

She felt Matt's frustration with her as she began to work again. It fairly radiated off him. But he'd have to get over it.

Millicent took shot after shot of the park, and anything else she found interesting, before turning to Matt once more. "Will it be all right if I get a few photographs of John and Elizabeth and your men?"

"I suppose so. I'll move your camera—"

"No, I'll use my Kodak for those. I don't want them thinking they need to pose. I'd rather get some more natural shots."

"Do you want me to bring your tripod and camera?"

She shook her head. What she wanted most was distance from Matt. "No, unless they're in the way. I'll just walk around—you don't need to keep watch over me. I'm not going anywhere close to the edge."

"Millicent, I'm responsible for your safety—"

"I know. And can assure you, I'm not going to do anything to put myself, or your job, in danger. I just want to get in an inconspicuous place to take photos of your crew at work, and to be truthful, you watching my every move makes me nervous."

Matt closed his eyes and sighed once more, and Millicent sensed she was pushing his patience to the limit but he did make her nervous. "I'll just stand right over there and get my shots." She pointed to a place near the elevator where she'd have a good view of the work going on.

"All right. But don't move from that spot without my knowing it."

"I promise."

Matt watched as Millicent took her Kodak out of her bag and walked over to where she could get the shots she wanted. The woman pushed his patience like no other. But at least over by where his men were she'd be safely away from the edge and he'd be able to keep an eye on her no matter where he was. He breathed a sigh of relief as she began to take her snapshots.

He really thought she might have been sick there for a minute, but he had to give it to her, the woman had grit. He went about his business, making sure the men who weren't speaking to John and Elizabeth were doing their jobs. It appeared they were trying, although they did occasionally glance over at Millicent. But if they caught his eye on them, they quickly got back to business.

She was very pretty. She wore a blue skirt and a striped shirtwaist of two shades of blue, and her light blond hair was covered with a white hat trimmed in those same shades of blue, making her eyes the color of the sky. He couldn't blame his men for looking at her; he found it hard to keep from doing so himself. However, keeping Millicent and the Talbots safe while they were up here was his main job, so *he* didn't have to keep from watching Millicent.

But when he looked over at her, he found her taking aim at him and he quickly turned and spoke to one of his men. This was turning out to be one of the longest mornings he'd ever spent up here. After about a half hour more, John came up to him and told him they were leaving for the day.

"I can't thank you enough for this, Matt. We got enough for our first article from talking to Burl and that new young man he's training. No need to speak to everyone today—not if we're coming every week."

"Good, I'm glad you got what you needed." They walked over to pick up Millicent's tripod and large camera and took them over to where Elizabeth stood with her. Matt released a sigh of relief that Millicent wasn't quite so pale now. Perhaps it'd become easier for her with time.

"Do you need me to help get any of your equipment down?" Matt asked Millicent.

"I don't think so."

"I'll take it," John said. "No need to disrupt your work any longer than we have. We'll get a hack and make sure Millicent gets home safely with it all."

"Well, I wouldn't be doing my job if I didn't see you all down safely." Matt joined them in the elevator for the trip down. "I think Millicent got some good pictures for you today."

"Oh, I'm sure she did. That's why we wanted her to join us. Millicent has a knack for finding the very best shots, some we'd never even think to get," Elizabeth said.

Matt set the elevator to go to the ground level and as it picked up speed, he looked over at Millicent to find her looking down and grasping the handrail that ran all the way around the elevator. Her knuckles were white, telling him that she wasn't any more comfortable in the elevator than she'd been on the top floor. Why was she putting herself through all this? If she was as good a photographer as John and Elizabeth claimed, there'd be other opportunities to get her photographs in the paper, to make a name for herself. It must be pure stubbornness on her part.

Still, something in the way she held herself made him want to put his arm around her, hold her up and protect her.

The elevator came to a jerky stop and he couldn't keep himself from grasping her arm. "Are you all right?"

She looked up at him, her eyes brilliantly blue in a face that'd gone quite white once more. She gave a brief nod. "I am, thank you."

"I should've warned you that going down is a faster ride than going up." Her eyes were huge and he felt horrible that he'd not told her sooner. Even Elizabeth looked a little pale.

Millicent gently pulled away and followed Elizabeth and John out of the elevator, leaving Matt feeling like a cad for giving her a hard time earlier. "I'll see you back at Heaton House."

She only nodded as John hurried to procure a hack for the group. Matt waited until they were on their way before going back up to where his men were working.

He pulled out his pocket watch. Only thirty more minutes and they'd break for lunch, then he'd have to wait the whole afternoon before he could go home and find out how Millicent was doing. He shook his head and sighed. Why hadn't he tried to talk his boss out of this harebrained idea?

Millicent went straight to her room when she arrived home, then to the bathroom to get a cool washcloth to put on her head. She lay down on the bed, covered her pounding forehead with the damp cloth and closed her eyes. *Dear Lord, thank You for getting me through this morning. Please help this pain disappear and let me not give away how horrible I feel at dinner tonight. I can't let Matt sense how much I dread going back. Please help me to get past this sick feeling. In Jesus's name, amen.*

Thankfully, she soon dozed off and was able to sleep the afternoon away. By dinnertime the throbbing pain had eased to a dull ache and she felt well enough to freshen up. She gave a little more color to her cheeks by pinching them. At least she didn't have to go back to Park Row for another week. Surely that would get easier as time went on.

She made it downstairs just as Mrs. Heaton was calling everyone to dinner and she was glad that she didn't have to join the others in the parlor. But Matt seemed to be at her chair before she was and as he pulled it out, he whispered, "How are you feeling?"

She forced herself to smile at him. "Better. Thank you for helping me find the shots I wanted and for putting up with us."

He seemed taken back for a moment before he smiled and said, "Only doing my job. I'm glad you're feeling well."

He looked as if he truly cared, and Millicent couldn't resist that smile. "Thank you. So am I."

Mrs. Heaton asked Stephen to say the blessing, and as Gretchen and Maida began to serve dinner, she turned to Millicent.

"How did your day go, dear? Was the view as wonderful as Matt claims?"

"Oh, the view is magnificent, Mrs. Heaton. It's all Matt's said and more."

"You didn't get dizzy?" Julia asked.

Dear Julia, she would ask a question Millicent didn't want to answer. But she couldn't evade answering—not with Matt sitting next to her. "I did a bit. I bent and turned too fast, but I managed. Barely."

"She toughed things out," Matt said. "But I thought for sure she was going to—"

"Matt! Not at the dinner table!"

He chuckled and shook his head.

"Did you let her get too close to the edge, Matt?" Julia asked.

"I did not. Nor will I. But the first time up that high can make a person a little light-headed."

"I'll get used to it," Millicent said. She had to.

"I think it's very brave of you to face your fears, Millicent dear," Mrs. Heaton said.

"I don't know how brave I am, Mrs. Heaton. But it's the chance of a lifetime for my career. This will enable me to open my own shop much sooner."

There it was again—her career, her business and her shop. He'd never met a more independent woman who was so determined to make her own way. His ex-fiancée wouldn't follow him to New York and wanted to go her own way, but he'd never gotten the impression she didn't want a man to take care of her, like he did from Millicent. From what he'd heard from back home, Carla had already found a man who owned his own business and was now planning their wedding.

But with Millicent's plans, there didn't seem to be any room in her life for a man who might want to make a living with her, take care of her. Not when she was determined to do everything herself.

Matt couldn't deny she'd been brave today and he admired her for it. She'd also looked very vulnerable and he'd wanted to hold her until the world stopped spinning for her. But she'd pulled away from him and made it clear she didn't need or want his help.

He sighed as he tried to listen to the conversations going on around the table. But he couldn't get his mind off the woman beside him. She still didn't feel well; he could tell because she'd only taken small portions of each dish and now she seemed to be just moving everything around on her plate.

A look of relief came over her face as others began to get up from the table and he pushed his own chair back to help her with hers. Everyone headed to the parlor, but Millicent hung back for a moment.

"You coming, Millicent?" Julia asked. "We could play a game of charades if you do."

Matt watched Millicent take a deep breath, as she seemed to draw on some inner strength. He was certain she wasn't going to let anyone know how bad she felt.

"All right. I'll play for a bit," she said, confirming his instinct. But that realization both vexed him and saddened him as she followed the others into the parlor. That she'd taken this assignment and was putting herself through unnecessary stress made him want to shake her. But the fact she did and was so resolute about keeping her word—even if it made her lose her appetite—made him want to comfort her. But that seemed to be the last thing she'd want from him—and that saddened him most of all.

Over the next hour she did seem to relax and enjoy herself and for her sake he was glad. Surely the worst was behind her. She'd gone up and faced her fear of heights even though it hadn't been easy. Maybe by next Friday she'd feel more comfortable. He'd pray she would. And that he wasn't so...tense when she was there. Perhaps his frustration wasn't with her at all but with himself.

Chapter Four

The next day Millicent woke up early, dressed and hurried up to the darkroom on the third floor to develop the photographs she'd taken at the Park Row Building. She'd slept better than she thought she would after napping most of the afternoon the day before, but then she and Julia and Emily stayed up late working on the albums for Mrs. Heaton. They'd definitely decided one wouldn't do—there were too many photos and too many years to put in it. And Millicent looked forward to taking more photographs to put in them over the coming years.

But for now she needed to concentrate on the ones she was developing. She placed the paper in the developer solution and began to grin as the first image became clear. She could tell it was a great shot. Millicent rinsed it, fixed it and washed it, then hung it up before going on to the next plate. By the time she'd hung them all to dry, she was confident Elizabeth and John would be pleased with the outcome.

She especially loved the ones of the Statue of Liberty and the others showing the landscape out from the top of Park Row. After she finished the developing, she cleaned up her equipment and left the photos to dry completely while she went down to breakfast.

Almost everyone was there and she hurried to fix her plate at the sideboard before joining them around the table.

"Slept in, did you?" Stephen teased.

"No, I've been working. I wanted to get the Park Row photographs developed before we take off for the day."

"Take off? Where are you all going today?" Joe asked.

"I have to work but Julia and Millicent are going to the Ladies' Mile and out and about," Emily informed him.

Millicent hoped Emily didn't mention the suffrage meeting she and Julia were going to before they went shopping. But Emily put her fears to rest when she turned the conversation around. "What are you men doing today? Got another ball game lined up?"

"As a matter of fact, we do." Matt's gaze caught Millicent's and his smile made her chest tighten. He seemed to be in a very good mood. "How did your shots turn out? I'd like to see them before you hand them over to John and Elizabeth."

"I'd be glad to show them to you once they are completely dry. I want to get them to the Talbots before Monday." And then she could forget about going back to Park Row for a few days at least.

"I'll be glad to walk you over, if you'd like," Matt offered.

Why was he being so nice? He didn't like any of this and it'd been obvious yesterday. "I'll telephone

Elizabeth now to ask if this evening or tomorrow will be better—unless you have plans?"

"No, after dinner or tomorrow will be fine with me."

Millicent nodded and hurried out of the room and asked the operator to ring through to the Talbots. Elizabeth picked up after only two rings and was quite excited to hear the photos would be ready that evening.

"Oh, please do bring them over tonight, if it's not too much trouble."

"Not at all. Matt said he'd walk me over, so we'll be there after dinner."

"Wonderful. We look forward to your visit."

Millicent hung up the receiver and turned around to find Matt standing behind her. She placed a hand over her rapidly beating heart. "Oh! I—"

"I'm sorry. I didn't mean to frighten you. Emily just left for work and Julia has gone upstairs to get ready for your outing, so thought I'd save you a trip back to the dining room. When did she say would be best?"

"This evening."

"Good. I'm sure they're eager to see them."

"I think so. I'm excited about showing them. You can look at them at the same time since you're escorting me over."

"That will be fine, as long as I get to see them." He grinned. "I'm sure you got some great shots. It was interesting to watch you at work."

"Really?"

"Really."

He seemed almost as surprised at his answer as Millicent was at his comments. She shrugged. "Well,

I do love what I do and I hope it shows in each photograph I take."

"I understand. That's how I feel about what I do, too."

"Millicent!" Julia called. "Are you down here? I'm ready to go when you are."

"Yes, I'm right here." Millicent hurried into the foyer, with Matt right behind her. "I'll go get my hat and reticule."

Julia looked surprised to find Matt with her. "Oh good. We don't want to be late."

She turned back to Matt. "Have a good day."

"You, too."

Millicent started up the stairs as she heard Matt ask Julia, "How can you be late for shopping? The stores are barely open."

Her steps slowed as she waited for Julia's answer. "We don't want to be late for any sales. Things fly off the shelves if it's a good one, and they usually are on Saturdays."

"Oh. That makes sense."

Millicent took a deep breath and hurried up the rest of the stairs. At least he didn't ask if they were going to another one of *those* meetings.

He'd been so agreeable this morning, she didn't want to start anything up about the suffrage movement. If she thought he'd listen, she'd gladly have a conversation with him, but Matt and the other men's minds seemed to be made up about it. And their stubbornness about it all was a reminder of why she needed to guard her heart from any man—and she must keep it in mind at all times. Particularly on those days Matt was so nice to her!

Millicent pinned on her favorite autumn hat, a brown straw trimmed with green-and-blue ribbon and peacock feathers, grabbed her reticule and hurried back downstairs. She breathed a sigh of relief to find only Julia in the parlor waiting for her. "Did the men leave already?" she asked.

"Yes. Although I don't know where they were all going, only that Stephen went to work and Joe and Matt were going to meet at the Polo Grounds for the ball game later," Julia said.

"Why is it they don't seem to think they need to tell us where they are going, but they want to know every little thing we're doing?" Millicent asked.

"Good question. I'd like to know the same thing."

"My dears, it could be my fault," Mrs. Heaton said, entering the foyer.

"Your fault? How could that be, Mrs. Heaton?" Millicent asked.

"Well, you know I opened this boardinghouse in order to give young women a safe place that felt like home away from home, but I wanted you safe when out and about after dark, too. That's the reason I opened it up to men, too. Julia can probably remember when there were almost no men living here except for my son Michael."

"Yes, I do. But it didn't last long, once I told you I was walking to the soda shop that first summer." Julia chuckled and shook her head.

"That's when I made the rule that women must be in a group or ask a man to escort them to and from wherever it was they wanted to go at night. Michael was called into service that night."

"And he was quite gallant about it." Julia chuckled.

"But he was only one man and there were around six ladies living here at the time. Soon thereafter—the next day, I think—you put an ad in the newspapers and that's when Ben and John and Luke arrived."

"Quite true, Julia. And I inform the men who live here of my rules when they move in and perhaps they think of themselves as your protectors."

"Maybe so," Millicent said, her heart sinking just a bit. If she were going to have a protector, she'd much rather it be because the man cared about her and not because he'd been asked to. But Mrs. Heaton's explanation made sense. "But we don't want them to know about the meetings, Mrs. Heaton. They get all riled up when they're mentioned."

"I understand, and I support you not telling them about the meetings you've been going to, as they are all in the daytime. But should you ever decide to go to one at night…" Mrs. Heaton's brow wrinkled as she paused. "I think it might be time I spoke to the men about all of this."

"Oh, Mrs. Heaton," Millicent said. "The last thing we want is for you to feel you must defend us or—"

Their landlady chuckled. "Dear ones, I think each one of you is capable of taking up for yourselves, but I don't think the men residing here quite understand your interest in the suffrage movement. Perhaps it's time for them to learn that even though they do not have to like it, they must learn to accept your interest in aspects of the movement."

"Would you like to come with us?" Millicent asked.

"Not today, I'm going to visit little Marcus. But I'd like to go soon. Let me know when the next one is."

"I believe there is another in a few weeks, but we should find out more today. We'll see you this evening."

Stephen took off in one direction and Matt and Joe took off in the opposite one. Then they split up at the next corner. Joe worked for Michael Heaton's investigative-protection agency and needed to finish up some paperwork. They'd all meet up later at the Polo Field for the last game of the season. For now Matt was off to explore the city. He loved looking at the architecture of the downtown buildings, the mansions on Fifth Avenue and the neighborhoods not far from Gramercy Park.

Much as Matt loved working on the high-rises, lately he'd been wondering what it would be like to work on remodeling the inside of an old structure or building new ones from his own design. He didn't want to work for someone else for the rest of his life, but he'd wanted to get all the experience he could before striking out on his own.

But with all Millicent's talk of opening her own business, he'd begun to realize he'd like to do the same thing—to be his own boss and be able to work on his own designs instead of someone else's. He'd put the dream off, but he'd been giving it more and more thought lately.

He was eager to get a look at the photographs she'd taken from the Park Row Building. The views were spectacular, the building was one of a kind and he wanted to see if she'd done it all justice. He knew Millicent was talented but wished she weren't so independent—way too much so for him to be thinking about her as much as he'd been doing. He didn't want to have feelings for such a strong-willed woman.

And yet, his chest tightened as he thought of her. In spite of his resolve not to care about her other than as a friend, her smile seemed to shoot straight through to his heart and just touching her hand to help her out of the elevator sent sparks up his arm.

Something about her made him want to be her protector—when she'd declare that was the last thing she needed. Still, as long as he was responsible for her at his workplace, she'd have to accept that he would be looking out for her. She had no choice. And neither did he.

Chapter Five

Millicent and Julia left the suffrage meeting more excited and hopeful than ever that one day they might get the vote.

They were in high spirits as they stopped at one of the small cafés, which catered mostly to women who were out shopping. They were given a menu and decided on the lobster salad with rolls and English tea.

Millicent looked around the room and smiled. "We don't have anything like this back home in Virginia. Most women don't go out for lunch at all. I think there's a tearoom, but that's all. After living in a small town where everyone knows what everyone else is doing, it's very refreshing to go shopping, even if it's mostly window-shopping, in so many stores in one trip. To be able take lunch out instead of rushing home."

"The only time constraints we have are those of Mrs. Heaton and they do make perfect sense when you think about it," Julia said. "This is a large city and many women do go missing each week. We just don't hear about all of them. Sometimes it makes the news, but then only if they're from a well-known family. Others seem to disappear never to be heard from again."

Millicent shivered at the thought. She knew dangers lurked in this city—there were times when Mrs. Heaton took in women as temporary boarders who had no place to go and paid nothing until they could decide what to do or where to go. And she realized, from talking to others, most boardinghouses were not run like Heaton House.

"I do hope she'll come to a meeting with us one day," Julia said.

"So do I. Wonder if any of our married boarders would want to go, too," Millicent asked.

"They might," Julia said. "I'd think Kathleen would be very interested and possibly Rebecca. I'm not sure about Violet or Elizabeth, but we could ask them."

"It will probably depend on how their husbands feel about the suffrage movement. Surely they wouldn't object to their wives getting the vote. But then, consider how Matt and the other men feel." Millicent looked at Julia. "They've made us very aware they don't like the movement."

"But perhaps it's not the voting they have a problem with. Some of the women want more than that…" Julia sighed. "I can understand why men aren't thrilled with the movement as a whole, but all we want is the right to vote and I can't understand why that would upset them so."

"It would help if they cared to find out what is truly important to us about it. But there's no sense in stirring up friction at Mrs. Heaton's. They're her boarders, too."

The waiter brought their lunch and after they finished eating they headed out to shop. Millicent loved going to the Ladies' Mile. Even if one didn't buy anything, they could find what the latest fashion was and try to adapt their wardrobe in the least expensive way. Sometimes a new accessory or some new trim to put on a hat would do the trick.

They headed for Macy's, where they spotted Emily from afar. She waved to them and hurried to keep up with the man beside her.

"Wonder who he is," Julia said.

"Probably her supervisor."

"Most likely. He's not bad looking," Julia replied. "No wonder she never seems to mind putting in long hours every once in a while," she quipped.

"Now, Julia, Emily is quite good-natured and she seems to truly love her work."

"That's true."

"Emily's hours will be longer as Christmas nears and they start on the window displays Macy's is known for," Millicent said.

"I worked some evenings when I first started at Ellis Island, but thankfully, once I was promoted, I've rarely had to work evenings or weekends," Julia said.

"At least Emily doesn't have to stay late now. I think she said November would be bad, but she seems to be excited about working on the window displays," Millicent said. "I'm glad she lives at Heaton House. At least she knows she'll have a warm meal waiting when she gets home." Mrs. Heaton always made sure her boarders were taken care of no matter what hours they got home.

As she and Julia visited the ladies department,

Millicent realized how blessed she was to be able to set her own hours. But there was a downside, too. She did need a regular income so as not to dip into the money her grandmother had left her. Money she was saving to use to set up her own shop.

"You've grown awfully quiet, Millicent. What's wrong?" Julia asked as the stopped in front of the lace collar display case.

"Nothing's wrong. I'm just hoping John and Elizabeth and their boss like the photos I'm taking of the Park Row Building. If I can make enough on this assignment, the extra money will go a long way in helping me be able to open my shop sooner."

"Do you like the photos you've taken so far?"

Millicent grinned. "I do."

"Then you don't need to worry. You're more critical of your work than anyone and their boss asked for you to be in on the assignment. I'm sure they'll love them."

"Thanks, Julia. I needed your encouragement."

Julia handed the salesclerk the lace collar she'd been looking at and paid for it. They waited while the young woman wrapped her purchase and handed the small package to Julia. Then she turned back to Millicent. "You're a silly goose, you know? How can you not realize what a good photographer you are?"

"I just want to be able to make a living for myself." They strolled over to the millinery department to browse the newest styles.

"I understand. Believe me, I do," Julia said. "I want to get married one day, but I don't know if I ever will and even if I do, I want to be sure I can take care of myself. I've seen too many women marry only to have a man to provide for them, and most of them aren't happy. Nor are their husbands, I'd think. When—if—I ever marry, I want it to be for love and I want the man I marry to respect me as much as I want to respect him."

"I feel the same way." But Millicent wasn't sure finding that kind of man was possible. Suddenly, Matt came to mind, and she was surprised that she thought of him when talking of marriage. They were as opposite as two people could be.

And yet, her heart quickened thinking about Matt taking her to Elizabeth and John's that evening. Would he like the photographs she'd taken? Why did his opinion matter so much to her? She wished it didn't, but for some reason only the Lord would understand, it mattered a lot.

"Ready to go back to Heaton House?"

"Mmm, yes, let's go home." They hurried to the El, hoping it would be quicker than the trolley.

"We'll be home long before the men get back from their game. They'll have no reason to question why we were late getting back for dinner," Julia said.

And unlike last weekend, there'd be no reason for any tension on the way to the Talbots' tonight. Millicent settled back in her seat and sighed with relief.

Matt and Joe came home just in time to freshen up for dinner. They were in high spirits—the Giants had won their game and they'd had a great day.

"How did your shopping go?" Matt asked as he held out Millicent's chair for her.

"Wonderful. Julia and I bought trim to dress up

our Sunday hats for winter after looking at the newest styles in Macy's."

"Oh, that sounds like fun," Mrs. Heaton said as Maida and Gretchen began to serve dinner.

As always it was quite good. Mrs. Heaton's menu tonight was fried fillets of halibut, shredded potatoes and slaw, with lemon cake for dessert. Filling, but not too heavy for this time of year.

Conversation covered the shopping trip and the baseball game before Mrs. Heaton said, "We have a new boarder joining us soon. Do any of you remember Georgia? She's the daughter of a friend of mine."

"The one who was Michael and Violet's houseguest?" Matt asked.

"Yes, that's her. She's a teacher and wants to find a position here in the city."

"I remember her," Millicent said. "She seemed very nice."

"She'll be taking Rebecca's old room. I'm sure you'll all welcome her."

"Of course we will. It's always fun to get to know new boarders," Julia said. "And it will be good to fill out the table once more. Especially when Emily and Stephen begin working longer hours getting ready for Christmas."

Millicent couldn't argue with that. "We'll do our best to make Georgia feel welcome, Mrs. Heaton. But she'll feel at home here from the start and that's because of you."

"Why, thank you, Millicent dear."

As everyone finished his or her meal, Matt turned to Millicent. "Let me know when you're ready to go to the Talbots'."

"I just need to get the photographs and we can go."

"So, you two aren't going to be here, either?" Julia asked as they all headed toward the foyer.

"We won't be gone long. We're taking the photos to Elizabeth and John. I'm sure we'll be back before Emily and Stephen get home. She had a meeting. He's escorting her home tonight, isn't he?"

"He's supposed to. I'm sure he'd telephone if there's a problem, and I'm needed," Joe said.

"He would," Matt assured him.

"I'll go get the photos and be right back." Millicent went upstairs, but took a quick moment to neaten her hair and pinch her cheeks before grabbing the photos she'd placed in an envelope earlier. She hurried back down to find Matt waiting for her in the parlor with Julia and Joe.

"Do you two want to go with us?" Millicent found herself asking. "I'm sure Elizabeth and John would be glad to see you."

"Want to go, Julia?" Joe asked.

Julie shook her head. "Not this time. They want to talk about the articles and if we tag along they might think they need to entertain us."

"Are you sure?" Millicent didn't know if she was relieved or disappointed that she and Matt would be alone on the way over and back to the Talbots'.

"What about you, Joe?"

"Nah. I'll stay and keep Julia company."

"We won't be long." Millicent turned back. "You tell Joe about our plan while we're gone and I'll tell Matt."

"That's a good idea—but they must promise to keep it secret."

"Secret?" Joe said. "Hmm, now my curiosity is up."

"I'll tell you, but maybe we should take a walk, though, so we aren't overheard."

"Julia, there's no one here but us and—" Joe broke off when Julia placed her finger over her lips.

"Shh. I'll tell you later."

"Well, I can't wait to hear what this is all about. Come on, Millicent, let's get going." Matt touched Millicent's elbow, sending a current of electricity flying up her arm as they headed toward the foyer.

"See you after a while," Julia said.

"Yes, later," Millicent said, giving a little wave as Matt hurried her out of the house and down the street.

"Now, tell me, what's all this secrecy about?"

"I will, but I might as well wait until we get to John and Elizabeth's, because we want their help, too."

"Their help? What is this all about?" Matt sounded almost impatient.

"You'll see." They turned the corner and she continued, "We're almost there and I'll only need to tell it once."

"Oh, all right. I suppose you're right."

Millicent giggled. "Why, Matt, did you actually admit I might be right about something?"

"I never said you couldn't be."

"No, but—" She shook her head.

"But what?"

"Nothing. It's not important." She didn't want to ruin the evening. He'd told her she was right—there was no need to rub it in. "Let's hurry so I can let Elizabeth and John in on the secret, too."

Matt grasped her elbow and did as she asked, causing her to pick up her pace to keep up with him. She was almost breathless when they arrived at the Talbots', but John opened the door as soon as she knocked and they were quickly welcomed inside.

Millicent and Matt were shown into the Talbots' parlor, where Elizabeth had tea ready to serve.

"How did you know when we'd be here?" Millicent asked. "I forgot to telephone and let you know."

"I took care of the task while you were upstairs." Matt grinned at Millicent.

"Thank you for minding my manners for me, Matt," Millicent said.

He chuckled. "My pleasure, I assure you."

"And I'm glad you put on the kettle, Elizabeth. I think I could use a cup of tea." Maybe it would calm her nerves. "But first, I want to give you these. I hope they'll fit your first article."

She handed the packet of photographs to John and he lost no time in opening it. Millicent watched as he looked at the first one and handed it over to Elizabeth. John did the same thing with each photo, all without saying anything. Then he and Elizabeth both looked up at the same time and grinned.

"These are wonderful, Millicent. It's going to be hard to choose which ones to use," John said.

"I was thinking the same thing," Elizabeth said. "I really like the one you got of Matt talking to his men, and the shot of John and I speaking to Burl—and the ones of Central Park and the Statue of Liberty from up so high. What a view!"

"Oh, I'm glad you like them. I was worried you might not find any that would work."

"May I see them?" Matt asked.

Millicent's heart began to hammer in her chest and only then did she realize it was his opinion that mattered most to her.

Elizabeth handed them to Matt and then began to pour their tea and pass around the tea cakes she'd made.

Millicent took her cup with trembling fingers as she watched Matt study each photograph. It was impossible to decipher what he was thinking. He began to nod his head and when he looked at her, there was an expression she couldn't read. She waited for him to speak.

"Elizabeth and John are right. These are very good. I'm glad I'm not the one having to make the decision on which ones to use."

His words soothed her jitters and surprised her at the same time. She looked at John and Elizabeth. "Maybe I don't need to take any more for a while?"

"Oh, no, you don't." Elizabeth handed her the plate of teacakes to choose from. "You aren't getting out of this assignment."

"Besides, there will be changes each time we go. Small or large, we want to capture the progress as it goes," John said.

Millicent chose a small iced cake, took a bite and sighed. She'd agreed to do this and she wouldn't back out—no matter how much she might want to.

She watched Matt take two small cakes and pop a whole one into his mouth. He grinned when he caught her gaze on him and this time she had no problem reading his expression. She'd seen it before. The glint in his eyes seemed to be challenging her to say something.

Millicent sat up a little straighter and took another bite of her cake.

"Are you going to tell us your secret before we leave?" Matt asked.

"Secret? What secret?" Elizabeth asked.

Millicent took a sip of tea before answering, "Well, it's something I and the rest of the ladies of Heaton House thought you might all like to be part of. I started an album for Mrs. Heaton as a Christmas present and then Julia and Emily began to help me with it and we decided this is something everyone could be a part of and we could continue to add albums to the collection through the years."

"Oh, that's a wonderful idea, Millicent. What do we need to do?"

"Well, between the photos I've taken since I've been there and those Julia has collected over the years, we thought it would be a good idea to get everyone to comment on the ones they're in, give a memory to the photo. Emily will write the captions in her beautiful handwriting and we'll add them throughout the album."

"How are you going to do all of this without Mrs. Heaton knowing?" Matt asked.

"It won't be easy—at least not with the first albums we give her. We want to get the photos to those who are in them to comment about and we can put them together upstairs of an evening or on a weekend. After we give them to her the first time, she'll know what we're doing and we won't need to be so secretive."

Elizabeth got up and freshened their tea. "Did you want the other couples to help?"

"Oh, yes. I'd love for them to."

"Why don't you plan on coming over here with the photos one evening—John and I can host an album making party and have you all over to work on them."

"That would be ideal!"

"Won't you need album supplies—paper and covers and those kind of things?" Matt asked.

"Yes, we will. We thought everyone could chip in on the supplies."

"I'd be glad to provide them. You and I moved in about the same time and, well, I'll only be able to comment on the photos that were taken since then, but I really do want to help with this project."

"I'll gladly let you help in that way, Matt. Thank you all. Elizabeth, would you mind letting the other couples know what we're up to?"

"Of course. And I'll get back to you soon as I find out what night might work best for everyone."

"Oh, thank you, Elizabeth! This is going to turn out even better than I first imagined and I am so happy everyone wants to help. Mrs. Heaton is so good to all her boarders and I hope she'll love this Christmas gift."

"Oh, yes, she will," Elizabeth said. "It will be so much fun working on this with you. I can't wait until Christmas!"

"Neither can I!" Millicent took a last sip of tea and set her cup down. "I suppose we should be going. Julia was going to tell Joe and if Emily hasn't told Stephen yet, we will."

Millicent and Matt stood at the same time and Elizabeth and John walked them to the front door.

"Thanks for bringing the photographs over, Millicent," John said. "I can't wait to let my editor see them."

"Nor can I," Elizabeth said.

"Please let me know what they think of them."

"We will. And I'll be in contact with you about the party, too," Elizabeth said. "Talk to you soon."

Matt and Millicent waved goodbye and he took hold of her elbow as they headed down the walk. He'd warmed her heart by complimenting her about her photos and then was so kind to want to contribute to the supplies for Mrs. Heaton's gift. The man never failed to surprise her.

Chapter Six

The air was a little cooler out when they left the Talbots, and the street lamps cast a warm glow as they walked back to Heaton House. But there were shadows in between and she was glad for Matt's company and the light grasp he had on her arm.

"I'm so relieved they—and you—liked the photographs, Matt."

"How could we not? You are very talented, Millicent."

"I— Thank you, Matt."

"I might not understand why you would put yourself through all the stress and nerves of this assignment when you are so good at what you do and could earn money for your shop without it, but I do admire your talent. Besides, once you marry, you won't have time for it, will you? But it could still be a hobby."

Millicent wasn't sure what to say next. She was aware Matt didn't comprehend her reason for wanting her own business, but she didn't think anything she said would help him to. It seemed obvious to her, but not to most men. And her heart gave a little twist with the knowledge that Matt had just proved her right with his statement.

However, it'd been a wonderful evening and she didn't want to ruin everything by getting into a debate with him. There were other things to talk about. "So, you liked the idea of giving albums to Mrs. Heaton for Christmas?"

"I do, very much. And I'm looking forward to seeing all the photographs that will go inside. Those you've taken and the older ones, too."

"I think it will be fun to read everyone's comments about the photos through the years. We'll gain more insight into each person, hopefully make others feel as if they came from a huge Heaton House family."

"The boarders are like a family, aren't they? I mean not totally, but…"

Millicent wondered what he'd been about to say. Julia and Elizabeth felt like older sisters to her, and Emily like a younger one. Joe and Stephen were kind of like cousins, and John sort of like a big brother. But Matt…Matt didn't fit either of those descriptions. There was something different about how she felt about him. She wasn't sure what to call the emotion or even how to describe it, but it certainly was not brotherly. "I think I know what you mean. But the best thing about Heaton House is that it feels like home to all of us."

They rounded the corner and the topic of conversation came into view. "Yes, it does," Matt said. "More so each day."

As they reached Heaton House, they could hear piano music.

"Stephen and Emily must've gotten home," Millicent said.

Matt chuckled. "Or Julia got bored waiting for us, let's find out which one it is."

They hurried up the steps and Matt threw open the door. Hurrying into the parlor, they found all the boarders and Mrs. Heaton, harmonizing along with Julia's playing.

Matt and Millicent grinned at each other before joining them in singing the popular song "Love Makes the World Go Round." Julia turned around and smiled when she heard their voices added to the mix.

"It's about time you two got home," she said as soon as she'd hit the last note. "A few minutes later and you would've missed our sing-along altogether."

"You aren't going to sing another?" Millicent asked.

"No. Mrs. Heaton has something she wants to tell us and we were all just waiting until you got back," Emily said.

Mrs. Heaton entered the room just then. "Oh, good. I thought I heard you two come in. I'm glad you're back. I wanted you all together to tell you the news." She took her own glass from the tray and took a sip.

"What news do you have?" Millicent asked. "Is Georgia coming in early?"

Mrs. Heaton shook her head. "No, not yet, but I visited with Mrs. Crawford, the lady next door, after dinner and she told me she and her husband are putting their home up for sale. They want to move back to Boston to be nearer their grandchildren and I can certainly understand that. But I will miss them. I hope whomever buys their home will be a good neighbor.

The Crawfords were so very nice when I moved in, and I'll try to welcome the new owners the way they welcomed me."

"Oh, Mrs. Heaton, they'll love having you as a neighbor as much as we love having you as a landlady," Julia said.

"Thank you, Julia, dear. Much as I will miss the Crawfords, I do hope, for their sake, they sell quickly so they can move closer to their children and grandchildren."

Millicent smiled. She would feel that way. It was obvious to anyone who knew her that Mrs. Heaton loved her family and her grandchildren. Her face lit up at the mere mention of them. But she also cared for her boarders and there wasn't one of them who would want to live anywhere else.

Millicent wasn't in any hurry to move out, but she did hope to find a building that could serve as a business downstairs and a home upstairs to help with her expenses. Maybe now was a good time to start looking. It might be a while yet before she could afford anything, but it'd be fun to see if she could even find something that would fit her needs.

"How did John and Elizabeth like your photos, Millicent?" Emily asked.

"They liked them."

"They loved them," Matt interrupted her. "She took some beautiful scenery shots and some really candid ones of my men at work."

Millicent was so surprised by his praise, she was speechless for a moment.

"I had no doubt they'd like them," Mrs. Heaton said. "You take lovely photographs, Millicent. I'm sure when you start your own business, you'll do very well."

"Thank you both. I certainly hope so."

"Well, I believe I'm going on up," Mrs. Heaton said. "I'll see you all in the morning. Good night."

"Good night," everyone called in unison as she left the room.

They waited only long enough to be assured she was out of hearing range before Julia broke the silence. "Did you tell the Talbots about the plan to surprise Mrs. Heaton? I told Joe, and Emily told Stephen."

"I did tell them. They love the idea and Elizabeth is going to contact Kathleen, Violet and Rebecca and ask if they and their husbands want to help. She's going to plan a party to get us all together to work on the album. And Matt has offered to pay for supplies. It's going to be great fun!"

"A party sounds wonderful! I can't wait," Emily said right before her smile faded. "I hope I won't be working that evening."

"I hope not, too. If you know your schedule ahead of time, perhaps we can make sure you don't," Millicent said.

"We're making plans for the Christmas windows already and I know I'll be working late some in November and in December, of course, but hopefully not until then." She yawned. "I think I'll follow Mrs. Heaton's example and call it a night. Thank you for waiting for me to get off work and escorting me home, Stephen."

"You're quite welcome. You really should think of coming to work at Siegel-Cooper. We wouldn't work you nearly as hard," Stephen teased.

Emily just chuckled and shook her head.

"I'm heading up, too." Millicent turned to Matt as the others seemed amiable to ending the evening and headed upstairs and down to their rooms. "Thank you for escorting me to the Talbots'."

"You're welcome. It was my pleasure. I'm glad you're letting us all take part in your surprise for Mrs. Heaton."

"I'm happy everyone wants to. Knowing we all helped will make the album even more special for her."

"Working together on her gift will certainly make it special for us."

The expression in Matt's eyes made Millicent's insides do a little twist and she wasn't sure why. She quickly said good-night and hurried up the stairs, her heart thudding with each step she took. What was there about Matt that made her feel so…tangled up inside?

Matt spent Monday trying to tell himself to quit thinking about Millicent, but it was easier said than done. He'd started out for work woolgathering about the weekend and accompanying Millicent to the Talbots'. They'd never really spent any time together—just the two of them—until this assignment with John and Elizabeth had come up, and he found her company very enjoyable.

Whether they were with the group as they'd been at church the day before, when he'd stood beside Millicent and the sound of her sweet alto mingled with his tenor, or walking alone to the Talbots', he liked being with her—a lot.

He managed to get his work done, but each time he looked off into the distance, he thought about the photographs Millicent had taken from where he worked every day.

She was gifted, no one could deny that fact. The view from up here was spectacular, but she'd somehow managed to take specific spots and bring them into focus in a way that stood out from everything around them.

And the candid shots were a study of human nature, the expressions she'd caught—John and Elizabeth's interest in what Burl said to them, and Burl's earnestness in whatever he was explaining. Then there was Ed, new on the job and just as interested in what Burl was saying as the Talbots were.

And the shot of him and his men that showed them concentrating on getting the job done—when had she taken that one? Matt had a feeling that this assignment would go a long way in cementing her reputation as a top photographer—and helping her set up her own shop. But where? Would she get a shop and still live at Heaton House? Or would she move out?

He didn't like the idea of her living somewhere else any more than he liked the idea of her having her own business. Suddenly he realized how unfair he was being. If Millicent were a man, he'd have no problem with him starting up a company of his own. In fact he'd be cheering him on and offering to help in any way he could.

The thought unsettled him and he turned back to his work, putting—pushing—*shoving* thoughts of Millicent and her plans out of his mind. It was none of his business what she did. He worked harder than any of his men that day, keeping those meditations at bay, at least until they took their lunch break.

"What's with you today, Boss?" Burl asked. "You're going at it like your life depends on it. Something wrong?"

"No, I—"

"You having woman troubles?"

The men around them chuckled.

"Maybe that lady photographer?" Henry grinned at him. "You sure watched every move she made the other day."

"I'm supposed to. I'm in charge of keeping them safe up here."

"Uh-huh."

"She sure is pretty," Ed said with a gleam in his eye.

"Yes, she is. And I don't want to catch any of you acting anything but gentlemanly around her. You hear me? You're here to do your job and when she's here, it's to do hers." Matt's voice sounded sterner than he'd intended, but his men's teasing bothered him more than usual today. Or perhaps he was just more irritable.

Whatever the reason, no one was happier about hearing the bell signaling the workday had ended than Matt was.

He waved goodbye to his men and headed toward the El, getting home just as everyone was gathering in the parlor. He barely had time to run down and wash up, but made quick work of it, and when he arrived back upstairs, the others were filing into the dining room. He followed them in and pulled out Millicent's chair for her. She appeared quite happy and he smiled. "You must have had a good day."

Her smile gave him an answer even before she spoke. "I did. How did yours go?"

It was full of thoughts of you. "Okay. But you look as though you had good news or something—"

"You're right. John's and Elizabeth's bosses loved the images and I have two new bookings to take wedding photographs. It's amazing how fast word of mouth travels. From taking photos of John and Elizabeth's and Ben and Rebecca's nuptials I received requests to take wedding and family photographs, and from those, I'm now receiving more. So yes, it's been a very good day."

So it wouldn't be long before she could afford to open her own shop. The thought didn't sit any easier with him than it had that afternoon and relief washed over him when Mrs. Heaton spoke, saving him from having to comment.

"I'm so proud of you, dear. I love the photographs you took of Rebecca's wedding. I'm sure the demand for your talent is only beginning."

Everyone seemed to agree with her.

"I'm happy for you, Millicent." Julia smiled from the opposite side of the table.

Matt wanted to be happy for her, too. But he felt so conflicted in many different ways. Millicent was an excellent photographer and deserved to be a success. But owning her own business, giving it all her attention, would mean she'd make no room for anything else—like a family—and he couldn't deny he did have a problem with that.

But Millicent looked at him so expectantly, he felt

he had to say something. "Looks like you're on your way."

His words seemed to satisfy her, for her smile grew and she said, "Thank you, everyone."

"You'll be setting up your own shop before we know it," Emily said.

Matt's heart tightened and he realized that was the crux of the matter for him. He didn't mind her making a living from her photography—but actually setting up a shop and perhaps moving out of Heaton House was something he didn't want her to do. He found himself holding his breath waiting for Millicent's answer.

"Oh, not for a while yet. But I do think I might start looking at suitable places, though. Just to have an idea of what I want."

The tightness in Matt's chest eased. She wasn't doing anything yet. Wasn't planning on moving out of Heaton House anytime soon. And yet, it shouldn't matter to him. He had no claim on her and with her independent ways, he never would. He'd learned his lesson from his ex-fiancée and he wasn't traveling the same road again. No matter how drawn he was to Millicent Faircloud.

Millicent was glad to stay busy over the next few days. It helped to keep her from worrying about going to Park Row or think about Matt's reaction to her good news earlier in the week.

He'd acted happy for her, and yet, from the things he'd said on the way home from Elizabeth and John's the other night and the tone in his voice when he'd told her she was on her way, she didn't really believe he was. She hoped she was wrong, but it was hard for her to trust the words of any man after Robert. He'd said all the right things until he found out she was serious about wanting to start her own business. She'd wanted him to embrace her dream and he'd made it clear he would not.

Now she doubted any man would truly encourage her in accomplishing her goal. She'd accepted that fact before she'd moved to New York City and, while she might wish for things to be different, she didn't believe they ever would be.

She'd hired a hack to take her to the home of her new clients and the driver was kind enough to help her get her equipment to the front door. She gave him a small tip and was thanked profusely as he hurried back to his vehicle.

Millicent rang the doorbell and waited only a minute or two before Mr. Evans appeared. His wife was right behind him, holding their toddler. A young couple, they were friends of Michael and Violet Heaton and she thought that if they were pleased with her work, she'd have clients for life.

"Good morning, Miss Faircloud." Mr. Evans took her camera from her. "We're so pleased you agreed to take our first family photographs."

"Yes, we've seen some snapshots you took of Michael's family and knew you were the one we wanted to take ours," his wife added.

"Thank you, I'm happy to do so. I really enjoy taking family photographs. And what a doll your little girl is."

"I fear Laurie may test your patience," Mrs. Evans

said. "But she's usually at her best this time of day, so hopefully it will go well."

"I'm sure she'll be fine." Millicent smiled at the blond-haired toddler. Her eyes were big and blue and her cheeks rosy when she smiled, and Millicent thought the photo shoot would go well.

Mrs. Evans led them into the parlor, which faced south and was light filled and beautiful.

"Do you have any idea where you'd like these to be taken?" Millicent asked.

"I thought perhaps with me holding Laurie in the chair by the fireplace and my husband standing behind us? But truly we'll let you decide. You know better than we do what will photograph best."

"I do like your suggestion and we'll certainly take several shots there. But I think there may be a few other places in this room that will work well, too."

She helped to get them settled for the first few shots, handing Laurie a new stuffed toy she'd bought and slipped into her bag. "It's new, so I hope it's all right that I brought it. I've found a new toy sometimes brings the kind of smiles you might want in a photograph."

Millicent believed that many people thought they shouldn't smile in a photo, but she tried to bring them around to her way of thinking. If they were happy at the time of the photo, then she believed they should be able to show it.

"I'd like to take some photographs with you in the traditional, serious pose. And then some a little different for the times, but something I hope will grow to be the norm. I'd like to get some shots of you both looking at Laurie and smiling at her like I've already seen you do. Perhaps a few shots of Mr. Evans smiling down at you and Laurie, Mrs. Evans? And maybe one of you and your husband smiling at each other?"

"That sounds wonderful, Miss Faircloud. I've never really liked those serious poses. Most times it looks as if the couple doesn't care for each other."

Just then she looked up and smiled at her husband, who quickly returned the gesture.

"Please, hold that pose!" Millicent said, quickly focusing her camera on the couple and taking the shot. "Oh, that is going to be wonderful! I'm so glad you like my idea. And if you do, perhaps we won't have to worry about taking those too-serious poses."

"Oh, perhaps just one, Miss Faircloud," Mr. Evans said. "We'll need to send our parents photographs and I'm not sure they're ready for anything other than traditional."

Millicent chuckled. "Of course. I'll develop them all and you can choose which ones you want for yourselves and them."

The rest of the morning flew by as she took first one and then another pose. Laurie was quite cooperative and Millicent felt sure that the Evanses would be quite pleased with their first family photographs. And if she felt a tug of longing watching them interact with one another, she pushed it aside. Not even to herself did she want to admit how much she longed for a loving husband who could accept her the way she was, and a child of her own. That dream was something she'd come to believe would never happen.

Chapter Seven

Friday dawned sunny and bright but lying in bed thinking about working on the Park Row Building again, Millicent's mood was anything but. Still, she told herself it wouldn't be as bad as the first time and forced herself out of bed and into the bathroom she shared with Julia to freshen up.

She dressed in a beige skirt and a blue-and-brown-striped shirtwaist before heading down to breakfast. Should she eat? Oh, surely she wouldn't get as queasy this time. She knew what to expect and she'd hold tight to the rail in the elevator. She'd be fine.

"Good morning, Millicent," Mrs. Heaton said as she entered the dining room. "Matt left a few minutes ago and said to tell you he'd see you later."

Thankful he'd left early, Millicent smiled at her landlady. "Good morning, Mrs. Heaton! Thank you for telling me."

She went to the sideboard and helped herself to a bit of fruit and a fluffy biscuit, then looked longingly at the sausages before joining the others at the table.

"You're taking photographs at Park Row again today, aren't you?" Julia asked.

"I am. Elizabeth and John will be calling for me soon." Millicent buttered her biscuit and added a small dollop of strawberry jam. She took a bite and waited to find how it settled before taking another.

"I'm sure you'll do fine this time," Julia said as if she realized Millicent was anxious about the day.

"Of course you will," Mrs. Heaton said. "But rest assured, if you're at all nervous about it, I'll be praying all goes well and you can enjoy taking your pictures."

"I will, too," Julia added.

"And so will I," Emily said, pushing back her chair and standing. "I've got to go but I can't wait to hear all about your day when I get home."

"Thank you all so much. I'll remind myself you're all praying for me while I'm up there. I hope you all have a good day, too."

Julia scooted back her chair also. "Thank you. I'm not too sure how good a day it will be, but it will be busy and that's the way I like it. See you all at dinner."

"Have a good day, dear," Mrs. Heaton said.

Only Millicent and Mrs. Heaton were at the table when the front doorbell sounded and Maida hurried through the dining room to answer it. From the sound of their voices, Millicent could tell it was Elizabeth and John, even before Maida led them into the dining room.

Millicent jumped up from the table. "Oh, I'm sorry. I didn't realize I was running late!"

"You aren't late at all," Elizabeth said. "John and

I thought we'd come early enough to visit with Mrs. Heaton for a bit."

"I'm so glad you did," Mrs. Heaton said. "Would you like something to eat?"

"Oh, no, thank you, Mrs. Heaton, although I will take a cup of tea, if I may?"

"Of course you may, dear."

"My lovely wife made me a great breakfast, but I might eat a sausage or two, if you don't mind," John said.

"Please help yourself, John. We've got plenty left. I'm so glad you and Elizabeth came for Millicent early. I've missed you two."

"We've missed you also, Mrs. Heaton," Elizabeth said.

"Well, I'm glad I wasn't running late," Millicent said. "Have a nice visit. I'm going up to gather my things and I'll be back shortly so we can leave when you two are ready."

She took her time going upstairs now that she didn't need to rush. She'd give them as much time as she could to visit.

Millicent gathered both cameras and took them down, then went back up to get her tripod, placing it at the base of the stairs. She went back up once more and straightened her hair before putting her hat on. When she came back down, it was to find Mrs. Heaton and the Talbots coming out of the dining room.

"Your timing is perfect, Millicent. I'll take the tripod and your big camera out to the hack." He grabbed them both and then kissed Mrs. Heaton on the cheek before going out the door his wife held open for him.

"It was wonderful to visit with you, Mrs. Heaton," Elizabeth said. "Thank you for the tea and sausages."

"Anytime, my dear. I'm so glad you were able to make time. We need to plan a big get-together soon. With the holidays coming, surely we'll be able to."

"That sounds wonderful," Elizabeth said. "Let's talk soon."

"We will."

"I love that idea, too." Millicent stuffed her Kodak into her bag and Mrs. Heaton followed her and Elizabeth to the foyer. She gave a little wave as they went out the door.

She and Elizabeth hurried out to the hack where John waited and their conversation centered on the upcoming holidays. It was only when the hack pulled up at the bottom of the Park Row Building that Millicent's thoughts returned to the thing she'd been dreading all week. Going back up on that elevator to the top. *Oh, dear Lord, please help me to get through this morning.*

Before Matt left what he was doing and took the elevator down to meet Millicent, John and Elizabeth, he did some straight talking to his men, warning them not to stare at the women and make them uncomfortable, but to watch out for them at the same time.

It was a lot to ask, but he expected them to follow his orders. As the men began to grumble, he said, "This wasn't my idea, you know. The boss gave the go-ahead for this assignment, not me. But he expects us to accept his decision and make sure they have access to what they need and stay safe up here. Understand?" He gave them the sternest expression he could muster and hoped it worked.

"We do, boss," Burl said, looking at the other men

as if daring them to say anything. "Sometimes we forget that while we answer to you, you're answerable to someone else. Which means we are, too."

"Glad you understand. I'll be back up with them shortly and I expect you all to be polite and watchful at all times."

"I thought you said not to look at those ladies," one of the younger men said.

Matt looked him in the eye. "You know what I meant. No ogling the women. But be mindful of their safety."

With nods, they all ambled off to do the work they were paid to do and Matt headed to the elevator. As the door opened, he was glad to see a hack pull up with Millicent and the Talbots. He kept telling himself they'd only be there for a short while and then he'd be left in peace for another week. Except that couldn't be true—he lived in the same house with Millicent and peace was not a word he would use to describe how he felt about being around her.

"Matt! Glad to see you," John called as he approached him carrying Millicent's camera and holding on to his wife's arm. Millicent followed behind with her small camera and tripod, which Matt took from her.

"Thank you." Millicent smiled up at him and Matt was glad she didn't look quite as nervous as she had the week before.

"You're welcome. It's a beautiful day up top."

"That's good," Elizabeth said as they entered the elevator.

"Do you want to stop at each floor again or go right to the top?"

"I think we have enough photos of the lower floors for now, let's go straight to the one you're working on," John said.

"That's fine with me. We can check the other floors out when they're nearer the finished stage."

Matt smiled at them all, but his gaze captured Millicent's. "Make sure you take a deep breath and maybe pretend you're on a ride at Coney Island. I can't guarantee it, but it might help." He set the elevator into motion and made sure he stood by Millicent as she gripped the railing beside her. He grasped her arm at the first jostle and smiled down at her.

Her eyes were closed and her hand white. Matt looked over at Elizabeth and she looked a little pale, too. But John seemed fine.

As the elevator headed straight up and the speed evened out, Millicent opened her eyes. "I think it's better not stopping at each floor."

"Yes, so do I," Elizabeth agreed.

They both chuckled and some of the tension Matt had felt since first thing that morning eased. Perhaps today would be okay after all.

But as the elevator came to a jerking stop, both women closed their eyes once more and clutched their midsections. *Dear Lord, please let them be all right today.*

Matt kept hold of Millicent's arm as they filed out of the elevator and whispered, "Take another deep breath. Or two. I don't think it can hurt."

She did as he suggested before glancing back at him. "Better. I think."

"Good. Where would you like your camera set up?"

"I thought I'd try to get a few shots of the buildings surrounding Park Row—"

"Are you sure?" He wanted to accommodate her, but—

"I'm going to need to at some point and I'll dread it more until I actually do it."

She made sense and he'd like for her to get over her fear if possible. He never felt jittery for himself, but he did for her. "If you're sure that's what you want, I'll set you up and stay beside you. I think you can get some good photographs without getting right to the edge, but there is a sturdy railing and I'll be right here if you need to get closer."

However, as he moved closer to the edge, Millicent's steps slowed. He turned to find her biting her lower lip and looking a little pale. "Are you all right?"

"I don't think I'm ready for this just yet. Perhaps I should just take photographs of your men at work and some different distance shots."

"Whatever you want to do is fine with me." He certainly didn't want her getting sick or dizzy. "How about on the other side of the building today? You should be able to get some good photos of Brooklyn and both waterways by just turning your tripod a little one way or the other." And that would hopefully keep her safely busy while he made sure John and Elizabeth got the interviews they wanted. He turned to see them speaking to Burl once more, but he needed to see who else they might want to talk to.

He led Millicent in another direction and put her easel up where she could get what he thought would be some good shots. "Think this will work?"

"Yes, thanks. When I'm done here, I'd like to take a few more candid shots, if that's all right with you."

"As long as you don't wander off where I can't see you."

"You don't have to worry. I'm certainly not going anywhere near the edge without you."

Something about the way she released a deep breath and looked at him sent his heart hammering in his chest and his protective instincts surging. "That's good to hear. I can promise you I'll be right by your side when you decide to try it. But there's no rush, you know."

"Not yet anyway." She dropped her gaze and set her camera on the tripod. "Please don't let me keep you from your work today. I'll be fine."

"Just call me if you need anything."

"I will."

With nothing more to be said, Matt turned and headed in the opposite direction. He had a feeling Millicent would be as glad to get this day's photo shoot over with as much as he would.

John treated both Millicent and his wife to lunch before taking her back to the boardinghouse. Then he brought her equipment into the foyer while Elizabeth waited in the hack and Millicent waved both of them off feeling much better than the week before, when she'd barely managed to make it to her room.

She was glad to get back to Heaton House and extremely thankful she'd made it through the morning with only a few bouts of nausea and those passed quickly. Even the elevator's speed going down hadn't been quite as bad as that first day.

Of course it could have been because Matt kept a good grip on her arm the whole while, and she'd been glad of his support even as his nearness made her heart beat faster. She'd caught him watching her throughout the morning and it wasn't easy to get candid shots of him, but she'd managed to get a couple without him knowing.

Today she was able to develop her photographs right away. She smiled as she hung the last one up to dry. She liked these as much as the ones she'd taken a week ago. The view from up so high was spectacular. She still didn't feel totally safe up there, but suddenly she looked forward to the day when she could take photos from near the edge. But only if Matt were right there with her and then only when she could make it to that spot without feeling all wobbly on the inside.

It might be a while yet, but for now she was happy that she hadn't come close to being sick. Feeling as if she'd accomplished what she'd set out to do that morning, she washed her hands in the bathroom and looked at the clock beside her bed. If she hurried, she might make it downstairs in time to join Mrs. Heaton for tea.

She was a bit surprised to hear voices in the parlor and wondered who'd come calling. She peeked around the corner hoping not to be seen if that were the case, but she recognized the woman with green eyes and dark brown hair Mrs. Heaton was speaking to right away.

"Georgia! Mrs. Heaton said you should be arriving any day now. How was your trip?"

"Millicent, isn't it?" Georgia Marshall smiled.

"Yes, that's it." Millicent returned her smile. Georgia and her family were friends with the Heatons, and Millicent wanted to make her feel as welcome as she'd felt when she'd moved in.

"Georgia surprised me right after you left, even though I'd been expecting her at any time. We got her settled in her room, which is the one across from you, Millicent, and then decided to come down for tea. You will join us, won't you?"

"Of course."

Mrs. Heaton poured her a cup and Millicent settled herself in the corner of one of the sofas. She loved this room done in gold and burgundy fabrics, both solids and stripes. There were photographs of Mrs. Heaton's family and of the boarders here and there throughout the room. And there were fresh autumn flowers in vases scenting the space.

"I've asked Michael and Violet, and Rebecca and Ben to come for dinner tonight."

"Oh, wonderful," Millicent said. "It will be good to see them."

"They will be bringing baby Marcus and Jenny, won't they?" Georgia asked.

"Of course." Mrs. Heaton chuckled. "They don't dare come to dinner without my grandchildren."

Millicent smiled. She and the other boarders all enjoyed Mrs. Heaton's family and especially the children. It was part of what made Heaton House feel so much a home.

"You know," Mrs. Heaton said. "I think I'll ask Elizabeth and John, too. And Luke and Kathleen. It wouldn't seem right not to. Excuse me while I go telephone them."

Millicent watched the older woman hurry out of the room.

"Oh, I hope my coming isn't making too much work for Mrs. Heaton," Georgia said.

"Mrs. Heaton loves having company and it's been a while since we all got together. I'm sure she's got everything under control."

"I feel like long-lost family coming home," Georgia said.

"And that's exactly how Mrs. Heaton wants you to feel. You're going to love living here, Georgia."

"I think I already do." Georgia smiled but there was an expression in her eyes that Millicent couldn't quite read. She looked a little sad, too.

Julia came home just then and greeted Georgia like an old friend, and Mrs. Heaton joined them, letting them know that the married couples would be joining them for dinner. It'd be good to have a big group at the table and Millicent found herself looking forward to it. She wondered how Matt might react to having Georgia there—she was pretty and she was a teacher, not someone who wanted to pursue opening her own business. Millicent pushed the thought out of her mind. It shouldn't matter to her how Matt responded to Georgia or any other woman. She had no hold on him.

Chapter Eight

An extra leaf was needed at dinner that evening, and it felt like old times with the married boarders joining them. As Matt laughed at something Ben said, he realized he'd missed this group more than he thought.

Miss Marshall seemed as nice as he remembered from her visit earlier in the year, but she did seem a bit subdued.

He looked around the table, glad to see that everyone seemed happy to be together again. His gaze caught Millicent's, who sat next to him. "I'm glad you made it through the day a bit easier than last time."

"Thank you. So am I."

"I'm pleased we're all together tonight," John said from across the table. "I wanted to let Millicent and Matt know that the first article on the Park Row Building will be in Sunday's paper, and from what my editor told me, it's going to be quite a spread."

"And my article will be coming out in the next edition of the *Delineator*," Elizabeth said.

"Oh, I do look forward to seeing both articles," Mrs. Heaton said. "We must get some extra copies for you two to be able to send the articles to your families."

"Millicent's photographs from the first week will grab attention to them, there's no doubt about that," John said, turning to her. "I meant to ask, when did you take the one from the street that you gave us? He's going to use that photo and asked if you could take one from that same spot as each floor goes up?"

"I'll be glad to. I took that one when I went to look at the building while trying to decide what to do. Thought I'd add it to the others, just in case."

"He also asked if you might take one looking down from up there, too, but I told him we aren't allowed that close to the edge yet," John said.

Matt sensed Millicent's relief as he heard her release a deep breath. He let out a small one of his own. The thought of her so close to the edge made him nervous.

"Thank you, John. Maybe one day I'll be able to get that close, but not yet."

"The Park Row? Isn't that the tall building going up now?" Georgia asked.

"Yes," John said. "Matt works up there."

"Really? We've even read about it back home in Ashville. It's to be the tallest in the city, isn't it?"

"When it's finished," Matt answered. "But I'm sure another, taller one will go up soon after."

"And you'll probably work on it, too," Luke said from the other side of the table.

"I don't know," Matt said, surprising himself with his comment. He shrugged. "We'll see."

"Well, by the time Millicent gets through with this

assignment, she'll probably be able to open up her shop—if not sooner," Elizabeth said.

"Oh, I don't know," Millicent said.

Then she seemed to realize she'd used Matt's same words. She laughed, looked at him and shrugged. It seemed they were both of the same mind for a brief moment, which caught him a bit off guard and warmed his heart at the same time.

"I do think I'll start looking at possible places, though. I don't think it will be easy to find just the right place for what I can afford. And I don't know if I'd be able to tell if a place needs a lot of work, either."

"I'd be glad to help you," Matt offered. "I enjoy looking at the different architecture in the city and I'd know if a place needed work to make it what you want." He wasn't sure who was more astounded by his words, him or Millicent—or the other people sitting around the table, who suddenly became quiet.

"Really? You'd help me look?"

He certainly couldn't tell her no now. He'd offered in front of everyone. "I will. When do you want to start?"

"Whenever is good for you."

"How about tomorrow afternoon? I have to work part of the day, but we've made good progress this week and I should be free by three or four. Will those times work for you?"

"Yes, either time will be fine. Thank you, Matt."

Conversation picked up once more around the table and Matt concentrated on the plate in front of him. He wasn't sure what prompted his offer to help Millicent find a place for her business. He'd never been in favor of her starting her own business. But if she was determined to open her own shop, he told himself, then he wanted it to be in a good building, something that she wouldn't need to worry about spending extra money on or that would drain her dry before she ever got started. But deep down he knew there was more to his offer.

Everyone headed to the parlor to play charades after dinner and it was great fun, having enough people for several teams. Even Rebecca's daughter Jenny played and her giggles had them all laughing. When they ended the game for refreshments, Millicent was surprised at the sudden longing she felt, seeing Jenny run to her mother and stepfather for a hug.

She'd never given much thought to having children of her own—what good would that do when she'd about given up ever finding a man who would accept her for who she was? But seeing Mrs. Heaton's daughter, Rebecca, and her husband, Ben, together with Jenny caused a twinge in her heart, and then an even deeper one as she watched Michael Heaton looking down on his wife and their baby boy, Marcus.

One could almost feel the love arching between them and Millicent released a deep but quiet sigh before turning her attention to Julia, who'd given in to Jenny's pleas for them to have a sing-along.

"Are you all right?" Matt whispered from beside her.

"I'm fine. Why?"

He shrugged. "You looked a little sad there for a moment."

"I was just—" Just what? How could she tell him she'd been longing for something unattainable?

Julia ran her fingers over the keys just then, saving her from answering. "What do you want me to play first, Jenny?"

"I love 'The Sidewalks of New York.' Will you play that one?"

"Just for you," Julia said.

But Julia knew it was everyone's favorite. Millicent's mood lifted the minute the group began to sing and she loved the way Matt's tenor blended with her alto. She was also pleased that he hadn't seemed to give Georgia any more attention than he gave the other women at Heaton House. She told herself it shouldn't bother her if he did or not. But deep down in her heart, she knew it did—no matter how hard she fought against it.

They sang several more songs before calling it an evening and after everyone took their leave, the boarders all decided to call it a night, too. As they all headed upstairs or down, Millicent was still confused at Matt's sudden change of attitude—of course he hadn't said he'd changed how he felt about a woman having her own business, he'd only offered to help her look. And he'd make sure any place she might find would be built sound and if there were any remodeling to do, what it might entail and how much the cost would be. Whether he'd changed his mind about anything or not, she'd be crazy to turn down his offer.

The next afternoon as she and Matt began their search for a place that might work for her photography shop, Millicent was still having a difficult time believing that he'd offered to go with her.

She could see him checking a building out once

she'd found something she thought might work, but to go with her at the beginning? There must be more to this than just his willingness to help her. She didn't believe he'd had a change of heart.

"Where were you thinking you'd like to set up shop?" he asked as they headed down the street.

"Somewhere there is a lot of traffic, where it'd be visible but yet a safe place to live, too."

"You're really going to live there?"

"Perhaps not at first, but it would help to have an upstairs apartment."

"You'd live by yourself?"

"Well, yes. Although I don't plan on leaving Heaton House yet, it's something I'd need to do at some point, don't you think? From a financial aspect?"

"I suppose. But—" Matt cut off his sentence. Then he glanced at her. "It might take some time to find the right building. Wouldn't it be easier for you to rent a space?"

"But then that would mean two rentals."

"Yes, but then you wouldn't eat into your savings until you were sure—"

"You think I will change my mind? Or regret my decision?"

"I don't know. It seems you *could*. And if you did, and you'd put a lot of money into it…" Matt shrugged.

"If I sold the building, I'd get it back."

"But it might take a while."

Millicent released a frustrated sigh. "Matt, why are you even going with me if you—"

"Because, if you found something and it wasn't in good shape, I'd feel guilty because I didn't check it out for you."

"Oh." His admission gave her mixed feelings. He was living up to his principles, but at the same time, he hadn't offered because he'd changed his mind or because he might want to spend time with her.

"So, back to my questions. Where do you want to go? I see you brought the newspaper. Did you find anything interesting?"

"I circled a few places." Millicent handed the paper to him. "They aren't too far from here, but in different directions. One is on Third Avenue and the other over on Fifth Avenue. I telephoned to inquire if we could see them between three and five o'clock and both owners said they'd be there."

"Well, let's go to the one on Third first." It was within walking distance and they were at that building in minutes.

It was a three-story building tucked in among taller ones and Millicent really wasn't sure it would work. "I don't think this has enough natural light for me. There's only this one window in the front and a smaller one on each floor above."

"I don't much like the looks of it, either," Matt said. "It doesn't appear to have been well cared for."

They knocked on the door and a middle-aged man opened it. "Miss Faircloud?"

"Yes, and this is my friend Mathew Sterling."

"I'm Edward Abernathy. Pleased to meet you both."

The two men shook hands and Millicent looked into what could be a reception area, but it appeared to be the only room with a window and as she suspected, the lighting wasn't good.

"What has this building been used for recently?" Matt asked as they went through the other rooms downstairs. A kitchen was in the back, but it wasn't well equipped and Millicent couldn't imagine how it would work for her needs.

"I'm an attorney and it's been my office building. But I've decided to move to New Jersey and want to sell. There are more rooms upstairs—I mostly used them for storage."

He led the way up the stairs and Millicent followed with Matt right behind her. The upper two stories were as dark as Millicent thought they might be and while one would work for a darkroom, she couldn't see herself living or working in a building this dark.

"What do you think?" Mr. Abernathy asked.

Millicent shook her head. "I'm sorry. I don't think it will work. I'm wanting something with a little more light."

"What kind of business do you want the building for?" Mr. Abernathy asked a bit defensively.

"She's a photographer and she needs something with a lot of windows."

"I suppose it wouldn't work, then."

"I'm sorry to waste your time, Mr. Abernathy."

"It's fine. I have another person coming to look at it. Perhaps it will be right for him."

"I hope so."

She and Matt hurried out into the daylight and Millicent released a deep breath. "Oh, I couldn't work in there, much less live in something so…"

"Depressing? Not to mention it hasn't been well taken care of. Those stairs were rickety and would need to be replaced. I'd be afraid for you to even touch a match to that dilapidated stove. The facade outside is crumpling. I would have discouraged you from buying it even if you liked it. I fear there is unseen damage everywhere and that it would cost too much to fix it all."

"Something tells me it's good I've started looking now. I don't think it's going to be as easy to find what I need as I first thought."

"Well, let's go see the next one. Hopefully, it will be better."

Millicent smiled at him. "I have to admit I'm glad you offered to come with me."

She didn't mention how awkward it would have felt to be in that building alone with a man she didn't know. She hadn't thought of it before today. Perhaps she wasn't quite as independent as she thought she was.

"I'm glad you took me up on my offer." Matt took her elbow as they headed down the avenue. When he'd made it, he'd never given thought to her being alone with men she didn't know as they showed her their buildings. Now that realization would keep him going with her. She might believe she was able to take care of herself, and in many situations she probably was, but she was a lovely woman and he'd seen how Abernathy appraised her.

The Lord must've nudged him to make his offer last night, knowing what Millicent could come up against in her search for a building that would work. Matt sent up a silent thank-you and then turned to her. "I hope you won't go inside any building you're interested in unless I'm with you."

"After seeing all you pointed out to me, I certainly don't plan on it. I wouldn't know what to look for, other than I want it to feel right to me."

Matt chuckled as relief settled in on him. It didn't matter why she agreed to let him go with her, as long as she did. She could be in as much trouble trying to find a place for her business as she'd be if she went out at night alone. He wasn't going to allow himself to think about her living alone. He could only pray that wasn't going to come about anytime soon.

They took a trolley over to Fifth Avenue to the next address she'd circled in the paper.

"Well, this building does appear better taken care of," Matt said, peering at the four-story structure.

"Oh, but it's much larger than I'd need and most probably more expensive."

"What do you want to do? Do you want to look anyway?"

"Well, I did tell the lady I'd be here. I hate to put her out." They could tell there were lights on inside. "I think it may be a shop of some kind. That would give me an idea of the layout."

"Let's go inside to make sure," Matt said. "You won't know until we do."

They entered the building to find the bottom floor being used as a millinery store. A nicely dressed lady came up to them with a smile. "Good afternoon, may I help you?"

"I'm Millicent Faircloud. I telephoned earlier about your advertisement in the *Tribune*. The building for sale."

"Oh, my dear, yes, I remember speaking to you. But I believe there might be some confusion. I'm only renting out the third floor to help with my expenses."

"Oh, I must've read the advertisement wrong."

Matt didn't think she had. He'd read it also. "So, are you renting space for a shop or—"

"No. Not a shop. I live on the second floor and the third is an apartment also."

"Oh, I'm not looking for a place to live. I need a place for a photography shop."

"Do you have that advertisement with you?"

The lady appeared as annoyed as Matt felt while she read the circled description and released a vexed sigh. "I'm so sorry for the mix-up. This is completely wrong. I'll telephone the newspaper right now and get it straightened out."

With that, the lady turned her back on them and hurried away. Matt glanced down at Millicent. "You might be right about it taking a while to find the right place."

"I think so. Next time, I'll ask more questions before I set up a time to see a property. I'm sorry to waste your afternoon."

"It hasn't been a waste. We'll take our time going back to Heaton House and you can point out some buildings that appeal to you along the way. Then I'll be on the lookout when I'm out and about, or going and coming home from work."

He really was such a nice man—most of the time. If only he didn't seem to disapprove of her dreams, her decisions. But he did. Still, they could be friends and that was what he was being to her now. "Thank you, Matt."

"You're quite welcome."

They walked up and down several streets and Millicent pointed out the places she liked. But there were no signs for rent or sale out anywhere. "I think it is going to take longer than I thought to find something."

"Perhaps. But at least I know what you like now and I'll know what to look for. Let's get back home and see what's for dinner. I'm getting hungry."

"So am I, as a matter of fact. Let's take a trolley."

They hurried to the nearest stop just as one pulled up. Several blocks down, as the driver stopped to pick up more people, Millicent spotted a sign in the window of a three-story building and grasped Matt's arm and pointed out the window. "Look! It says Space for Rent. I can't read what's under it. Do we have time to—"

Matt hurried out into the aisle and grabbed her hand. "Come on. It shouldn't take long."

Millicent giggled as she followed him. She hadn't thought he'd be so agreeable. But she appreciated his kindness as they got off the trolley and hurried across the street, dodging first one vehicle and then another.

Once they reached the building, they found it wasn't open. There was only the sign and the smaller lettering only said, "Inquire by telephoning this number."

Millicent quickly pulled a small notepad out of her pocketbook and wrote it down, then turned to Matt. "I'm sorry to waste even more of your time. I'll pay for the next ride."

"You will not," Matt said, grabbing her arm and hurrying back across the street to wait for the next trolley. "I pulled you off the trolley. I could've said no, but that building is one I've passed several times and I wanted to see it."

"Oh…but—"

Matt turned to her and placed two fingers over

her lips. Millicent caught her breath at his light touch while he said, "No buts, Millie."

Their gazes met and something in Matt's expression sent her pulse racing. He quickly took his fingers away and looked in the direction their trolley would come in. And for once in her life, Millicent was at a total loss for words.

Chapter Nine

By the time Matt and Millicent arrived back at Heaton House, they had little time to freshen up for dinner and hurried to do just that before Mrs. Heaton called them in. It was Saturday evening and they usually dressed up a bit more.

Matt changed into a fresh shirt and cravat before pulling on a dinner jacket. He looked in the mirror and combed his hair before heading back upstairs to gather before dinner.

As he took them two at a time, Matt was still trying to forget the way his heart had hammered as he and Millie had gazed at each other for those few brief moments. He'd enjoyed the day with her...very much. And he hadn't missed the envious looks from other men on the street. They'd looked at her and then him, as if wondering what was so appealing about him. There was no denying Millicent was a beautiful woman and any man would be proud to have her at his side.

But much as Matt had enjoyed the day, he was still as determined as ever to ignore the growing attraction he felt for her. He wasn't willing to chance having a broken heart again, and he had a feeling Millie could turn his inside out—if he let himself care for her more than he already did.

He'd felt protective of her since the first night around Mrs. Heaton's dinner table. Impossible as it seemed, and hard as she'd fought to appear independent and afraid of nothing, he had the impression she was as innocent as could be. Seeing the expression in her eyes as she seemed to realize that, without him with her today, she would have been in an empty building with a man she knew nothing about only confirmed his opinion. She was naive. And the sad thing was she didn't even know it.

He joined the others as they came out of the parlor and headed to the dining room. Everyone looked very nice, and Millicent looked fresh and prettier than ever in a deep blue gown that brought out the color of her eyes.

He pulled out her chair for her and couldn't resist inhaling the scent of her hair as he pushed her nearer to the table. He took his own seat beside her as Julia asked, "Did you find anything that might work for your shop, Millicent?"

Millicent gave her head a little shake. "Not today. The advertisement was wrong on one—the lady was renting a room, not selling a building. And the other, well, it wouldn't work at all. I think I'll be looking for a while, but I certainly do appreciate Matt going with me. I did learn that I don't know enough to pick out anything without his input."

She smiled at him and Matt wasn't prepared for the way his chest tightened and his pulse began to race. He was going to have to be on his guard to make sure this woman didn't work her way into his heart.

Mrs. Heaton asked Matt to say the blessing and he readily agreed, thanking the Lord for the beautiful day, for Mrs. Heaton and her boardinghouse and for the food they were about to eat. At the end, everyone echoed his amen.

Maida and Gretchen began to serve their meal of veal cutlets and mashed potatoes and gravy, along with shelled beans, and talk turned to the others and their day.

"How is the planning for Macy's Christmas windows coming along, Emily?" Mrs. Heaton asked.

"Wonderful. I never realized how much work went into them, but they are going to be magnificent. I can't wait for you all to see them!"

"We can't wait to," Julia said. "It really seems like Christmas is coming once those windows are revealed."

"I can't believe we're into October already. Where do the days go?" Julia asked.

"They certainly speed by this time of year. Thanksgiving will be here before we know it and then Christmas! I am very excited to begin my shopping soon. What a blessing to have my grandchildren nearby. I'm sure Jenny is going to love those windows, Emily!"

All the talk about the holidays reminded Millicent that they still hadn't gotten together as a group to work on the albums. She'd need to speak to Elizabeth about the party soon.

Millicent threw off her covers and hurried into the bathroom to freshen up for the day, then came back into her room and picked out her favorite Sunday dress, a blue-and-green plaid.

She put her hair up, pulled out a few strands around her face and added her straw, still trimmed with the blue-and-green ribbon and peacock feather because she hadn't gotten around to changing it out. Maybe she'd buy a new straw to add the new trim to. She did still like this one and it matched her dress perfectly.

She turned first this way and that in front of her mirror and then, feeling happier than she had in a long while, Millicent hurried down the stairs to the dining room.

After serving herself a plate of waffles, eggs and bacon at the sideboard, Millicent took her place at the table.

Mrs. Heaton picked up the paper beside her and held it up. "You must see this, Millicent dear. It's John's article and your photographs of the Park Row Building. I am so proud of you both."

Her landlady passed the paper to Matt and he handed it to her. "It is a good article," he said. "I read it earlier."

Millicent took the paper and was more than pleased to see the first article about the Park Row Building on the front page of the *Tribune*. Her photograph from outside the building was an attention grabber, as John thought it would be. The article he'd written was wonderfully entertaining—something Millicent hadn't expected. Excerpts from his interviews with some of Matt's men gave one even more respect for those working up so high.

She really liked the photograph of Matt with his men and even he seemed pleased with the write-up.

However, she couldn't tell how he felt about the photo she'd taken of him being in the paper.

But everyone else thought they were wonderful and by the time she arrived at church with the others, Millicent felt truly blessed as she stood to sing hymns.

Matt stood on one side of her and Emily on the other. Georgia sat in the row behind them with Julia, Joe and Stephen. Mrs. Heaton sat with her family in the row in front and Millicent felt gratitude that her parents had only allowed her to come to New York City if she agreed to board with Mrs. Heaton.

The sermon that morning gave Millicent much to think about. She'd always loved the saying "To thine own self be true" from Shakespeare's *Hamlet*, but scriptures made it clear that it was the Lord, *not* herself, that she should strive to be true to—His teachings, His will.

Here she was thinking that Matt, or any man, should accept her for herself, and accept that she was independent and wanted her own business—but had she stopped to ask God if what she wanted was in keeping with *His* will for her? *Dear Lord, please help me to know.*

She was still mulling the lesson over when the last prayer was said and everyone began to file out into the aisle.

Matt fell into step with her. "You seem lost deep in thought. Is anything wrong?"

This was the second time in less than two days that he'd asked that question. Once again, Millicent glanced up at him and gave a little shake to her head. "I was thinking about the sermon today. It was a good one, don't you think?"

"I do. And I've found that if I go home thinking about it, and how it applies to me, I might have gotten that nugget of truth that the Lord wanted me to."

"Yes. That's how I feel, too."

They made their way outside, and as the Heaton House group spread out to walk back to the boardinghouse, Millicent inhaled deeply of the crisp cool day. "It's beautiful out, isn't it?"

"It is. Did you have a chance to see if there were any new advertisements in today's paper? Maybe we could take a stroll and see if there are any signs out."

Millicent was taken aback by his suggestion. What was going on with Matt? He seemed quite eager to help her find a place and that didn't fit with how he'd acted ever since she'd known him.

"Why…ah…no, I haven't read the ads yet. But I will after Sunday dinner, and if you're sure—I would like to see what else might be out there we could look at."

"I'm sure." He took her arm as they crossed a street and smiled down at her, causing her pulse to gallop straight to her heart. She'd thought she had Matt figured out a long time ago. But now she wasn't so sure.

Matt wasn't sure what had come over him the past few weeks—he seemed to be offering to help Millicent with something on a daily basis. He didn't know what surprised him most, his offering or her accepting. Especially about taking him up on his offer to help her find a place.

Matt thanked the Lord that he'd been with her at Abernathy's place and shuddered inwardly at the thought of her running into that kind of situation again. She wouldn't, not if he could prevent it.

Now that he thought about it, he realized that much as he'd tried to ignore his growing feelings for Millicent, he couldn't deny them. He tried to tell himself that it was because they'd lived at Heaton House and he cared about her the way he cared about the other boarders, but it didn't ring true to him.

"What did you think of John's article and Millicent's photographs, Matt?" Michael Heaton asked as they entered the parlor to wait until dinner.

Relieved to have his mangled thoughts interrupted, Matt answered truthfully. "The article was great and so were the photographs—although, I could have done without my mug in the paper. But Millicent can get some great shots, there's no doubt about it."

"Your boss will be thrilled with it. She caught you doing your job. What more could he ask for?"

"I certainly hope that's it." Matt thought getting his work done while trying to make sure Millicent, Elizabeth and John stayed safe on the building was enough for a workday, but one never knew.

Mrs. Heaton called them all into the dining room and they filed in, taking their normal seating. Extra leaves had been put in and everyone just moved down a bit, leaving Mrs. Heaton's family to sit nearer her.

Matt always enjoyed Sunday dinner at Heaton House and today was no exception, as everyone talked first about how good the sermon had been, then the article in the newspaper and how nice the weather had been.

After Sunday dinner, everyone usually went their separate ways and today was no exception. Michael and Violet took baby Marcus home for a nap, and Rebecca and Ben had promised to take Jenny to Central Park for a bit. The other boarders headed back to their rooms or out for the afternoon.

"Did you still want to take a stroll and look for possible shops with me?" Millicent asked Matt.

"Yes, if you want to. Did you have a chance to go over the classifieds?"

"I found one or two that we can look at from the outside to find out if it's worthwhile to make an appointment to see the inside. They're not too far away. I'm sure we can walk to them. I do need to run upstairs first."

"All right. I'll meet you in the parlor in about fifteen minutes, if that works for you?"

"That'll be fine."

Matt watched Millicent hurry upstairs and then took the downstairs two at a time to freshen up a bit himself. He looked forward to spending the afternoon with her far more than he should and he'd have to keep reminding himself that he was going along to help her, not to enjoy her company. She was determined to open her own shop, determined to be independent—her interest in the suffrage movement told him that.

And those thoughts reminded him that what she wanted seemed to leave no room for any man in her life—most especially not him. He didn't mind a woman having a mind of her own or even dreams of her own, but he wanted to think she would put him and any children they might have first. He wasn't sure Millicent would ever be willing to do that.

Matt headed back upstairs, his earlier good mood

dampened a bit at the realization that he must continue to remind himself that he could only be a friend to the one woman who made his pulse race and his heart thud in spite of their differences. *What to do, Lord? Please help me to know.*

Chapter Ten

Matt seemed subdued when he met Millicent in the parlor and she couldn't help but wonder why. Maybe he'd decided he didn't want to go with her after all. But he was the one who'd brought it up.

"You ready?" he asked.

"I am."

"Let's go." He did smile as he opened the front door and motioned to her to go first, but still she wasn't sure he was as enthusiastic about their stroll as he'd seemed to be earlier. She told herself there was no need to borrow worry. Her moods had been up and down the past few days, too.

It was lovely out and seeing God's hand at work in the changing colors of the leaves, and the sound of birds as they found the nearest tree, it was near impossible not to be in a good mood.

She handed Matt her folded up paper so he could see where the two other places she'd circled were.

"These would be in good spots, but you know, if you could get something near to or in the Ladies'

Mile, that would be better. There's so much traffic there."

"True, but because there is, I'm afraid it's going to be more difficult to find something I can afford."

"That could be. Something will come up that will be right for you, but there's no need to make a rash decision, is there? You do have a darkroom at Heaton House and so far that's working, isn't it?"

"Yes, for now. And no, there isn't a rush and I'm glad. Now that I've started looking, I realize I might not find the right place for a while. But then again, it might be just around the corner." She grinned as they turned a corner and headed toward the city center.

"It could be."

As they strolled down street after street, Millicent pointed out first this building and that and Matt offered his opinion on the architecture of each one. It was an enlightening few hours at the least. And decisive in ruling out each of the two places Millicent had circled in the newspaper.

One was much too large for what she wanted and the other was hidden on a side street. "I'm sorry I wasted your afternoon, Matt."

"You didn't waste it. I'd probably have taken a stroll anyway. I do like to study the city's differing structures when I'm off."

"Have you thought of starting your own business, Matt? Building your own designs?"

He looked a bit surprised by her question but she truly wanted to know. She'd wondered about it ever since she'd seen him at work.

"Actually, I do think about it. I have an architectural degree and plan to put it to use one day. But right now, I want the experience of working on the Park Row—you already know how much I enjoy it."

"I understand why, now that I've been up there." And she did, although she still feared getting near the edge. But as a photographer, and in spite of that fear, Millicent found she wanted to get close enough to get some magnificent shots from the top floors. But she couldn't help but wish Matt didn't work up so high. It was a dangerous job, and while she could choose whether or not to get near the edge—with Matt beside her—he had no choice. And she worried about something happening to him.

She was sure he'd laugh if she told him, but the simple fact was, there'd recently been an article in the paper about a man falling to his death while working on another building—one not near as tall as the Park Row.

And she did realize that accidents happened every day, even on the streets of the city. People got run over by runaway vehicles or by running out in front of a trolley. But that didn't stop her from worrying about Matt and his men and—

She pushed away her morbid thoughts and gave her head a little shake before changing the subject. "Are you looking forward to the holidays? I am. I can't wait to see Mrs. Heaton when she opens our present. Julia and Emily and I have been working on the albums, but we need to get together with the others soon so everyone can add their comments."

"That should be lots of fun. I can't wait to see Mrs. Heaton's reaction when she opens her present. I am looking forward to Thanksgiving and Christmas at Heaton House. My family would like me to come home to Ashland for at least one of holidays, but they have a houseful every year and I'd really like to stay here."

Millicent hoped that he would. Her parents were going to visit her two married sisters for the holidays this year—one for Christmas and the other for Thanksgiving—and that'd made Millicent's decision easier. Neither sister had a lot of room, and besides, she wanted to have Christmas at Heaton House this year, especially because of the gift they were making for Mrs. Heaton. She'd been quite relieved that her family didn't seem too disappointed.

She and Matt chatted about this and that until they neared the soda shop where they'd met John and Elizabeth to discuss the articles.

"Want to stop and get an ice cream before we go back home?" Matt asked.

It was still a few hours until suppertime. "I'd love it. It'll be getting too cold for it soon."

Matt held the door open for her and then asked, "What do you want? Chocolate like the last time?"

"Yes, please."

Matt gave their order and they watched while the proprietor made their cones. Matt paid for them both and handed hers to her. "Do you want to sit here or eat them on the way?"

"Let's eat them on the way."

They headed out the door and down the street. "Too bad we don't have a key to Gramercy Park with us. We could sit there in the shade and enjoy our cones," Millicent said.

"Oh, we'll have them eaten before we get there," Matt said. And as fast as they seemed to be melting, he was right. Good thing he'd grabbed extra paper napkins!

The ice cream was melting even faster than she thought it would and they were both having a hard time keeping it from dripping on their clothes.

"Matt, do you have one more napkin? I'm making a mess."

Ice cream was dribbling down her chin when he reached out just in time to keep it from dropping onto her blouse.

"Thank you! That was close."

She giggled as he wiped her chin once more. But his eyes darkened as she took the napkin from him and their fingers tangled. Millicent caught her breath at the spark of electricity that shot up her arm and into her chest.

She jerked back as their gazes met. Had he felt the same thing? They were only yards away from Heaton House and she hastened her steps, running up to the front door ahead of Matt.

He quickly joined her and opened the door for her. She hurried in and headed for the stairs, but she turned at the first step. "Thank you for going with me again today and for the ice cream."

"You're quite welcome. See you at supper."

Millicent nodded and hurried on up the stairs. She let out a deep breath as she entered her room and flung herself down in the chair by her bed. Had Matt felt that jolt of…of whatever it was that shot straight to her heart? Or had it only been her who felt it?

The expression in his eyes…had she read it wrong? It was as if— Millicent shook her head and jumped up from the chair. No! She wasn't going to let herself think about it. And indisputable or not, it didn't matter how drawn she was to Matt. She could not, would not, let herself care more for him than as a friend, a fellow boarder. She couldn't let whatever feelings she had for him grow. For if she did, Millicent was certain heartbreak would follow.

Millicent stayed busy over the next few days, trying to keep her mind off Matt. She used the excuse of going through photos and trying to organize them somewhat in her room of an evening so that she didn't have to spend time in the parlor. It didn't get her out of sitting beside him at the table and wondering if he'd felt the same jolt that she'd sensed on Sunday, but it did give her something more to occupy her mind.

The paper had used three more of Millicent's photographs in John's article and she'd received several telephone calls asking her to take family photographs. Her calendar was filling up nicely.

Elizabeth telephoned her to let her know the album party had been set for the coming Saturday evening. They'd have a buffet dinner and then get to work afterward.

"That sounds wonderful, Elizabeth," she'd said. "Thank you for planning it."

"I'm glad to. It'll be fun for all of us."

"I wonder what we should tell Mrs. Heaton if we're all going to be gone." She didn't want her landlady to be upset that she wasn't included.

"Just that I'm having a get-together," Elizabeth said. "Rebecca and Violet are going to ask Mrs. Heaton to take care of the children and you know she'd much rather do that than have dinner with all of us. Time with her grandchildren will win out every time."

Millicent chuckled. It was common knowledge that Mrs. Heaton took every opportunity she could to spend time with Jenny and baby Marcus. "I'm sure you're right."

She'd relayed the information to the other boarders and was quite relieved when Mrs. Heaton joined them in the parlor to let them know she wouldn't be going to Kathleen's outing—she was going to enjoy her grandchildren that night. The glow on her face assured Millicent her landlady was totally happy with the arrangement. Her heart felt lighter and she looked forward to Saturday.

On Friday she found she wasn't quite as nervous as she'd been the first two times when Elizabeth and John picked her up. Instead, she was looking forward to taking more photographs from other directions up on Park Row. However, she was a bit fluttery about having Matt nearby. They really hadn't talked much since last Sunday, and she wondered if he'd been trying as hard to avoid her as she'd been doing to avoid him.

And then her thoughts returned to that shot of electricity that flowed between them and— She forced herself to think of other things. How her business was growing and her excitement about making the albums for Mrs. Heaton for Christmas and the life she'd made for herself since coming to New York City. She had many blessings to count and she needed to concentrate on them and not the things she wished for. *Dear*

Lord, please forgive me wanting more, when you've already given me so very much—a wonderful place to live, good friends and work to keep my dream alive. Thank you for my blessings. In Jesus's name, amen.

As in the past, Matt met them at the base of the building and helped get her camera and tripod into the elevator. His smile tripped her heart into beating rapidly.

Millicent smiled as the elevator came to a grinding stop and she realized her stomach hadn't lurched this time. In fact she felt fine when she stepped out. She wasn't sure if Elizabeth did, though. She looked a bit pale, but she smiled as she held John's arm fast.

"John, feel free to interview whomever you want," Matt said. "I'm going to get Millicent set up."

Millicent glanced around and then surprised herself by asking, "Do you— Would you help me get a little closer? I think I'm ready to try to take a shot with my camera aimed more down to what's below."

"Are you sure?"

"No. But I'd like to try."

Their gazes met and held for several moments. "All right. But let me get your tripod and camera over there. Remember there is a rail to hold on to and I'll be right next to you."

Millicent nodded. "I'm counting on it."

Matt picked up the tripod. "Let me know when I'm close enough."

Millicent swallowed hard as Matt stopped about two feet from the edge and glanced back at her.

"This good?"

She moved to where he was standing and glanced

down and across to Ellis Island. Then she looked at the guardrail. It did appear sturdy and she trusted Matt would keep her safe. "I think I'd like to see the view from the rail now."

Matt looked at her closely and then grasped her arm and led her over to the railing.

Millicent gazed out and then down at the city. It was…exhilarating and terrifying all at the same time. "Oh, I must get photographs. Can you bring my camera closer?"

She turned too quickly and stumbled backward. Suddenly the world whirled around her. Dizzier than the first day, she lifted a hand to her head. "Oh, I—"

Matt's hold on her arm tightened and his other arm went around her, pulling her close to steady her. "Are you all right? Are you feeling faint again?"

She gave a short nod, but it wasn't the dizziness that took her breath away; it was being held in Matt's arms, her pulse racing, her heart pounding and—was it his heart or hers she felt?

Matt's heart seemed to be hammering from one side of his chest to the other. Could it be both his and Millicent's he felt? Would she run from him again as she had on Sunday after that electric current arced between them? She had to have felt it as strong as he had and she'd seemed to have been trying to avoid him ever since. He lifted her face to his and gazed into eyes the same color as the sky. "Are you feeling any better?"

"I—" she glanced around, appearing a little dazed before her gaze met his eyes again. "I think so. I just moved too fast and lost my balance for a moment. I do want to take photographs from here, if I can."

"All right. Tell me when you're ready." He didn't want to let go of her. Wanted to hold her until she stopped shaking. She might say she was all right, but he felt her trembles. "There's no hurry."

"Hey, boss!" Burl hollered from across the way. "Is everything all right? You need any help?"

The grin on the big man's face told Matt he'd probably never live this day down, standing there with Millicent in his arms in view of everyone, but he didn't much care. She felt so soft, looked at him as if he were her hero or something. "No thanks. Miss Faircloud just stumbled a bit. She's fine now."

He could have bit his tongue as Millicent moved away from him, color rushing up her face, as she seemed to realize everyone was watching them. Great. Now she'd probably try to run away from him again.

Matt moved her camera to where she was standing and stood right beside her while she went about the business of taking her photographs. The woman had spunk and he'd never been so proud, knowing she was fighting through her fears, probably through dizziness, to do this. He'd never known a woman like her and—

"I think I've taken enough from here for today," Millicent said. "And now I won't be so afraid to take them from wherever I need to. Thank you, Matt."

She might not be afraid now, but the very thought of her falling off this building had him rethinking whether she should even be up here. "Only if I'm with you or give you the go-ahead to be by yourself. Agreed?"

He saw that stubborn little chin lift as she glinted at him. But he kept his stance and stared right back into those beautiful blue eyes until she blinked and nodded.

"Agreed."

"Good." He picked up her tripod and camera and they headed in the direction of where John and Elizabeth were standing, speaking to a couple of his men.

He noticed that Elizabeth looked a little pale and wondered if she'd been afraid for Millicent, seeing her so close to the edge. "I can't believe you were so near the edge, Millicent," Elizabeth said. "I don't think I'd be able to do that."

Millicent shrugged. "It was time. And I knew Matt wouldn't let anything happen to me."

Matt's chest swelled to almost bursting at her confidence in him. He'd do everything in his power to keep her safe.

"Are you ready to go for today?" John asked.

"Yes, if you are. I can get more photographs next time."

Next time. Matt found himself looking forward to the next time, to standing beside her as she worked, being there to hold her should she turn too fast once again. And he was more than happy that he didn't have to wait until then to see her again. He only had to wait until the end of his workday—and pray she wouldn't run upstairs right after dinner as she'd done all week.

"I'll take Millicent's tripod and camera and go

down with you all. You take care of Elizabeth, John. She seems a little under the weather."

He saw the smile John and his wife exchanged and glanced at Millicent. The expression on her face seemed to reflect the way he was feeling…at least he thought it might—if only he could find the words to describe it.

Chapter Eleven

Matt hurried downstairs to the dining room the next day. He'd be working on Saturdays in the upcoming weeks because it was nearing the time of year when the weather would prevent them from working. High winds, snow, rain—not to mention freezing temperatures—would soon disturb their workweeks.

He always worried about his crew when they couldn't work. It affected his men's bank accounts more than it did his—he'd managed to put a good bit in savings, which only grew the inheritance he'd been left by his grandfather. Besides, he didn't have a family to support. He was glad for the work while the conditions remained mild. Even though he'd rather have the day off to look for buildings with Millicent.

But from the chatter at the breakfast table it seemed she wouldn't be doing that today—at least not this morning. It appeared Millicent and Julia were going to another one of those suffrage meetings. They hadn't mentioned one in a while and he'd hoped their interest had waned. Apparently he'd been wrong.

And since he was the first man at breakfast that

morning, and the way they quieted as soon as he walked to the buffet to make his plate, he sensed they didn't want him to know about it. While he wasn't happy they were still interested in the movement, he didn't like the idea of them not bringing up the subject in front of him and the other men.

He plopped a big spoon of scrambled eggs onto his plate and grabbed several pieces of bacon, some sausage links and a couple of waffles before taking his seat.

"Good morning, ladies. I have to work today. What do you all have planned?"

"We're going to run downtown to get some supplies for some projects we're doing," Millicent said.

"Oh, I thought you mentioned a meeting you were going to."

"Oh, we did," Georgia said.

Matt almost chuckled at the sigh Millicent let out. Evidently, Georgia hadn't been told the meetings were a touchy subject between the men and the woman at Heaton House.

He wouldn't make much of it with Mrs. Heaton there. She didn't want or deserve discord at her table. So he just asked, "What kind of meeting is it?"

"We were talking about the suffrage movement we're going to next week," Georgia said. "It's my first one here in the city, although I've gone to several back home and I'm looking forward to—" Georgia stopped as Julia shook her head.

Joe and Stephen entered the room and everyone greeted them, probably in hopes of changing the subject. But once they made their plates and took their seats, Mrs. Heaton brought up the subject on her own.

"The ladies are going to a woman's suffrage meeting next week, gentlemen. You are welcome to go along, I'm sure. Many men do support the movement, you know."

Her announcement left the men speechless and Matt felt kind of bad, considering they probably all knew he'd overheard them talking before he came into the room and he'd been the one to ask.

"I don't like friction at my table, as you all know. But this time, I am bringing the subject up because I don't want any of you feeling you can't speak freely. I do ask that the conversation is cordial, and there is no speaking down to one another, as if your view is the only one that is right."

"But those meetings—" Joe began.

"Forgive me for interrupting, Joe," Mrs. Heaton said, "but I must tell you I do support women getting the right to vote, which is primarily the concern of the meetings these young women go to and the topic they most want addressed."

"Yes, that's it," Millicent said. "We work for a living like you do. We feel we should have a say in how our government runs and our futures. Is that really so hard to understand?"

She was looking into Matt's eyes and seemed to be imploring him to understand. But he'd heard so much about this movement—and knew some women wanted much more. "Perhaps not the right to vote. I think I can understand your desire for it. But we've all heard many women want more rights than the voting one."

"Yes, some do," Mrs. Heaton said. "But I would suggest you all go to a meeting with the ladies at least once so you'll know what it is *they* want to work for."

"When is this meeting and what time is it?" Matt asked.

"Next Friday evening at eight o'clock," Millicent answered.

"A night meeting." He looked at Joe and Stephen. "Perhaps we should join them."

"I'll go if you two do," Stephen said.

"None of you need to go. We're quite capable—"

"Of taking care of yourselves," Matt finished for Millicent. "Of course you are. But Mrs. Heaton suggested we go and even though you'll be in a group, it is at night."

"I think I might go, too," Mrs. Heaton said. "And I would appreciate you men accompanying us. I know there's been some trouble at some of the evening meetings and I'll feel better if we have a man or two with us."

Matt could tell Millicent's smile was forced and she wasn't very happy at their landlady's suggestion, but there was little she could say about it now. And he wasn't sure what he could do to ease her discomfort. He certainly didn't want to upset Millie any further.

A quiet tension seemed to settle around the table. Someone needed to say something and he'd brought the subject up, so Matt supposed it should be him. "We'll be glad to escort you ladies there. I suppose we haven't been very fair by not going to one and seeing for ourselves what the movement is all about."

"I think that's a wonderful attitude, Matt," Julia said. "We'll be glad for you all to join us."

Matt looked at Millicent. What was she thinking?

Now she seemed not to know what to say. Her glance met his and Matt could tell she didn't necessarily like the turn of the conversation. And he felt she blamed it on him. He took one last swig of coffee and stood. "For now, I need to get to work. See you all later."

He moved back his chair and as he bent to scoot it back to the table, he whispered into Millicent's ear, "If you follow me to the door, I'll give you some money for those supplies."

"I can get them," she whispered back.

"No. I don't want you buying them. I promised to pay for supplies and I mean to keep my word."

He seemed to have taken her by surprise and he watched her expression turn from stormy to something else he couldn't name as she let him pull out her chair and stood. At least her eyes didn't seem to be shooting daggers at him as they had earlier.

As they walked into the foyer, Matt pulled some bills from his money clip and forced them into her hand. "If this doesn't take care of what you buy, let me know and I'll give the rest to you tonight."

Finally, she smiled at him and said, "Thank you."

"You're welcome. Thank you for accepting my help." He put on his jacket and turned back to her. "I'm looking forward to this evening's gathering."

Her smile grew and he smiled back, suddenly realizing he hated to leave for work with her upset with him.

"Yes, so am I," Millicent said. "It should be a lot of fun. Have a good day."

"You, too." He opened the door to air that felt brisk and quite cool, but he felt warm inside as he hurried to the trolley stop.

* * *

Julia and Georgia were on their way out of the dining room just as Millicent hurried back in to pour herself another cup of coffee to take upstairs.

"I'll be ready in about half an hour. Meet you down here?" she asked them.

"That'll be fine with me," Julia said. "What about you, Georgia?"

"Works for me. See you both back down here."

Millicent quickly poured her coffee and went back upstairs, careful not to slosh any. Matt had been kind to give her money so that she didn't have to dip into her own, proving that he was a man of his word. How was it that man could change her moods quicker than she could keep up with them?

She was sure he had no real desire to go to a suffrage meeting and yet, he was going. Hopefully, he'd find out enough truths that he wouldn't be so against them any longer. She wasn't sure being at a meeting would actually change any of the men's attitudes about them, but there was at least a glimmer of hope that they would.

Dear Mrs. Heaton. She wanted the men to understand as much as anyone and now she'd forced their hands in a most genteel way. And they no longer had to worry about the subject being brought up for her sake. But it would need to be a civil conversation and Millicent was all for that.

She took a sip of her coffee while she neatened up her hair and put her hat and a lightweight jacket on. The mornings were cooler now, but the afternoons warmed up nicely and they'd be inside most of the time, except for the trolley rides. There was no need for anything heavier.

Then she looked at her supplies to see what more they'd need and made a list. She tucked it into her purse, took the last sip of coffee and headed back downstairs.

She hurried down the hall and took her cup and saucer to the kitchen before meeting up with Julia and Georgia in the parlor.

They hurried to the trolley stop in high spirits, all three looking forward to the party that evening. As they found seats together, Georgia smiled. "I am so excited to be part of this, although I have no photos to add to the album yet, but I'll help in any way I can."

"Oh, I'm sure we can get a photo or two of you," Millicent said. "In fact, I think I took one or two when we all went on the sleigh ride when you came to visit last winter."

"Oh! That would be wonderful, Millicent."

"We'll try to find them soon as we get back."

They got off the trolley and headed toward Macy's. Millicent was sure they'd find the supplies they needed in the stationery department.

"Maybe we'll see Emily today," she said. "Although I think a lot of her work is done out of sight I can't wait to find out what they're doing with the windows this year."

"Neither can I," Julia said. "One of the highlights of the Christmas season is coming down and seeing them, especially at night. We should plan to come as a group this year."

"That'd be fun," Georgia said.

They reached Macy's and took their time getting

to the stationery department. There was always new merchandise to see each time they came.

"We should go to Siegel-Cooper if we can't find what we need, here," Julia suggested.

"Or perhaps because we haven't been there in a while. Seems kind of disloyal to Macy's, as it's been here longer, but I'm sure Georgia would like to see what Stephen's store is like, too," Millicent said.

"Oh, I would. If there's time. I know it's a bit early but I need to start thinking of what to get my family for Christmas."

"Are you going home for Christmas?"

Georgia shook her head. "Not this year."

"I'm not, either. I went home last year, but my family is going to my married sisters this year—one for Thanksgiving and one for Christmas—and I'm excited about staying here for both," Millicent said.

"What about you, Julia?"

"My family lives in Brooklyn and I'll be going there for part of those days, but I'll be at Heaton House the rest of the time."

"Has Emily said what she's going to do?"

"Oh, I don't think she has time to go anywhere for Christmas—they'll start redoing the windows as soon as it's over, I'm sure," Julia said. "But Mrs. Heaton decorates so beautifully and we all get to help. And there are outings and get-togethers during that time. I'm sure we'll all have a wonderful Christmas here."

"I wonder about the men. Will any of them be here?" Georgia asked.

"I believe they will be," Julia said.

Millicent hoped they would so they'd be there to watch Mrs. Heaton open her gift. Deep down she knew it was more than that. It'd be her first Christmas at Heaton House and she hoped she'd be able to share it with Matt…

As the women dressed for Elizabeth's party, they hurried from room to room to ask each other's opinion on what they were wearing and what to put in their hair. Once they were ready, Millicent collected her small camera and one bag of supplies, while Julia was in charge of the box of photographs. Emily carried another bag of supplies and Georgia carried several empty scrapbooks. Millicent hoped they'd be heavy with photographs when they returned.

They were all excited as they headed down to the parlor to meet the men, who took charge of their bags and boxes.

Mrs. Heaton had left earlier; she was keeping the children at Michael and Violet's since baby Marcus would go to sleep early, and Rebecca and Ben were bringing Jenny over there. Gretchen and Maida had the night off and they seemed to be almost as excited as the boarders.

They were going to have dinner with their family and then come back and enjoy relaxing in the sitting room Mrs. Heaton recently had made for them on the third floor. They loved working for her and it suddenly dawned on Millicent that she should also include photographs of the two maids in the albums.

She explained what they were going to be doing at Elizabeth and John's that evening and that she wanted them represented, too. "Would you mind if I take some photos of you two now and then when I can from time to time?"

Both women seemed taken aback for a moment and then they smiled and nodded.

"Oh, how nice of you to include us, Miss Millicent!" Gretchen said. "Of course you may take some photographs of us."

Millicent took her camera out of its bag and turned to the two sisters. "Let me get several of you all dressed up. And later, I'll try to get some candid ones."

Both women blushed and giggled a bit as Millicent instructed them to turn this way and that, and suggested they smile instead of looking so serious. But they did as she asked and she was happy with the shots she got.

As soon as she finished, Matt seemed to be right beside her and he took her camera and put it back into its bag and slung it over his shoulder. "Those are going to be a great addition to the album, ladies."

The two maids blushed even more and thanked him before hurrying into their coats and on their way.

Then Matt helped Millicent on with her jacket while the other boarders put on theirs and they all headed out the door. The air was crisp and the sky star laden and bright as they set off for Elizabeth and John's.

Joe now had charge of the box of photos and Stephen had been given the bags of album supplies to carry.

Matt took hold of Millicent's arm and leaned near her ear. "I think I got out light, just carrying your small camera bag, Millie."

Millie again. Only, for some reason, she didn't seem to mind him calling her that so much anymore.

"It's the least they could do," she whispered. "You paid for the supplies."

"Oh, that. Did you have enough money? If not—"

"I did. In fact I had several dollars left. I'll give it to you—"

"You will not. I'm sure something will come up even if it's paper and ribbon to wrap them in. But I have a feeling you'll need more supplies before you're done. If so, let me know and I'll give you more money."

"Thank you, Matt."

"I'm just glad to be contributing to it."

"Well, have no doubt you are. I'm so glad this has turned into a group project!"

"I can tell. Your eyes are shining as bright as the stars above."

His smile and the way he looked at her as he was doing now made Millicent's heart do a kind of jump and dive, and she told herself she was reading things into his expression and that the warmth she felt from it meant nothing other than they seemed to be becoming good friends. And that couldn't be a bad thing, could it?

Chapter Twelve

Millicent's pulse began to race as Matt grasped her arm a little firmer and pulled her nearer as he whispered, "It was very thoughtful of you to take photos of Gretchen and Maida."

"Thank you. I feel bad that I didn't think of including them before now. I hope they're in some of those photographs that were taken before I came to live at Heaton House."

"Surely they will be. They're part of the daily life at Heaton House and I can't imagine them not being in any of the photos. But if not, you'll make sure they are from now on."

"I'll try. But you give me too much credit."

"I don't think so. All of this was your idea after all."

His words warmed her heart and Millicent looked up at him and smiled. "I'm so looking forward to seeing Mrs. Heaton's reaction to the albums."

"She's going to love them," Matt assured her.

Millicent stumbled over a rough place in the walk and Matt quickly used both hands to steady her, sending her pulse racing faster and her heart slamming against her chest.

"Oh, that was close. I wasn't watching where I was going very well."

"It's dark out. I should have been paying attention."

"You two coming or what?" Joe called as they stood gazing at each other.

Only then did they realize the others were a half block ahead of them. "We're coming."

Millicent felt a flush of color she was glad no one could see as Matt hastened their pace so that they caught up with everyone quickly when they turned the corner. Two more turns and they were on John and Elizabeth's street. The house was lit up, as if expecting company, and they all hurried up steps to the front porch.

John opened the door wide and welcomed them in as Elizabeth joined him.

"Come in," she said from over her husband's shoulder. There seemed to be an extra sparkle in her eyes tonight. "We're so happy to welcome you all to our home. I don't think we've had everyone over since our housewarming last winter."

"Come join us in the parlor," John said. "The Roths and Heatons arrived a few minutes ago."

They all headed to the parlor, where the married couples and present boarders all greeted each other as only close friends could, and Millicent sent up a silent prayer of thanksgiving that she was living at Heaton House and counted so many as treasured companions.

Millicent glanced at Matt and found him looking at her and once again her heart fluttered deep inside. Matt was her friend; there was no doubt about that.

But her heart didn't feel as if it were taking flight when she looked at any of the other male boarders. Her pulse didn't hasten at their smiles as it did the one Matt flashed her. So what exactly did she feel toward this man that made her reaction to him so different?

"Come on into the dining room, everyone," Elizabeth said. "Please help yourself from the sideboard and then take a seat at the table. After we eat we'll clear everything off and get started on the albums."

Everyone lined up and Millicent joined in the small talk as she waited in line to fix her plate. Elizabeth had gone all out, although she wouldn't take credit, saying her aunt had sent her maid Amanda over to help. But the buffet was filled with all manner of tasty treats.

She joined the others at the table, which, with the addition of two leaves, was much longer than when she'd eaten there last. Matt took the empty seat beside her and Millicent was pleased more than she thought she should be.

Once everyone was seated, John asked them to bow while he prayed. "Dear Lord, we thank You for the friendships that have grown over the years and for new ones being made with the new Heaton House boarders. We ask you to bless this project we are all honored to be part of for Mrs. Heaton, and we thank you for the food we're about to eat. In Jesus's name, amen."

"We really are so happy you've included us in this album project, Millicent," Rebecca said from across the table. "My mother is going to love it for years to come."

"You're welcome," Millicent said. "Your participation will make the gift even more special for her. But, oh! Before we all start eating, I'd like to get a shot of you all at the table. Please excuse me while I get my camera!"

"Of course, but if you brought your Kodak, would Amanda be able to take the photo, so that you could be in the picture, too?" Elizabeth asked.

"Of course, it's very easy. I'll show her how," Millicent said.

Matt stood and placed a hand on Millicent's shoulder. "Let me get your camera. I know right where I put it."

"I—" But he was on his way to the parlor before she had a chance say anything more. Matt seemed to be getting more thoughtful of her with each passing day and Millicent wasn't sure what to make of it. All she knew was that her attraction to him was growing, too, and she must fight against it.

Matt came back with her camera bag and Elizabeth went to ask Amanda if she would mind taking their photographs. It took only a few minutes to show her how to use the camera and then she began snapping photos from both ends of the table to be sure to get everyone. Then Amanda handed the camera back to Millicent with a smile.

"Thank you, Amanda." Millicent slipped the camera back into her bag, and knowing Elizabeth wouldn't mind, she hung it over the back of her chair.

"Thank you all for waiting. I'm sure you're all starved. I won't take any more photos until we begin work on the albums. I just want to make sure Mrs. Heaton will be able to see that everyone wanted to do this for her."

They all began to eat and conversation flowed easily. Rebecca and Ben Roth were trying to get their home ready to be able to offer a room to one of the young women in need Ben worked with while teaching business at the college and the YWCA. They also wanted to provide a gathering place for those young people who were out on their own for the first time and occasionally needed encouragement. They planned on being able to open their smaller version of Heaton House after the first of the year and were looking forward to their first Christmas as a married couple.

"Normally, it might seem a bit early to be thinking so much of Christmas," Julia said. "But when you're working on a present as special as this one, it's impossible not to."

"Oh, you should hear all the talk about the holiday at Macy's," Emily said. "The planning for this year's windows began even before I started working there."

"It's the same at Siegel-Cooper," Stephen said. "We've been in planning mode for months now."

"I think I'm looking forward to Christmas more than I have in a long time," Georgia said.

"So am I," Matt said.

"Have you decided if you're going home or staying in the city yet?" Millicent asked.

"I'm staying here. I can't wait to see Mrs. Heaton when she opens this present!"

"It's going to be the best Christmas ever." Elizabeth looked down the table at her husband and gave a little nod as she smiled at him.

John cleared his throat and stood, walking around to stand behind his wife. "Elizabeth and I have an announcement to make. Some of you have noticed she's been a bit pale lately and expressed concern for her, but we want to assure you it's been for a very good reason."

Elizabeth reached up and clasped his hand on her shoulder as she smiled and looked back at everyone. "And I'm feeling much better, as you can tell."

The couple looked at each other once more and John grinned. "We're thrilled to tell you all that Elizabeth is expecting our first child in the spring!"

Everyone burst into a chorus of "Congratulations!" followed by clapping and laughter. Millicent joined in, as joy for her friends flooded her along with a stab of envy she tamped down as hard as she could. Oh, how she longed— No! She couldn't let herself start thinking of what she truly wanted. She'd already accepted her lot in life.

Matt watched as differing expressions passed over Millicent's face. She looked so wistful for a moment he wondered if she were feeling much like he did.

He'd been surprised by the depth of longing he'd felt as John looked at his wife and made their announcement. How was it he knew four men who'd found true love and seemed to have everything he wanted, but didn't believe the same would ever be in his future? He held no hope after the break with his fiancée. Although he realized now that he hadn't loved her enough to stay and make a living back home, either.

But it'd taught him a lesson about falling for the wrong kind of woman. At least he'd thought it had, but as Millicent smiled at the happy couple and then glanced at Matt, his chest tightened and he knew he'd become more drawn to her with each passing day.

If possible, she was more independent than Carla had been, yet, hard as he tried to fight it, something about Millicent drew him like a moth to a flame. He told himself he should stop spending as much time with her, but he was getting nowhere with that. In fact, he'd begun to look for opportunities to be with her.

"Thank you all," John said. "We've known for a while but wanted to wait until tonight to let everyone know. We think of you all as family and this party seemed to be the perfect time."

"And now that we've told you, we're going to get to work on Mrs. Heaton's album," Elizabeth said. "Please go back to the parlor and get all your things together while Anna and I clear the table."

"I'll stay and help," Millicent said. "It'll go faster that way."

The other ladies did the same and Matt was pretty sure they wanted to congratulate their friend without all the men watching. He followed John and the others as they headed toward the parlor but in only minutes they were called back. They gathered up the supplies and took them to the table.

As everyone took a seat once more, Millicent stayed standing. "I really can't thank you all enough. This gift is going to be so much better than I'd originally planned with you all helping. Julia has so many photographs and I know some of you brought some, too. With those and what I've taken, I think we'll have enough to fill several albums."

"I'd say so," Matt said as the photographs were

pulled out of boxes. "Are we going to be able to get this done in one night?"

"I don't think so," Millicent said. "I believe the best thing we can do right now is to put them all out—probably starting with Julia's, as many of them were taken when some of us weren't boarders. We can pass them around the table along with a sheet of paper for you to write down your memories of when the photo was taken. When we get them in the album, Emily has offered to write in your comments in her lovely handwriting. We'll do what we can tonight and maybe we can get together again."

"That shouldn't be a problem," Kathleen Patterson said. "I'd like us to start doing this more often even after the albums are full."

"Yes, so would I," Rebecca said.

"I love that idea. And I am certain with all your help, we'll be done by Christmas." Millicent clapped her hands. She loved these people!

Millicent placed a batch of photos at each end of the table and on each side. "Please choose a photo and comment if you're in it or if you have a special memory of the day it was taken, and then pass it to the person next to you. Not everyone has to comment on each photo, but it'd be great to have two or three with each one."

Matt watched as everyone picked a photo from the nearest pile. He took one as Millicent continued with her instructions.

"When the photo gets back around to the person who had it first, please wrap the paper around it and put it back in the empty box in the center of the table."

Millicent sat back down beside Matt and everyone took a photo. The one he picked was taken before he came to Heaton House and he passed it on to Millicent, who passed it on to Luke, who was on the other side of her. He chuckled when he gazed at it and began to write.

Soon others were laughing or saying "Aww" or "Oh, look! Remember this?" to the person next to them.

"Maybe I should pull out photos from those I've taken for you and me and the newer boarders," Millicent whispered to Matt. "What do you think?"

"I think you're right," he said. "Otherwise we're going to be sitting here doing nothing but passing photos to the others."

With his encouragement, Millicent stood once more. "Everyone, I wonder if you'd mind if we line up around the table with the newer boarders, starting with Matt and me, on one side of the table and then the boarders who were there before all of us on the other side? That way some of us could begin working on photos taken by me, and the first boarders can do the ones before that time. Then, if we run across photos others are in, we can pass them around to the other side. I think we might be able to get more done if we do."

"That's a great idea, Millicent," John said. "Come on, everyone, let's change places. Older boarders come sit on this side, newer on the other side."

After a few moments everyone got settled in their new places and the photos were passed around once more. Millicent leaned over and whispered to Matt, "I love hearing their comments as they look at the pictures. I can't wait to read some of the notes they're writing."

"Neither can I," Matt said, smiling as they watched Luke and Kathleen put their heads together over a photo and then pass it on to Violet.

"What if one of us doesn't particularly like the shot of us and doesn't really want it in the album?" Emily asked.

Everyone chuckled. "I wondered the very same thing," Julia said. "Some of the photos I took weren't the best."

"Just put them to the side—maybe write *don't use* on the back and we'll gather them up after we're through," Millicent said.

"Oh, thank you," Emily said. She sounded so relieved, one couldn't help but laugh.

"You're welcome. None of us want bad photos of us for all to see. I'm sure some of my shots weren't that great, either," Millicent said. Then she pushed her chair back again, stood and grabbed her camera. "But I must get some photographs of us working on this. Please continue what you're doing and I'll walk around and take some shots."

Everyone did as she asked but would look up if she asked them to smile for her. She was like a little whirlwind, going around and snapping shots. After making her way around the table, she took her seat once more, looking quite happy with herself. She truly seemed to love what she was doing and Matt had no doubt the photographs would be great.

Then Julia excused herself and came back to the table with her own camera. "My pictures won't be as good as yours, but we need a few with you in them, Millicent. So I'll take them and you can develop them."

"Thank you, Julia. I'll be happy to."

"That's a great idea, Julia," Matt said. "I'm glad you thought of it. Since Millicent took so many of these later ones, she isn't in them."

"Well, I've taken a few with her in them," Julia said, stopping by her seat to pull a few photos from her pile. She handed them over to Matt.

Millicent looked at them with him. Matt wondered if she liked the one of them skating together last winter as much as he did. It was the day had Rebecca sprained her ankle and what they all thought of as the beginning of her and Ben's romance.

But this photo showed him and Millicent smiling at each other as they skated. Matt's chest tightened as he saw the expression on both their faces. There was something…

"I really like this photo of us." Matt leaned near her and whispered as they looked at the photo. "That was a fun day—at least until Rebecca took her fall."

"Yes, it was." Millicent met his gaze and smiled.

Matt picked up the next photo. "Oh, look at this one."

Millicent bent her head toward him and then Matt heard the click of a camera and looked up to see a grin on Julia's face.

"That was a great shot. I think you'll both like it," Julia said before heading to the end of the table and snapping another of the whole group.

"Will you make an extra copy of the one Julia took of us?" Matt asked.

"You want one for yourself?" she asked as she looked into his eyes.

"Yes. I do. If it's not too much trouble."

"It's no trouble at all."

Matt felt as surprised as Millicent looked at his request. The words had just popped out of his mouth but he didn't want to take them back. He wanted a photo of them together. But why? And how would having a photo of the two of them help him distance himself from her? And did he even want to do that now?

He picked up another photograph. This one Julia had taken when they'd all gone to Central Park one day. Again, it was of him and Millicent, and it appeared they were sparring a bit. They were grinning at each other, but Millicent's eyebrow was raised as if challenging something he'd said. He'd seen that expression on her quite often in the past year and if truth be told, he'd enjoyed bringing it about.

"I like this one, too," he said as he showed it to Millicent.

"Looks like we were at it again, doesn't it?"

"That's what I like about this one. You look quite feisty."

"Oh, you!"

Elizabeth stood and asked, "Is everyone ready for a cup of tea or hot chocolate? I asked Anna to prepare some for us. She'll put everything on the sideboard and you can help yourselves and bring it to the table. Just make sure not to spill anything on these wonderful photographs."

Matt held back as others went to get some refreshment and then slipped the photo he'd been so intrigued with into his shirt pocket. Surely no one would miss this one. After all, there were a few set to the side that someone didn't want included. He wouldn't mind this one being used, but he'd rather keep it for himself. He patted his pocket and went to get a cup of hot chocolate.

Rebecca and Ben, along with Michael and Violet, were the first to leave so that they could relieve their mother of her babysitting duties.

"We're going to pick up Jenny and Mama and we'll drop her off at Heaton House," Rebecca said. "When should we meet again?"

"Luke and I will gladly have it at our home next time," Kathleen said. "Check your calendars and I'll telephone you all and try to come up with a date that will be good for us all."

"If we need another album party before Christmas, Ben and I can host it," Rebecca said.

They'd made good headway for the first album but there were many more photos to go through. "That sounds like a good plan. I do hope it's not too much trouble for all of you."

"It's not a problem at all, Millicent," Elizabeth said. "This has been so much fun and brought back a lot of good memories."

"Oh, yes, it did," Violet added. She glanced at her husband and smiled. "Some were pictures of Michael and I when we were beginning to fall in love."

Once again Millicent felt an ache deep inside. What was wrong with her lately? She'd planned her future and it didn't include marriage or a family. So why did she seem to long for those very things right now?

She began gathering their supplies as the three couples put on their wraps and left. The boarders helped pack things back up and John and Elizabeth walked them to the door. Millicent gave her friend a hug. "Thank you so much, Elizabeth. And I am thrilled about your news. I hope this didn't tire you out too much."

Elizabeth shook her head. "It didn't. I'm feeling wonderful now."

Matt helped Millicent on with her wrap and after they all said their goodbyes, the boarders headed out into the chilly night.

It wasn't all that late and they decided to walk back to Heaton House. Matt fell into step beside Millicent, her camera bag slung over his arm, and he held her arm lightly as they followed the others.

"Everyone had such a good time. This whole idea has been great for us, giving us a reason to get together more often and even find out a bit more about each other than we knew before."

"In what way?" Millicent asked.

"Well, hearing the older boarders reminisce about their time at Heaton house and special outings. Not to mention the photos that reminded them of falling in love."

"Yes, that was special, wasn't it? Hearing them comment on their romances was quite…"

"Romantic?"

She giggled and nodded at the finish Matt gave her thought and when her gaze met his, there was a light in his eyes that sent her pulse racing.

Matt cleared his throat. "I wonder who the next couple will be to fall in love at Heaton House."

Millicent's heart seemed to do a little flip as she

looked up to see his gaze on her once more. If only…
No! She couldn't start thinking of what-ifs.

"I don't know. Julia shows no sign of being attracted to anyone. But maybe Emily and Joe or Stephen? Or Georgia and one of them?"

Matt gave a little shrug. "Could be any of them, I suppose."

"Are you two telling secrets back there or what?" Joe asked from up ahead. "You keep falling farther and farther back."

"We're coming," Matt called back as he picked up his pace and gave Millicent no choice but to keep up with him.

They quickly caught up with the others as they rounded the next corner. They could see the lights of Heaton House down the street.

"I hope Mrs. Heaton isn't back yet. We don't want her to wonder what's in these bags!" Millicent said.

"Oh, right!" They all hurried the rest of the way, hoping they beat Mrs. Heaton back.

Millicent and Julia quickly took off their outer wraps and Matt and Joe hung them up while the women rushed upstairs with the photographs and supplies. Millicent breathed a sigh of relief when they came back down and entered the parlor, just as Mrs. Heaton came out of the kitchen.

She met them in the foyer. "Rebecca and Ben just dropped me off. She said you'd all had such a good time reminiscing about old times and new ones."

"Oh, we did," Millicent said. Mrs. Heaton must have arrived home about the time they did, but thankfully, she seemed to have no clue of what they were up to.

"She also said she thought you might get together

more often," Mrs. Heaton said. "Happy as they all are in their married state, I do believe they miss everyone. I assured her and Michael I'll gladly do babysitting duty anytime."

Her eyes were shining so, Millicent was certain she was telling the truth and she was very happy that Rebecca had paved the way for more album parties. But they needed to find a way to get the supplies out of the house and back in without Mrs. Heaton knowing what they were doing.

Chapter Thirteen

Millicent wanted to go look at possible places for her shop on Sunday afternoon but it was very breezy, and instead, she stayed in and developed the photographs she and Julia had taken. And Julia was right. Millicent loved the photo she'd taken of her and Matt. She gazed at it again. They both appeared happy. What was the photograph they'd been studying so intently when she took it?

Then she remembered. Matt had just pulled it out of the pile. It was one taken when they went skating at Central Park. They'd looked happy that day. But then he'd pulled out another one that had been snapped at the park and it appeared they'd been sparring as they still did, though mostly during those first few months after they'd moved in. Matt wore a teasing expression and grin on his face and from the height of her eyebrow, he'd said something she didn't like and she'd responded in kind with whatever it was he'd said.

That man. What was it about Matt that could both irritate her one moment and turn her heart to mush the next? And make her pulse gallop and her heart hammer all at the same time?

Millicent sighed and glanced at the photo once more before shaking her head and taking the others down from where she'd hung them to dry. She couldn't let herself think about any of that now. It would only serve to feed her longing for things to be different.

But she hadn't changed. She was still independent, wanted the vote and to set up her own shop. All things men did not want in a wife. And she was pretty sure that Matt was no different.

She gathered her photos together and took them down to her room, where later she'd write comments on the party and what everyone was doing.

Right now, it was teatime and she hurried down to join Mrs. Heaton and the others, who were sure to be in the parlor enjoying a cup.

They heard the front door open and Matt and Joe peeked into the parlor. "Ah, teatime. Any chance there's enough left for us?"

"There's always enough. But I'll have Gretchen bring in a fresh pot, unless you men would rather have coffee?"

"Well, now you mention it, I wouldn't mind having a cup of coffee," Matt said.

"Neither would I," Joe added. Mrs. Heaton headed for the kitchen and the men joined them in the parlor.

"Is it still breezy out?" Millicent asked.

"Yes. Not too bad at the moment, but the papers have said we might be in for an Atlantic storm sometime in the week," Matt said. "I hope not. It's not fun when it's windy on the floor we're working on.

There's nothing to block it and if it gets too bad we'll probably be ordered to leave work."

Millicent's heart seemed to stop for a moment at Matt's words of being ordered to leave. She'd never thought how windy it could get on the top of a skyscraper. A shiver coursed down her spine at the thought of what that might mean for the men working near the edge. But Matt grinned at her as he took a seat and her heartbeat returned to normal.

"Will you have to work tomorrow?" she asked.

"If the wind gets worse, probably not. But they'll let us know tonight or in the morning."

"Do those inside work when the winds are bad?"

"Depends. If the windows are in place, the inside work can usually continue. And if there's a lot to do, those of us on top just work on the lower floors, helping where we're needed, but if there's not that much to do, we don't work."

"And you don't get paid if you don't go in, right?" Joe asked.

"Right. But that's why we work when we can on Saturdays. This time of year especially, one never knows what the weather will bring."

Millicent felt that shiver of apprehension again. She hoped that storm out in the Atlantic stayed there.

The next week the papers were full of dire predictions of a severe storm hitting the East Coast and everyone seemed on edge. Matt worked each day but the consensus seemed to be that the winds would pick up over the weekend and shipping companies were warned to keep their ships in harbor.

"It's not too bad up top," Matt said on Thursday.

"But the boss said to tell you and John and Elizabeth not to come tomorrow. Hopefully, things will be better next week."

"If it's bad enough that we can't go, will you have to work tomorrow?"

"I won't know until tomorrow," Matt said. "But the boss is just being cautious."

Millicent only nodded, while she prayed Matt wouldn't have to work the next day.

But as it was only breezy the next morning, Matt did work and the group gathered to go to the suffrage meeting as planned on Friday evening. Although Matt wasn't really looking forward to it, he'd decided it might be a good distraction from all the talk about the weather.

Mrs. Heaton had called for an omnibus to take them all to the meeting and he was a bit surprised to find that Kathleen and Luke, along with Elizabeth and John, were accompanying them, too.

"I didn't know you were interested in this movement, Luke," Joe said.

"I'm going mostly because my wife is. She wants the vote and I certainly can't say I don't think she should have it. Kathleen is one of the smartest women I know."

"And I suppose you're covering it for the paper, John?" Matt asked.

"Well, I might write an article about it," John said. "But no, I'm going because my wife wants to go. Her aunt Bea, who is now her stepmother, and her father will be there, but I don't want her going without me. These meetings can get heated at times and this one is at night. But the big question is, why are you men going?"

"Mrs. Heaton convinced us that it might be something we should know more about before we get all steamed up about it and, well, she made sense. Besides, with it being at night, we didn't want the ladies out by themselves for the same reason you're with your wife. It could be too dangerous," Matt said.

They were let off at the home of a Mr. and Mrs. Alfred White. It was an affluent part of the city and Matt hurried to help Mrs. Heaton and then Millicent down from the omnibus. The architecture of the home told him it'd been built by the best craftsmen around, and he couldn't wait to see the inside. They were all greeted by the butler and then directed to a ballroom. The woodwork and inside finishes were exquisite and Matt knew right away that the Whites must be quite wealthy.

As they entered the huge room filled with chairs, Matt was quite surprised by the turnout and so, apparently, were the other men. "My goodness, this is where wealthy and poor come together, it seems."

"Yes, it does." John turned to his wife, who was pulling at his jacket sleeve.

"There is Aunt Bea and Papa, over there." She pointed to the side of the room and waved. "They said they would save seats for us all."

The group hurried over to where Elizabeth's family had indeed saved them seats and as everyone settled down, a woman came to a built-up stage of sorts and began to speak.

"My husband and I welcome you to our home. I'm so pleased at the turnout tonight. I want to introduce you all to Mrs. Rachel Foster Avery, who will be speaking to us tonight about working to get women the vote."

A nicely dressed woman stepped up onto the platform and turned to Mrs. White. "Thank you and your husband for opening your home for this event and for your support in our endeavor, Mrs. White."

Then she turned to the audience and smiled. "And thank you all for being here. It is such an encouragement to us working to get the vote for women. Many of you are new to these meetings and many of you have been coming to them for quite a while now, not giving up, bringing others, getting the word out that we must never quit in our goal of attaining a woman's right to vote!"

Matt sat up a bit straighter and sighed. He hoped this woman didn't begin a tirade about how men kept women under their thumbs and it was time to fight.

"For those of you who have daughters, wives, mothers and sisters who've had no voice in what our government does, the time to help them is now," Mrs. Avery said imploringly. "We don't want to take the vote away from men, but we do want it for ourselves. Is that so terribly wrong? I don't think so and I don't think you do, either."

Matt felt as if she were speaking directly to him as he thought about his mother and his sisters. He glanced at Millicent, who seemed to be hanging on to every word, as were the other women from Heaton House. Would it really be so bad if they had a say in how they were governed? What if they had the vote and men didn't?

Whoa! Where did that come from? He'd never really given much thought to it.

"For you men out there. What if the women you love and care about have no one to take their interests to heart, or lost the man who did?"

She had his complete attention now. He'd never, ever thought about things in that way. By the time the meeting ended, Matt was overwhelmed with all that he'd never considered. And a bit ashamed that he hadn't.

He waited with Joe and Stephen while the women of Heaton House hurried to meet the woman who'd just given the men of Heaton House much to think about.

When they arrived back at the boardinghouse after dropping off the married couples, Mrs. Heaton asked for hot chocolate to be brought in, and as they waited for it, Matt actually apologized for being so judgmental without ever going to a meeting.

"I'm still not sure how I feel about all this. I've heard many of these groups want to fight for other rights I'm not in favor of at all, but I heard nothing about that tonight."

"You're right, Matt. There are other groups wanting rights for all manner of things," Millicent said. "But the most important one in our opinion is getting the right to vote."

"Well, this meeting certainly gave us much to think about," Joe said.

"Then it was worth your time, wasn't it?" Mrs. Heaton asked.

"I believe so," Matt conceded.

Their landlady was one smart woman and Millicent appreciated her more every day.

"I'm just glad I don't have to keep quiet about going to the meetings any longer," Emily said, making everyone chuckle.

"So are we all," Julia said.

"We are sorry about that, aren't we?" Matt turned to Joe and Stephen.

"Yes. We didn't realize we were being so hard on you all. But we'll be better from now on."

"That's all we want—for you to have an open mind when we bring these things up. That's not too much to ask, is it?" Millicent asked.

"No, it's not. And we do want to know when you go to the meetings. Sometimes there is trouble at them and it wouldn't hurt for us to be with you, if that ever happens," Matt said. "Will you agree to tell us?"

Millicent looked him in the eye. "I will."

He grinned. "Thank you. That's all I ask."

She smiled back at him. It truly was a relief not to have to keep the fact that they attended the meetings secret any longer.

Chapter Fourteen

The weekend was quite enjoyable in spite of storm warnings for the area. Matt did work on Saturday and reported that the winds seemed to be picking up and ships were staying put. But they all stayed in that evening and enjoyed a good meal after Mrs. Heaton asked Matt to say the blessing.

He prayed for those at sea to get to shore before the storms hit and for there not to be too much damage. After dinner they retired to the parlor and Julia played the piano while they sang along. At least it helped drown out the gusts of wind that hit the windows from time to time.

On Sunday, the wind forced them to take the trolley the few blocks instead of walking to church. There, the minister prayed about the weather and asked the Lord to keep everyone safe.

It was a bit calmer out when they left church and they decided to walk, but by the time they got back to Heaton House for Sunday dinner, it'd picked up again. Still, it was hard to believe there was a huge storm only a day or so away.

Monday morning the winds were no worse than the day before and Millicent began to hope that the forecasters had been wrong all along. She and Georgia spent most of the day working on Mrs. Heaton's album and after lunch they made a quick trip to Macy's for more supplies. But the winds had picked up by the time they got back to Heaton House and they were both glad they'd made it in time for tea.

"Oh, I'm glad you girls are back. It's getting bad out there," Mrs. Heaton said. "Michael telephoned a short time ago and said he'd heard we were in for several days of really bad weather."

"Is there anything we should be doing?" Georgia asked.

"If it gets too bad, we'll close the outside shutters, but I think we're fine tucked in here in Gramercy Park. Those living right on the coast might have some problems, though. I think we should pray and trust the Lord to get us all through."

Millicent sent up a silent prayer that Matt would be home soon and that he and his men were safe as Mrs. Heaton poured their tea. The women tried to ignore the gusts that rattled the windowpanes and pounded against the door.

Suddenly, the door flew open and they ran out into the foyer to find Matt pushing it shut. When he turned around, it was obvious that something had happened. He was pale and looked almost dazed.

"Matt, you look— Is something wrong?" Mrs. Heaton asked.

"I'm afraid there is. They told us to leave early but to secure things before we left. The winds had gotten worse and we were trying to tie everything down best we could when—" Matt shook his head, closed his eyes and rubbed his forehead.

"One of my men…" He cleared his throat before continuing in a husky tone, "Tom O'Riley lost his balance and fell… He died."

Millicent hurried over to him and placed a hand on his arm. "Oh, Matt, I'm so very sorry."

Mrs. Heaton and Georgia were right behind her, murmuring their condolences, as well.

"But we're thankful you got off safely," Mrs. Heaton said. "I'll get some coffee for you."

She was already down the hall when Matt said, "Thank you. I'll just hang up my jacket and—"

He seemed very shaken and Millicent's heart twisted in pain for how he must feel. "Here, let me help you off with your jacket. I'm so very sorry about Tom. He seemed a very nice man."

As Matt just stood in the entry, Georgia took his coat from Millicent and hung it up, while Millicent put her hand through his arm. "Come on into the parlor. Mrs. Heaton will be back with the coffee in a few minutes."

Matt only nodded as she led him into the parlor. How devastated he must feel that one of his men had died in such a way.

He sat down on the sofa and Millicent took a seat beside him. She wasn't sure if he wanted to talk about it or not. All she knew was that she wanted to be there for him.

Mrs. Heaton came in just then and poured him a cup of coffee while Gretchen brought in a pot of tea and freshened up the ladies' cups.

"I'm sorry to hear about your coworker, Mr. Matt."

"Thank you, Gretchen."

The maid quickly left them and quiet fell on the parlor as Matt took a sip from his cup.

Then he finally spoke. "He was one of my best men. I rarely had to tell him what to do—he just knew."

"Did he have a family? Was he single?" Mrs. Heaton asked.

"He was married and had two small children. He spoke of them often. I know the boss was going to let them know, and we'll be taking up a collection for them, but I need to visit his family. In fact that is what I should be doing now!"

He jumped up and Millicent stood, too. "Would you like me to go with you?"

"I— Would you mind? I'm not sure—"

"I don't mind at all," Millicent said. She couldn't let him go alone. "I need to go upstairs and gather up some things, but I'll be right back down."

"Thank you, Millicent."

She rushed to her room and quickly went through the photos she'd taken of Matt's men. She ruffled through them until she found the two she wanted and tucked them into her purse. Then she hurried back down.

Matt had evidently gone downstairs and changed because he was coming up as she reached the first floor.

"Are you sure you want to do this?" he asked.

"I don't want you to have to go alone."

His gaze met hers for a moment. "Thank you. I don't want to go alone."

Mrs. Heaton came out of the kitchen just then. "I arranged for a hack to pick you two up. It's far too windy to be going by foot or standing at the trolley stop waiting for it to arrive."

"Thank you," Matt said. He put his jacket back on and turned to Millicent.

"I brought some photographs I'd taken and I'd like to give them to Mrs. O'Riley, if you think she might want them," she said. "Or I can give them to her later if you think that would be best?"

"Bring them and we'll see how things go. It might be better to wait. I just don't know. But you'll have them just in case."

This was a side of Matt she'd never seen—one who seemed unsure and needed someone to lean on, if only for now. Once again Millicent slipped her hand through his arm as he opened the door and they went out to the hack. She'd never seen him like this and all she wanted to do was help. But how?

Matt gave the driver the address to take them to and helped Millicent into the hack, thankful that she'd offered to go with him. This wasn't something he wanted to do. In fact, if he had his way, he would have run down to his room and locked himself in for the rest of the day and night.

But he was a man and that kind of action was something only a boy would do. Still, he'd never dreaded anything more than having to face a wife and kids he'd heard so much about in their time of grief. But he had to do it. He still couldn't get the vision of Tom disappearing over the side of the building out of his head. His heart had seemed to stop beating even as his feet had begun to run to the elevator with the other men.

The ride down to the ground floor had seemed to take forever, and when the door opened, they'd hurried out to find their coworker and friend covered with a tarp and heard the bells of the ambulance as it made its way toward them.

Matt's first instinct had been to see how bad it was, but one of the men who worked on the lower floors, and had evidently covered Joe, grasped his arm and shook his head. "You don't want to see. If it's any comfort to you at all, he died on impact."

It'd been no comfort and Matt knew it was only by sheer will and prayer that he hadn't lost his lunch right then and there.

The ambulance had arrived and taken Joe away, and the owner of the Park Row Building gathered everyone together inside. Matt couldn't remember all of what he'd said before he sent them home, only that he looked as shaken as the rest of them.

I need to go back up and make sure it's all secure, Matt had said.

I'll go with you, his supervisor had replied and together they, along with the other men who normally worked on the top floors, had gone up and made sure nothing would be flying off to hurt anyone below. Then they took the elevator down and he'd taken a trolley to Heaton House.

Millicent's hand squeezed his arm, bringing him back to the present. "Matt, I think we're here."

Only then did he realize the hack had stopped in front of a modest house in an older neighborhood. He helped Millicent out and started to pay the driver, but the man shook his head. "No, sir. Mrs. Heaton put it on her account."

Matt nodded and felt the sting of tears behind his eyes at the kindness he'd been shown by the women at Heaton House, including the woman beside him, who clutched his arm as he turned to her.

They made their way up the walk and Millicent was the one who knocked on the door.

Matt had only seen Tom's wife once. She'd been a pretty woman, happy and glowing as she'd looked up at her husband that day. One could tell she loved him and was very proud of him. But the only word that came to mind now as she opened the door to them today was…devastated.

"Oh… Mr. Sterling, how kind of you to come. I—Please come in."

Matt and Millicent stepped into her home, small but clean and well cared for. It was full of family and friends and for that Matt was extremely thankful as he took her hands in his.

"Mrs. O'Riley, there are no words to tell you how very sorry I am about your loss. It happened so fast, there was no time for any of us to get to him in time and I—"

"It's not your fault, Mr. Sterling. It was a horrible accident. But Tom died doing what he loved and I… I've been told that he died instantly. I am glad he didn't suffer long." She seemed to stifle a sob and Matt squeezed her hands once more. He felt like an interloper and didn't know what to say next.

"Mrs. O'Riley. I'm Millicent Faircloud and I've been taking photographs of the building of Park Row. I…I took a few of your husband and I wondered if you might want them."

Tom's wife didn't hesitate for a moment. "Oh, yes! Please."

Millicent took the photos out of her pocketbook and handed them to Tom's widow.

She looked at the first one and then the others, smiling as tears flowed down her cheeks. "This is *my* Joe. Smiling, laughing, the way I knew him. I don't have any photographs like these. Thank you so very much, Miss Faircloud."

"I am so very sorry for your loss."

"Thank you both for coming. And for bringing these. It means more to me than I can say," Mrs. O'Riley said. She wiped at her tears and smiled once more as she held the photographs close to her heart.

Only then did the tightness in Matt's chest begin to break up. *Dear Lord, thank You for Millicent.* Why was he only now realizing that while Millicent might be more independent minded than any woman he'd ever known, she was also one of the kindest and most humble women he'd ever met.

"You're more than welcome. Please know that you and your family are in our hearts and prayers," Millicent said and then quickly gave the woman a hug before they left.

It was nearly dark out and Matt was glad the hack had waited for them—probably at Mrs. Heaton's request—because he hadn't thought of it. He helped Millicent in and then took his seat beside her. They both released a big breath at the same time and only then did Matt realize it must have been as difficult for Millicent as it had been for him.

As the driver made his way through end-of-day traffic and the wind gusts that shook the vehicle, Matt turned to the woman by his side. "I can't thank you enough for coming with me. And for speaking when I didn't know what to say next, Millie."

"I'm glad I came with you. I didn't want you to have to come alone and it's never easy to know what to say at times like this, Matt."

"And the photographs. Your instinct to bring them was perfect. I think somehow those comforted her in a way I don't think I could have."

"I'm so glad I caught some images of her husband that somehow seemed to bring her comfort."

Matt looked at Millicent as they passed by a street lamp and her eyes looked watery, while his stung as he thought about his friend and coworker's family and the loss they'd suffered.

When Millicent slipped her hand through his arm, Matt had a feeling she knew he was having a hard time keeping his emotions in check. He looked down at her and she smiled at him. Then, suddenly, those emotions moved him to cup her chin in his hand and tip her face up. He murmured, "Thank you for being here for me, Millie."

And then he did what he'd wanted to for weeks—what he couldn't keep from doing now. He lowered his head and simply kissed her. Lightly and for only a few brief moments, but long enough to know her lips were sweeter than he'd ever imagined.

Millicent wasn't sure what to do or say as Matt's lips left hers and he raised his head. First, the tone in his voice as he thanked her and called her Millie had made her realize that not only did it not bother her for him to shorten her name any longer—it made her feel

special when he did. And then he'd kissed her. Softly
and long enough to take her breath away—something
she was having a hard time getting back. And why
had he kissed her?

But as she got her breathing under control, she
told herself that he'd thanked her just before his lips
found hers, and she could only assume that was all
the kiss meant, a thank-you for being there for him.
There was no need to make too much of it, although
her pulse raced and her heart hammered deep inside.
And yet, he shouldn't have kissed her at all! But he
wasn't himself today. He'd just witnessed a horrific
accident and she had a feeling he was still in shock
because of it.

"I—probably shouldn't have done that, Millicent.
But I—"

Oh! She didn't want him to say he was sorry!
"Matt, I understand. You've been through a lot today
and I'm glad I could be of some help. We'll forget this
ever happened and go on from here."

"I don't—" The hack jerked as the driver pulled
up and stopped at Heaton House, leaving Millicent
to wonder what he'd been going to say. But as Matt
tipped the driver and helped her out, she thought it
might be best if she didn't know.

True to her word, Mrs. Heaton had dinner waiting
for them when they arrived back at Heaton House.
The other boarders had been told what happened and
as they expressed their sorrow about it all, Matt was
relieved that he didn't have to tell everything all over
again. All he wanted was to block out thoughts of seeing his friend go off the side of that building.

He forced the memory out of his mind as everyone filed into the dining room, and he pulled out Millicent's chair for her and took his own seat beside her. She'd requested they forget the kiss he'd given her and go on from there. But how did one forget something so sweet? Or the fact that for a brief moment he'd felt the pressure of her lips as she kissed him back. Or had he imagined that she'd responded? No. Surely not. It wasn't as if he'd never kissed a woman before. He knew what a response felt like, even if it had been light as a feather.

"Joe, would you say the blessing, please?" Mrs. Heaton asked.

"Of course. Please bow with me." He waited a brief minute before continuing, "Dear Lord, we thank You for our many blessings and for this day, but we are sorrowful tonight for the O'Riley family and their loss. Please give them the comfort only You can. Please be with Matt as he deals with losing his friend and coworker, and please show us how to help. And Lord, please be with those who are in the path of the storms that grow ever closer. Please keep them safe and we pray the damage is minimal. Thank you for this food and for the close friendship we all share around this table. In Jesus's name, we pray. Amen."

"Amen." Matt added his to everyone else's and hoped he could get through the meal. All he really wanted to do was go to his room and try to get a grip on all that had happened that day, but everyone had gone out of their way to make him feel better and the least he could do was stay through the meal Mrs. Heaton had put off until he and Millicent got back.

But Mrs. Heaton was a very intuitive woman, and

she swiftly began a new conversation as Maida and Gretchen began to serve one of his favorite meals of roast beef with rich gravy, potatoes, green beans and rolls. It'd always been a comfort meal to him and the fact that she seemed to know touched his heart.

"I'm so looking forward for this weather to move out so we can get back to our normal autumn weather. Thanksgiving will be here before we know it. If there are any special dishes any of you might like, please let me know."

The thought of spending the holidays here with these people—especially Millicent, who'd been there for him so solidly that day—gave Matt something to think about and look forward to in the coming days.

By the end of the meal, Matt felt somewhat better, although when he thought of Mrs. O'Riley and her children, his heart ached for them and he wasn't sure how he felt about going back to work. But as a gust of wind hit the window in the dining room, he had a feeling it wouldn't be tomorrow. Still, it didn't matter when it would be. He'd still have to deal with the loss of Tom and working in the very place where he lost his balance and fell.

Matt swallowed around a knot in his throat as he glanced at Millicent. Would she ever go back up? He certainly couldn't blame her if she didn't. And he wasn't sure he even wanted her to. His heart twisted at the thought of something happening to her up there. Maybe, after this, his boss would put an end to them coming up on top. There were still many floors to go and Matt had a feeling Millicent would be there for each floor, even if she was afraid after what happened today. She had grit, that woman did. And…she had the softest, sweetest lips he'd ever kissed.

He forced his gaze off those lips and watched a warm pink color flood her cheeks as his gaze captured hers. Could she be remembering, too?

Chapter Fifteen

The weather was some of the worst anyone at Heaton House could remember having that time of year in a very long time. But thankfully, it proved to be better than they all first feared. There seemed to be a collective sigh as the winds finally died down and weather seemed to revert to their normal autumn.

Matt and his men had attended O'Riley's funeral together and Millicent was relieved to know he could soon start healing from that loss. There was still sadness in his eyes that tugged at her heart and all she wanted was to see them sparkle with orneriness once again.

He was back at work by the end of the week and Millicent was almost relieved when John telephoned and let her know that they were asked to put off going back until further notice.

Yet she might as well be at the Park Row, for she couldn't get Matt out of her mind, and she prayed off and on all day that the Lord would watch over him and bring him home safely. She couldn't imagine how difficult it must be for Matt and his men to go back to work as if nothing had happened.

She began to watch for him to come home an hour before he usually did, one minute worrying about him, the next telling herself to quit thinking of him. For when he was in her thoughts for more than a few minutes, they inevitably strayed to the kiss she'd suggested they forget ever happened.

Something she hadn't been able to do—something she'd relived all day and night since it'd happened. How had she possibly believed she could forget the sweet gentleness of Matt's lips and put the kiss behind them?

Every time she looked at him it was all she could do to keep her gaze from landing on his lips. They'd been soft but firm on hers, sending an electric shock straight to her heart.

No! She had to quit doing this. Matt had only been thanking her for going with him, for being there to support him that day. It meant nothing more to him than that and she had to accept it.

After all, he hadn't brought it up again and if it'd meant more to him, surely he would have, wouldn't he?

She looked at the clock at the same time the front door opened and she hurried into the foyer to find him taking off his coat. Relief washed over her in waves as he hung it up.

He turned and smiled at her just then. "I made it. Now you can quit worrying."

"How did you know?" There she went, giving away her feelings.

"From the look on your face—and I just had a feeling you would be."

When had he become able to read her mind? But she wasn't going to deny it. "I think it's a natural reaction after everything that happened to your co-worker, don't you?"

"I do." Matt walked over to her and looked deep into her eyes. "I appreciate you being concerned. To tell the truth, we all dreaded going back up there, but we did it and hard as it was, hopefully it'll get easier from here on out."

"I wish you didn't…" Millicent clamped her mouth shut to keep from saying more.

"I know. You wish I didn't work up so high. But it's my job, Millie. I can't just quit when it gets difficult. You don't quit going to places you don't want to go in order to get the photos you know you need to take, do you?"

"Why, no, but my job isn't as dangerous as yours."

"No? You take pictures from the top of the building. You even took some from near the edge last time you were up there."

"Well, those may be the last I take from that position."

"Are you going back up when the boss gives the go-ahead?"

"I don't know. I was glad that he told John we shouldn't go up this week."

"So was I. The thought of something happening to—"

The door burst open once more, bringing in Joe and Julia, Stephen and Emily. Their chatter effectively put an end to whatever it was Matt had been about to say. And perhaps it was for the best. Millicent's feelings for him in the past few weeks had undergone a change she wasn't sure she understood and she wasn't ready to delve too deeply into them. Not now and maybe not ever.

She greeted the others just as Matt did. He'd made it to the top of the Park Row and back down and home again. The Lord had answered her prayers and she'd be thankful for that.

Matt didn't know whether to be relieved or frustrated that the boarders had interrupted his and Millie's conversation. And as he glanced over at her, he couldn't tell how she felt about it, either. His insides had been topsy-turvy ever since he'd kissed her. But at the same time, thinking about that kiss had gotten him through the rest of the week, kept him from thinking too much about seeing his friend fall. And he welcomed the distraction from the sorrow that washed over him every time he remembered about that day.

Yet, contemplating about that kiss brought with it a whole other set of problems. Millicent had suggested they forget it but he hadn't been able to stop thinking about it. Was she having any better success of putting it out of her mind than he was?

Something told him she wasn't, but was that only because it was what he wanted to think? After all, he didn't believe that most men would want a woman to forget their kiss—no matter how short and sweet it was.

He hurried down to freshen up for dinner. All thinking about that kiss seemed to do was make him want to repeat it!

* * *

As the next few weeks passed with Matt coming home safely each day, Millicent kept telling herself that what happened to Mr. O'Riley had been a horrible accident, and those didn't happen that often, did they? Surely not, or no one, not even Matt, would want to do that kind of work.

Still, she found herself praying for his safety off and on every day. She had to quit dwelling on what might happen and remember he was a professional who'd been working at what he did for a long time without ever being hurt. When she wasn't worrying about Matt, she was thinking about how her feelings had changed toward him.

While their relationship seemed much the same as usual, Millicent knew it wasn't. She could no longer deny that the attraction she felt for him was real. Thinking of Matt as merely a friend was impossible now. And that was not good.

Especially as she had no idea how he really felt and as they'd never talked about that kiss—if she brought it up after insisting they forget it, he would know that…well, he might be able to tell that she didn't want to forget it!

Oh, dear Lord, please help me with this. I feel so mixed-up and I don't know what to do. Please keep my feelings from growing for Matt. I—

The front door opened and she jumped before hurrying into the foyer to find Matt. He turned to smile at her, but her heart twisted at seeing the sorrow still in his eyes. She knew he was having a hard time with all that had happened, but he tried not to let it show.

She wondered if he ever did that with his feelings about other…things.

"How was your day?" she asked as he took off his jacket and hung it up.

"Not bad. Has Elizabeth or John telephoned you?"

Millicent shook her head. "No. Should they have?"

"Well, my supervisor told me the big boss said you could all come back up this Friday, if you still want to."

Go back up? Someone fell off that building and died. And every day she waited for Matt to come home because she worried about the same thing happening to him. She'd been fighting her fear of heights from the beginning but now how could she go back? This Friday? Millicent felt almost sick just thinking about it. Could she actually do it? What was she thinking? She had to. She wasn't turning away from her commitment.

"I suppose they'll be telephoning anytime now."

"And? What are you going to do?" Matt's brow furrowed.

Was he challenging her? Or was he concerned? It didn't matter. Her answer would be the same either way. "Go up and do the best I can, just like you do."

"But going up is my job, Millicent. You've taken a lot of photographs. Surely John and Elizabeth have enough."

"But these articles are about the changes each week brings, Matt. They're about the building of Park Row," she reminded him. "It can't be adequately told without the photos to accompany the article."

He closed his eyes and shook his head. "I know. But, Millie, I don't want you up there."

"I'm going. Your boss gave the go-ahead."

Matt gave a short nod, but she could tell he wasn't happy. "But remember this. I'll be in charge up there. If you get *anywhere* near the edge—no, if you think you're going anywhere *at all* without me by your side, or watching your every move, you're wrong. I'll escort you back down immediately and you'll never go back up."

His voice had never had that kind of edge to it before and the knowledge that he truly feared for her safety sent a flood of warmth racing through her, while his authoritative tone irritated her at the same time. How did he do that? "Do you really think I'd do that? I'm not even sure I'll get near the edge again, with you near me. You don't need to worry. I'll take the shots I can from a distance I feel comfortable with and that will have to do, or they'll have to get someone else to take the photographs. But I don't think there will be any pressure to put anyone in danger."

"Surely not," Matt said, his voice sarcastic.

The telephone rang and Maida came out of the kitchen to answer it.

She peeked around the corner. "It's Mrs. Talbot for you, Miss Millicent."

Millicent hurried to the alcove and picked up the receiver Maida had left on the table. "Hello, Elizabeth. Matt told me you or John might be calling."

"Yes, we've been given permission to go back up this Friday. I just wanted to check and see if lunchtime would work for you. I'm not at my best first thing of a morning, right now."

"Of course noon will work for me as long as Matt thinks it will." She turned to see him right behind her and at his nod, she said, "I don't think he's happy about us going up, but he says it will work."

"Oh, good. Tell him thank you for us and we'll pick you up around eleven-thirty."

"I will. See you Friday." Millicent hung up the receiver and turned to Matt. "She said to tell you thank you."

"I heard." He grinned. "Actually, that might work best now. It's pretty cool up there of a morning and it'll be easier for John to interview while my men are on lunch break."

"Good. And hopefully, I can get some more candid shots—for them to have, you know?" While she prayed none of them would ever have an accident, she'd not forgotten how thankful Mrs. O'Riley had been for the photographs she'd given her. Now she would develop extra copies of her candid shots of Matt's men so their loved ones would have them. Especially when they were smiling or laughing like the ones she'd taken of Tom O'Riley that'd given his wife such comfort.

By the time Friday arrived, Millicent was surprised that her nerves about going up Park Row weren't for herself. She mostly wanted to see how Matt and his men were handling working there after what happened to their coworker.

As usual, Matt met them outside the building and went up to the top with them, picking up Millicent's tripod and camera. It was only when the elevator shuddered to a stop and they stepped out that Millicent realized they'd moved to a new floor, bringing them near the halfway mark of the height the Park Row Building would be when finished.

"When did this happen and why didn't you tell us?" John asked.

"Just last week, and I thought I'd surprise you all. To tell the truth, we're a little relieved to be up another floor and off the one below."

Millicent could certainly understand that. She looked out in the direction of the harbor and beyond, realizing she could see just a bit farther than on the floor below. The thought of how far one would be able to see from the top once the building was finished took her breath away.

"So, what do you want to do? The men are just breaking for lunch and they're all willing to talk to you two. I know you want to interview them about Tom's accident, but just don't press if they don't want to continue."

"I won't," John said. "And if they aren't ready to talk about it, that's fine, too. I don't have a problem relating that they aren't ready to think about it right now. I think my readers will understand."

"I know mine will," Elizabeth added.

"I can't expect more than that, so feel free to ask whatever you want. I've told them they don't have to answer everything." He grinned at John and Elizabeth before turning to Millicent.

"Do you know what you want to photograph and from where?"

"You know, I think I'd like to just get what I can from a safe distance with my big camera, and I want to get some shots of your men when they aren't expecting it with my small one, kind of like the ones I gave Mrs. O'Riley."

"That'd be great, Millicent. I was hoping you'd

do that. Not that I expect anything to happen to any of them, but—"

"I know. And I don't, either. I'm going to make extra copies for them to have now for their families to enjoy. Who knows? Maybe some of them will want me to take a family photo shoot for them. My prices are very reasonable, you know."

"I'll pass that information on."

"Good. I did receive several telephone calls this week from friends and family of the O'Rileys'. They saw the photos I gave Mrs. O'Riley and asked if I'd take some of those 'happy' photographs of their families."

"That's wonderful, Millicent."

She nodded and smiled. His approval seemed to mean more to her each day. "I think that's what I want to be known for most—my ability to take photographs of people being themselves and not just some unsmiling, unfeeling vision."

"If that's what you want, I have no doubt that's what you'll be known for. Along with talent for capturing many things no one else sees. I'll set up your tripod wherever you want it and let you get to work."

"Thank you. I think right here is good. After I get what I can, I'll just walk around and try to capture some good shots of John interviewing and your men at lunch. I promise I won't go anywhere near the edge."

That seemed to satisfy him, in spite of his rant a few days ago. He set her camera up and left her to do her job, and Millicent took what she thought were some good shots of the beginnings of a new floor and some out to sea. She hoped the ships she saw would be clear when she developed them. Once she had what she thought she needed, Millicent took up her small camera and began to walk around, gradually getting nearer to Matt's men, and Matt himself, joshing with one of them. They all seemed to relax while they took turns speaking to John and Elizabeth and then going back to finish their lunch.

She couldn't wait to develop the photographs and prayed they were as good as she thought they were. She took a few more then zeroed in on Matt. Just watching him talk to his men did funny things to her heart, making her feel all fluttery inside. She focused in on him one more time as he stood there, hands on his hips, thinking he didn't see her.

But just as she began to snap the shot, he turned and winked. Millicent almost dropped her camera, and when Matt chuckled and grinned, her pulse took off like lightening. Oh, this was one photo she was keeping just for herself.

Chapter Sixteen

As Millicent and the Talbots returned to their Park Row assignment, things seemed to go back to normal for Matt. He was still heartbroken over Tom's death. The accident had given him much to think about, and he prayed for Tom's family every day. But finally, he began to feel more in control of his feelings and his life.

Except when it came to Millicent. He seemed to have no say over his thoughts where she was concerned. The memory of the kiss they'd shared was never very far away and seemed to pop into his mind whenever his glance fell on her. And lately, that was more often than not. Especially when she smiled at him like she was doing when he pulled out her chair at dinner that evening.

"Matt, I had a telephone call from Mrs. White this afternoon."

"Mrs. White? The lady who hosted the suffrage meeting we all went to?"

"Yes. She's hosting another one this evening and even though I hadn't planned on going to this one, she wants me to come as a photographer to take photos that can be used in their flyers. I thought I might need my professional camera. Who knows? It might bring me more clients and I wondered if you'd mind escorting me and helping me with my equipment."

"I'll be glad to help in any way I can." Not that his choice of being with her was at one of those meetings, but the one he'd attended hadn't been all that bad, and he and the other men had offered to escort them there and back anytime. And he certainly didn't want anyone else escorting Millie.

"Oh, thank you. The meeting is at eight and I'd like to be there by seven forty-five in order to set up, if possible. We might need to leave before dessert."

"That's fine. I'm sure Mrs. Heaton will excuse us if we leave early."

"Of course I will. I'm glad you'll be there to help Millicent. This should be the last meeting before the first of the year, shouldn't it?"

"I hope so," Millicent said. "With Thanksgiving nearly here and Christmas coming, it's hard to make time for them during the holidays."

"True. We have even more things to fill our time," Julia said.

"Yes, like the party Luke and Kathleen are hosting tomorrow evening," Mrs. Heaton said.

Her words reminded Matt of the album meeting planned for the next evening at Luke and Kathleen's. With all that had happened, he'd nearly forgotten. But they'd all had a good time at the last one and he was looking forward to this one.

As the meal progressed, pleasant conversation took them through to time for dessert. "I suppose we should be going now," Millicent said as she placed her napkin beside her plate. Matt stood and helped her scoot her chair out.

Millicent ran upstairs to freshen up, but she'd brought her camera and tripod down before dinner and Matt telephoned the livery for a hack, then put on his coat and took hers off the hook so that he could help her into it.

She was back down in a flash and smiled as he held out her jacket. That smile of her's warmed his heart.

"Thank you for doing this. I know it's cold out and I'd rather have stayed in myself tonight."

"I understand. This could be a great opportunity for you. But why weren't any of you planning on going to this one?"

"We don't go to all of them. And this is a new speaker. We've not heard of her before. If there's any fresh information, I'll tell the others."

The hack pulled up just as they reached the street and Matt put in Millicent's tripod and camera and then helped her inside before giving the driver their destination and taking a seat beside her.

"Matt, did you call for the hack?"

"I did. It's cold out and the streetcar is bound to be full. No sense worrying about something happening to your equipment with all the jostling."

"Thank you. I'll pay you—"

"Millie, you've got to stop saying that. It was my idea and well worth the money. I didn't want you shivering before you even got there and we'd still be standing at the trolley stop like those people are."

He pointed to the group waiting for the next trolley to come by.

"They do look quite cold."

"They do. So let's just enjoy the fact that it's a bit warmer in here."

He wished he had the right to move nearer to her, to put his arm around her, to— *Whoa.* He had to quit thinking that way. After all, there was no way to know what she was thinking and the last time they were in a hack together, he'd kissed her. No wonder she was cuddled up in the opposite corner.

They arrived at the meeting just in time for Millicent to set up her tripod and camera. Mrs. White greeted them both and instructed her to set up at the side of the room, near the middle.

"I appreciate you doing this at such short notice, Millicent. We've been enjoying your photographs of the Park Row and my husband suggested that you be the one we ask to take photos for our new flyers."

"How very nice of him. I'm glad you contacted me, Mrs. White," Millicent said.

The older woman smiled at them both and hurried up to the front of the room to speak with the lady Matt supposed was the speaker. He helped Millicent set up and then took a seat near where she'd be taking her photographs. The room had quickly filled up in those few minutes and the chatter grew louder until Mrs. White stepped up to the podium and introduced the guest speaker.

Matt was more interested in watching Millicent take photographs of the two women than in listening to what they were saying. As the meeting got under way, she would turn her camera in different angles to get the audience, too. Most were listening intently, but a few were fidgeting in their chairs.

Suddenly the woman at the podium raised her voice a notch or two. "Ladies, we cannot let the men we care about control our lives! We should have the same rights they do and we don't have to put up with being mistreated or put down in any way! We should have the right to our freedom should we marry a man who wants only to rule us! We must stand together for the sake of our daughters. We don't want them marrying someone who won't take their interests to heart!"

"Hold on there!" a man in the audience yelled. "There are men here who support the right for women to vote, but you're going too far, madam—accusing us of such things!"

Millicent gasped and looked at Matt, confusion clearly in her eyes. He looked around and saw several women and men leaving and at the same time he heard footsteps advancing on the ballroom.

Someone from the audience said, "And we've been photographed! I don't want my photo attached to this kind of meeting!" Several people headed their way, but the crush of others going in the opposite direction slowed them down.

"We've got to go, Millie! I don't know what's going on, but let's get your camera and tripod and get out of here. Hurry!"

Millicent put her camera in its bag while Matt broke down the tripod. Mrs. White seemed to be at their side right away, leading them to a side door. "I am so sorry about this, Millicent. Please, go right in the hall and take the stairs down to the kitchen and go out that way. This was not the meeting we expected.

We don't get into domestic rights at our meetings. I'm so sorry."

She didn't wait for an answer and Matt was glad as he hurried Millicent down the stairs. The kitchen staff looked quite surprised to see them, but one of them led Matt and Millicent to the back door, making Matt wonder if this kind of thing happened often. He could hear other people clamoring into the kitchen as he and Millicent went outside and made their way through the backyard and then to a street over, where he hailed a hack.

He told the driver where to take them as he threw Millicent's camera back in and then lifted her and her tripod into the hack. The driver took off as soon as Matt shut the door but as he turned the corner, they saw policemen hurrying up the steps of Mrs. White's place.

They both let out the breath they'd been holding and turned to each other.

"We made it," Matt said once he could speak.

"But from what? What was going on there? Why were they yelling so?"

Matt began to laugh as he realized Millicent had been concentrating so much on taking her photos, she really didn't know.

"Why are you laughing? I don't think police raiding Mrs. White's home is a reason to laugh!" Millicent said. She wasn't sure what had happened, but obviously it wasn't good and she had a feeling her photographs would not be used. And she sincerely hoped her reputation as a photographer hadn't been ruined because she was there!

"You're right, Millicent. It's just that neither of us was paying much attention to what was being said. You were concentrating on taking your photographs and I was watching you. It wasn't until the speaker began to rant about…wanting more rights than just voting that the group got a little riled. By the time you realized something was going on, it was time to leave."

"What was she saying?" Millicent needed to know. Mrs. White had apologized and as far as Millicent knew there'd never been an incident of any kind at the meetings she'd hosted.

"I didn't hear it all, either, but I think she was saying a woman should be able to leave her husband if…he was too, I don't know, Millicent. If he took his interests more to heart than hers?" He shrugged. "I know that some of these groups push for the right for a woman to divorce her husband for nearly any reason, but I'm not sure…"

Millicent let out a sigh. "There are those groups. And they aren't helping the ones who are most interested in getting the right to vote. With that, hopefully there will be ways to get more rights. I for one don't believe in divorce, but yet, I know there are women out there who are being severely mistreated. Kathleen's sister Colleen's husband nearly killed her before the cops shot him. For these women I wish there were a way they could get out of that kind of situation, I guess. But if a husband and wife would only take each other's interests and feelings into consideration, and if the couple looks to the Lord for guidance, I don't think there would be a need to leave. Do you?"

"I— No. But most of the couples I know have

never even thought about leaving one another. My parents listen to each other and make most decisions together. And should my father make one my mother isn't pleased with, he explains why. I've never heard them argue."

"My parents are like that, too. But I do know that not all couples are. And there are men who…" What was she doing? Matt didn't approve of her wanting to have her own shop any more than Robert had.

"Men who…?" he asked, his voice sounding husky in the darkened hack.

Millicent sighed. "Men who don't want an independent-thinking woman and certainly not one who might want a business of her own."

"Maybe they only want one who would put her husband and any family they might have first and are afraid she might not make time for them if she's busy with her own business."

"Well, why do they *assume* that one wouldn't put her family first? Why do they think they'd be ignored instead of realizing that she would work her business around her family? Couldn't one talk about those things before putting one's foot down and saying absolutely not?" Millicent could have bitten her tongue once the words were out. Matt was the last person she should be talking to about all of this! She'd never voiced her feelings in this way before.

"Millicent, I… You make a very good point. Have you— Did your father put his foot down about you coming here?"

"No. In fact he was very supportive and felt bad about encouraging Robert—"

"Robert?"

Millicent closed her eyes and shook her head, glad it was dark inside the cab.

"Who is Robert?" Matt pressed.

Well, she'd asked for it; she might as well get it out. "Robert Baxter was a man back home whom I almost married. Until I found out that he was strongly opposed to my continuing with my photography at all, much less opening my own shop. He knew that was my goal when he started courting me, but evidently he thought marriage to him should be my only objective, waiting on him, wanting only what he wanted, working with him to fulfill his dreams with no thought at all to mine."

"Did you assure him—"

"I did. But it didn't seem to matter. He didn't want children right away, if at all. He wanted all of my attention to be on him and his desire to run for office one day. He didn't love me for who I am, but for what he wanted me to be. So I broke it off." Millicent clamped her lips shut. She hadn't meant to tell Matt so much about herself and her past.

"Sounds like a wise decision to me, Millicent. But surely you know that not all men are like him? Look at Michael, Luke, John and Ben—they're very supportive of their wives…"

"But they are not the norm, Matt."

"And you decided this because of one man?"

"No, of course not. But be honest—you and Joe and Stephen made up your minds about the suffrage meetings before you ever went to one. You didn't give much thought to why we were going to them. And you've made it known since we first met that you don't approve of my starting my own business."

"Millie—you can't read my mind. You don't know—"

"Matt, I don't have to read your mind. You've made it quite clear how you feel."

"But all the women at Heaton House work. They have no man to take care of them and—"

"Exactly. And once they are married and have a husband to take care of them? You don't think they should work, do you?"

"Millicent, Elizabeth still works, as does Kathleen. John and Luke don't seem to have a problem with it."

"And as I said, they are the exception, not the norm. Tell me the truth, Matt. If you married you'd expect your wife not to work, wouldn't you?" She wished she could see his expression, for that would be the most telling of all, but even as the hack pulled up outside Heaton House, it was too dark to have any idea what Matt might be thinking.

"I—" The hack jerked to a stop right outside Heaton House and Matt didn't know whether to be relieved or disappointed at first.

"I suppose you've been saved from answering, but only for now. I do want an answer to that question one day."

Relief won out at her words and as Matt realized he didn't know how to reply to her question. Had she asked him a month ago, he knew what he'd say, but now…

He helped Millicent out of the hack and paid the driver before grabbing her camera bag and tripod. Once they opened the front door, they could tell everyone was in the parlor as they took off their coats and hung them up. They hurried in to see what everyone was laughing about and found them just ending a game of charades.

"Oh, good, you're home," Mrs. Heaton said. "I'll go ask Maida to bring in dessert for everyone—they wanted to wait until you got home."

"Oh, that was nice of you all," Millicent said.

"Well, we wanted to hear how the meeting went, too," Julia said. "Did you find out anything new tonight?"

Matt looked at Millicent and they both began to chuckle, then burst into laughter.

"What happened?" Georgia asked.

Mrs. Heaton came into the room just then. "Did something happen at the meeting?"

"You could say that," Millicent said. "Matt actually saved me from being mobbed and my reputation as a photographer being ruined, I think."

"Mobbed!" Joe said. "Tell us what happened."

"You tell them, Matt. I was concentrating so much on getting good shots and I wasn't paying a lot of attention to what was going on around me."

Maida came in just then with a loaded tray and they each took a slice of Mrs. Heaton's coconut cake and a cup of tea or coffee, and then, as they all settled down, Matt explained what went on at the meeting. He finished with "If we hadn't gotten out of there when we did, I'm not sure what would have happened. Policemen had been called to the house and were hurrying up the steps when our hack rounded the corner."

"Oh, my," Mrs. Heaton said. "I'm sure Mrs. White is distraught over it all. She's never had anything like that happen at any of her meetings that I know of."

"She was quite apologetic to Millicent," Matt said.

"Mrs. White was very sweet and if not for her, we wouldn't have gotten out before I was assaulted by those people who wanted to make sure their photographs don't show up anywhere. But I wouldn't do that to them. I'm not sure I'll even develop them!"

Matt hated that her opportunity had turned into such a debacle. She looked so forlorn he wanted to make her feel better. "I'm sure Mrs. White will pay you anyway. It wasn't your fault her speaker caused such an uproar."

"Oh, I think she will, too, Millicent," Mrs. Heaton said.

"I'm not worried about the money. I just don't want this to affect my professional reputation."

"I don't see how that can happen if the photographs aren't developed," Matt said. "And truly it shouldn't anyway. You were asked to be there. It's not like you stood up and just began taking photos on your own."

"Nevertheless, I will telephone Mrs. White tomorrow so she can assure anyone who inquires that the photos won't be developed or used in any way."

The woman never failed to surprise him, in all kinds of ways. Her questions on the way home had made him realize he had much to think about.

Chapter Seventeen

Millicent's remarks had shown Matt a side to himself he wasn't proud of, and that evening he did more soul searching than he'd done in years. He'd tossed and turned most of the night and his thoughts were still all over the place when he woke the next morning.

While he shaved and got ready to go upstairs, his mind went back to what Millicent said about his disapproval of her having a business of her own and to the question she'd asked just as the hack pulled up at Heaton House, about him not wanting his wife to work.

He tried to put it all out of his head as he went up to breakfast. But when Millicent smiled and said, "Good Morning!" it came back to mind all over again and he knew he was one confused man.

"John telephoned this morning and said he'd been called out on assignment and they wouldn't be going up to Park Row today, so I thought I might wait until next week, too, unless—"

"Things are moving pretty slow right now, with the

colder weather. You won't miss much." And he'd have a reprieve from looking at her sweet smile. Maybe he could actually get some work done.

"I'll wait until the next time John and Elizabeth go again."

How could a person be relieved and disappointed at the same time? It didn't make any sense, but that was how Matt felt.

"I'm sure you've plenty to do, getting ready for tonight's get-together at Luke and Kathleen's anyway."

"Yes, I do have some things to keep me busy. I think I need to go downtown to pick up a few more items. Want to go, Georgia?"

"I'd love to. Perhaps we'll run into Emily."

The closer it came to Thanksgiving, the more Emily worked. She'd gone in early so she could get off in time for the album party that night.

"She says the windows are going to be spectacular. I have to admit, with Thanksgiving only a week away, I'm looking forward to experiencing Christmastime in the city," Georgia said.

"Yes, so am I," Millicent said. "You're going to love it!"

"I think we should all go down to see the Macy's window unveiling together," Mrs. Heaton suggested.

"That's a wonderful idea," Millicent said. "Emily will be tickled."

"Well, I'm game," Joe said.

"Me, too," Stephen added.

"So am I," Matt said. "And I'm looking forward to tonight, but I suppose I'd better get to work for now."

"I've got to go in for a while, too," Stephen said. "Macy's isn't the only store preparing for Christmas.

I'm sure Emily will be as happy as I will be to have these long hours over with. You all have a good day." He headed out of the dining room right behind Matt.

"I think I'll go into the office for a while, too," Joe said. "I've got some reports I need to get in. Looks like you ladies will have to do without our company today."

"We'll try not to be too bored," Julia teased, as they all seemed to be through with breakfast at the same time.

Matt scooted Millicent's chair out and leaned down to whisper, "Do you need any money for supplies?"

She shook her head, sending the scent of whatever it was she wore into the air. "I think I'm good, but thank you for asking."

"You're welcome." Matt inhaled as much of the delightful fragrance as he could without being obvious. They joined the others in the foyer and he put on his coat, as Joe and Stephen were doing. He had a feeling he was looking forward to that evening way more than he should.

The ladies saw them off and the men headed to the trolley stop. They were none too early as they got in line and then jostled for places once they got on. Matt was almost glad he had to find a seat by a stranger, giving him time to collect his thoughts before he got to work. He'd decided to put Millicent's question out of his mind for now.

But once he and his men donned their work gloves to ward against the cold metal they'd be working with, her question popped up again, as if it'd been sitting on the edge of his thoughts waiting until he began his workday. *Tell me the truth—if you married you'd expect your wife not to work, wouldn't you?*

If she'd asked a couple of months ago, Matt would have said of course—he wanted to take care of his wife. That was what husbands were supposed to do, wasn't it? But he'd also have to admit he would want her to put him, and any family they might have, before any business of her own. He couldn't imagine how that kind of relationship could work.

It didn't mean he wouldn't take his wife's wishes and dreams into consideration like that Baxter person she'd nearly married. Still, Matt had to admit he hadn't given much thought to the actual compromises being married might entail. Probably because after his fiancée had refused to move to the city after they were married, he didn't want to be disappointed in love again. And he'd begun to think most women were like her—as Millicent seemed to have lumped most men into being like Baxter. It appeared they might both be wrong. And something stirred deep inside him at that thought.

Was it—could it—be possible for a woman like Millie and a man like him to get past their differences?

Matt rubbed a hand over his chin and looked out over the city. Then he shook his head. There was no sense in hoping—or in pursuing that line of thought. He'd been hurt before and he'd vowed never again. He must keep his pledge in mind now that he knew deep down that Millie had the ability to hurt him more than his fiancée ever had. No matter how much his feelings for Millicent grew, no matter how much he wanted to kiss her again. None of that meant a marriage between the two of them could work. Marriage to Millie? What was he thinking? Where did that thought come from?

He knew. Last night Millicent, independent as she was and as determined as she was to open her own business, had surprised him. She'd said her husband and children would come first in her life—said that she would work around her family.

Ever since he'd met her, he'd thought she was one of those "modern" women, wanting to make decisions on her own, to have her own business so that she didn't have to depend on a man to support her. Suddenly he'd realized that what she meant all along was that if she ever did marry, it would have to be for love and not because she needed a man to take care of her.

Even more food for thought. He wanted to be loved, not looked at as just a breadwinner for his wife. With Millicent, that would never be the case.

But if what she'd said last night were true, then it appeared Baxter had taken care of her wanting to ever fall in love again. But could those plans ever be changed?

Everyone seemed to be in high spirits as they took off for Kathleen and Luke's place. Millicent and Georgia had taken the album supplies over there that afternoon, so Mrs. Heaton wouldn't suspect anything. They'd leave them there that night for the same reason.

"I'm getting even more excited about this," Millicent said as Matt fell into step beside her. Stephen and Emily were up ahead of them and Joe was enjoying the company of both Julia and Georgia several steps behind.

"I think we all are. It promises to be a great Christmas, being able to give Mrs. Heaton something we all believe will mean a lot to her."

"It won't be long now. Thanksgiving is next week and the days always seems to fly after that!"

Millicent was glad Matt had decided to stay in the city for Christmas. He'd been so willing to help and she wanted him to see Mrs. Heaton's reaction as much as she wanted to see it. She wondered if she'd get up enough nerve to ask the question she'd asked him the night before—or if he'd just answer it on his own one day. He had looked a bit taken back by it, but he'd also surprised her when he said she couldn't read his mind. Was it possible she'd been wrong?

"Do you think another album party will be needed before Christmas?" Matt asked.

"I'm not sure. Depends on how much we get done this evening, I suppose. Part of me wants it finished, but it's so much fun to get together with everyone, I almost hate to see it come to an end."

"We'll come up with something to get us all together. There's always skating in the winter," Julia said from behind them.

"That's true. We'll think of something." They turned the corner to Luke and Kathleen's street and were soon welcomed into the couple's cozy home.

Because it was so cool out, Kathleen had chosen to serve clam chowder with a green salad and crackers or crusty rolls for their meal. She'd made a beautiful four-layer chocolate cake for dessert.

It was over their meal that Violet brought up an idea for a future get-together. "I've been hearing about something called a progressive dinner party and I thought it would be fun to try that sometime in mid-December, if you all like the idea."

"What is a progressive dinner party?" Millicent asked.

"Well, it's where each course is served at a different home. We'd need anywhere from four to six—depending on what we want to serve and how many times we want to move from one place to another."

"Oh, that's something Mama could enjoy, too," Rebecca said. "We could end up at her home for dessert and I'm sure Maida and Gretchen would be willing to watch the children for us."

"It does sound like fun," Julia said. "But that would put all the work on the married couples and Mrs. Heaton."

"Mama will love it and I don't think any of the married couples will mind, will we?" Rebecca looked around the table.

"No! I think it sounds lovely!" Elizabeth said.

"So do I," Violet echoed.

"And I do, too," Kathleen said. "If we don't enjoy it, we won't do it again. On the other hand, it could become a Christmas tradition for us all."

"That's true," Elizabeth said. "John and I will be spending Christmas Eve at Heaton House so we can be with you all when you give Mrs. Heaton her gift, but we'll be spending Christmas day at Papa and Aunt Bea's."

"And Luke and I will be doing the same, but we'll

be having Christmas with Colleen and the boys," Kathleen said.

"What do you men think?" Rebecca asked.

"I like the idea, but you already know that," Ben said, grinning at his wife.

"Sounds great to me," Michael said.

"I certainly like the idea," Matt said, while the other men at the table chimed in that they did, too.

By the time the meal was over, and the table cleared so they could get to work on the albums, everyone seemed quite happy about the possibility of a progressive dinner.

Because Millicent and the ladies at Heaton House had been working when they could on the albums, everyone was quite pleased with their progress and they enthusiastically began work on sorting and writing their comments on the rest of the photos.

Millicent took more photos of everyone while they laughed and reminisced as they looked at the photographs and wrote their comments. She got one of Matt when he was unaware she was watching him as he seemed to be studying one particular photograph. His expression made her wonder who was in the photo and she hurried around the table, under the pretense of taking photographs of people on the other side.

When she glanced down to see which photo he was holding, her heart seemed to melt inside. Matt was looking at a photo Julia or one of the others must have taken of her and him laughing at something one of them had said in the parlor of Heaton House. They seemed to be wrapped up into each other and whatever it was they were talking about. Millicent knew she enjoyed Matt's company…too much to her way of thinking. But he looked as if he were enjoying hers, too. The longing that suddenly enveloped her took her breath away and she brought her camera up to hide her reaction to the photograph.

She snapped away, not knowing or caring what she was aiming at, and then slid into the chair next to Matt's.

He looked at her then as if he only now realized she were there. "Do you know when this photo was taken?"

She took if from him and shook her head. "I have no idea."

"We seem quite…amused at whatever it was we were laughing about."

"Yes, we do." She held up the photograph. "Julia, did you take this photo?"

"I did. It was just a few months ago, but I can't remember why I took it. I thought you two might know so you could comment on it. Interesting, isn't it?" She grinned at the two of them and then went back to writing a note for the photograph she'd been looking at.

"Well, she certainly wasn't any help, was she?"

Millicent chuckled and shook her head. "No, she wasn't. Maybe it will come to us one day."

"Possibly. It's a nice photograph, though. Do you want to add it to the album?" Matt asked.

"We don't have anything to comment about it."

"How about just 'Matt and Millicent having a good time'? We do that from time to time, you know."

"We do."

Matt wrote on the back of the photo and handed it to her. "It'll work."

His smile was contagious, but when his glance landed on her lips, she found her own gaze straying to his. Would she ever forget that kiss? Could she?

Chapter Eighteen

By Thanksgiving Day the album was almost finished. Millicent wanted to add a few more pages and fill them with the photos she'd take today.

She hurried down to breakfast to find Matt joining the others around the table. She took a plate and began to fill hers with bacon and French toast, a special treat for the day.

He smiled at her and pulled out her chair as she made her way to the table.

"Thank you." Millicent endeavored to keep her attention on setting her plate down on the table and greeting the rest of the boarders without glancing at Matt.

Mrs. Heaton came in from the kitchen just then and made her way to the sideboard. "Good morning, everyone. Happy Thanksgiving!"

"Happy Thanksgiving to you, too, Mrs. Heaton. It's a beautiful day."

"It is. I think this is my very favorite holiday," she said. "And I am ever so thankful to have you all as boarders."

"And I know I can speak for all of us when I say we're very thankful to have you as our landlady," Matt said.

"Matt is right, Mrs. Heaton. I can't imagine living anywhere else," Millicent said.

Everyone else chimed in with agreement.

"Oh dear, you're all going to make me tear up if you don't stop. I'm so glad you'll all be here for dinner later, along with my children and grandchildren. I feel very blessed!"

"The first of December our Holiday Opening begins the Christmas season for Macy's. I can't wait for you all to see our windows," Emily said. "And the Santa Claus is wonderful! The children are going to love him."

"I'm sure they will," Mrs. Heaton said. "I know that my children are planning a trip to take Jenny and baby Marcus to see him. Of course, I'm going to tag along. I can't wait to see their faces."

"That will be such fun for you all," Millicent said. "And, Emily, we're all going to make a trip to see those windows."

"Don't forget to also visit Siegel-Cooper," Stephen said. "We've decorated our store quite magnificently, too. And we have more room to move around in." He grinned at Emily and she chuckled.

"You do have us there," she said. "It's a beautiful store and very big."

"Do you need any help with the meal or anything, Mrs. Heaton?" Millicent asked.

"We have everything covered, I believe. You all enjoy your day off. We'll be eating our dinner around five today, but if you get hungry before then, just come to the kitchen and we'll make sure you have something to tide you over."

"Oh, we should be fine," Millicent said.

"That's right. It won't hurt us to wait a bit—not for the spread you're planning," Matt said.

Mrs. Heaton chuckled and stood. "You all have a good day. I'd best go see how things are going in the kitchen."

As everyone began to leave the dining room, Millicent turned to Matt. "What are you going to do until dinnertime?"

"I thought I'd take a walk. Want to go with me? We haven't looked for places for your shop in a long while. Have you been looking at the classifieds?"

"I have. But there's not much in my price range."

"Well, maybe we'll find something with a sign out that hasn't been put in the paper yet. Come on. It's nice out. Chilly but not windy, and if you get cold, I'll treat you to coffee or hot chocolate somewhere."

Millicent hesitated for only a moment. She should say no, but Emily, Georgia, Joe and Stephen had already disappeared.

"Sure. But that cool air is only going to feed our appetite, you know." She took her coat off the hook in the foyer and Matt helped her into it.

He chuckled. "True, but that's the only way we'll be able do to justice to Mrs. Heaton's meal later."

He donned his own coat and held the door open for Millicent. The sun was shining and the sky bright blue as they went down the steps to the walk. "It is nice out. Where are we heading?"

"Well, I still think somewhere near the Ladies' Mile would be nice for your business. Women are the ones who usually plan for family photo sessions and if your shop was near where they shop and have lunch, I think you'd be bound to draw clients."

The man continued to surprise her with how considerate he was regarding her business. Perhaps he was right. She didn't know what he was thinking now. It seemed Matt was changing his mind on several things. Her heart skittered. If that were so—how in the world was she going to keep her feelings for this man from growing?

Matt was glad Millicent had agreed to go for a walk with him. He'd done much thinking over the past week and the truth was, Millicent had been right. He hadn't liked her independent ways when they'd first met, but he now realized it was because he'd been drawn to her from the very beginning. And her independence and determination to make her own way in the world had gone against everything he'd thought he'd wanted in a woman.

And yet, she was so sweet and caring, he couldn't help but like her. So he'd bantered and argued with her over this and that, trying to ignore the attraction. And it'd worked for a while—before they got to know each other better, before she began taking photographs from the Park Row, before he'd begun to feel protective of her and before…she'd claimed part of his heart by always being there for him. Before that unforgettable kiss.

But now…he didn't feel the same way as he had then. The Lord was working on him, of that Matt had no doubt. He knew he'd been judgmental and stubborn in his thinking—without really knowing Millicent and what kind of woman she was.

"It's a nice day for a walk," Millicent said interrupting his thoughts. "It's so quiet and peaceful out."

"Yes, it is. Seems the only traffic is coming from those who must work and people traveling to Thanksgiving dinner somewhere. Do you miss your family, today?"

"Not too badly. I do wish I could see them more often, but I'm glad I'm staying here for the holidays this year. It's Emily's and Georgia's first Christmas in the city and I'm looking forward to seeing their reactions to it all, too. And it's my first actual Christmas Eve and day at Heaton House, since I went home for those last year."

They turned a corner and headed for the Ladies' Mile. Usually there were masses of people shopping in the area and although there were others out and about, it almost felt as if they had the city to themselves.

They passed several residential neighborhoods before they reached the beginning of the shopping area he thought would be perfect for Millicent's shop. They strolled up and down Fourth Avenue looking for signs in the windows of buildings that looked as if they might have living areas on the upper floors. Many of the smaller shops would be the most likely to fit Millicent's needs.

At Union Square, they crossed the avenue to peek at the displays of Tiffany's jewelry store, only to find the window empty.

"Of course they locked everything up. Can't say I blame them," Matt said.

Millicent laughed. "I don't think I could afford even the least expensive jewelry there anyway."

"Want to go to Macy's?"

Millicent shook her head. "Most of the windows are covered and there won't be much to see now."

"All right, we'll head down Fifteenth Street to Fifth Avenue and then on to Sixth Avenue and see if there are any signs."

They passed by Siegel-Cooper. The building was on Sixth Avenue and Eighteenth and was six stories high and a block long.

"My it *is* huge, isn't it?"

"It is. And it's very beautiful inside," Millicent said.

"I've never been inside, but I suppose I'll need to go in before Christmas so Stephen will know I have. The outside is beautiful, though. I do love the elaborate beaux arts architecture." He pulled out his pocket watch. "It's near lunchtime. I suppose we should get that hot chocolate or a sandwich or something to hold us until dinnertime, if we can find something open."

They strolled down to Twenty-first Street and found a small café open. Matt opened the door and they took a seat at a table overlooking the street. He pulled out a chair for Millicent and then took one across from her.

"Good day," a waiter said. "What can I get you? Our clam chowder is very good."

"That sounds good to me," Millicent said.

"I'll take the same," Matt said.

"What to drink?"

"Tea?" Matt asked Millicent.

At her nod, he turned to the waiter. "Two teas, then."

There were several other customers in the café and it was warm and clean inside. Millicent looked around. "I wonder why I've never noticed this place before."

"Probably because you're usually on one of the main avenues where most of the shops are. And that's why you need to look for a place very near the busiest thoroughfares. But this area has a lot of smaller shops, too, so it might work well."

"I'm not sure I can afford something in either area."

"I understand. But you never know. Perhaps you will. You haven't actually been looking very long."

"That's true."

The waiter brought their meal—the chowder with crackers and their tea in a teapot.

"How nice, a whole pot to share," Millicent said as she poured the tea for them. "I like this place. I'll have to tell the others about it."

Matt took a sip of the chowder. "This is very good. I'll let my crew know about it, too."

Their light meal was very good and it warmed them up for more walking. When the waiter came to check on them, Matt surprised himself by asking, "Say, do you know of any building similar to this one that also has a living area above it near here?"

"As a matter of fact I do. The building two doors down is for sale. It used to be a haberdashery but closed a few months ago. It's a nice building. The owner moved away but there's a sign in the window with all the particulars. You can't miss it."

"Thank you so much!" Millicent grinned at Matt. "And you for asking."

He smiled back and paid for their lunch. Her excitement was contagious. "Let's go take a look."

The small three-story building tucked in between an alterations shop and a bakery on the other side was just the style Millicent had wished for. It had a big window to the left of the door, just perfect for showcasing her work. But with no lights on inside, they couldn't see much else. Still, hope filled her heart when she read the sign. It said, "Building for sale. First floor is ideal for retail shop, top two stories comprised of living space." It gave the name of a broker and the telephone number to contact him, but no price was mentioned.

Millicent quickly pulled out a small notepad and pencil and wrote the information down. "Oh, Matt, from the outside it looks just right."

"I agree. It seems to be well built from what I can tell, but I'd need to get inside and poke around to make sure."

"I'll telephone first thing tomorrow and see when we can take a look. You will check it out for me, won't you?"

"You know I will."

"Oh, I'm sure I won't be able to afford it, but it seems to be a dream come true. Both a shop and living quarters!" Then her heart sank. "Although, I'm not sure I'm ready to leave Heaton House just yet. I know I would miss everyone so much."

"You wouldn't have to move in until you had it just as you liked and got used to being there. Nothing says you couldn't continue to live at Heaton House for a while."

"That's true—if I can afford to do both."

"Maybe whoever is selling it wants to be rid of it and will give you a very good price."

"Wouldn't it have already sold by now if that were the case?"

Matt grinned at her and shook his head. "You won't know anything until you contact the broker. But there's no need to give up before you do, is there?"

Did Matt have any idea of how much he'd changed? Or was it she who had undergone a change? It seemed that perhaps she'd misjudged the man. Here he was encouraging her to hope and not give up. Saying just what she needed to hear.

"No. There isn't. Thank you for the reminder."

"We'll keep looking on the way back to Heaton House, but I think the location of this one might work. Look, several more people have stopped at the café and more are across the street window shopping."

Millicent's heart filled with happiness—that she'd found a place that might be perfect for her shop and that Matt seemed almost as excited about it as she was.

They took their time going up and down the avenues and side streets of the Ladies' Mile and did find a couple of other buildings, but both were farther from most of the shopping. Still, Millicent wrote down the information for each one and would telephone about them the next day, too.

By the time they arrived home, mouthwatering aromas were filling the air and they both sniffed appreciatively.

"Oh, I'm glad we didn't have too much for lunch," Millicent said.

"Lunch? I've already forgotten about it." Matt's stomach emitted an unmistakable growl, eliciting a chuckle from them both.

"Oh, I'm sorry." He grinned.

Millicent's gave a small answering gurgle, sending them into a gale of laughter. "Evidently my stomach forgot, too. I wonder where everyone is."

They looked into the parlor but no one was there.

"Maybe they went out to get something to tide them over instead of bothering Mrs. Heaton about it."

"Probably. Or they're upstairs getting ready for dinner. I suppose I should go up and dress for it, too. Thank you for giving me your opinion on the buildings, Matt."

"You're welcome. See you at dinner."

As she went upstairs, Millicent marveled at how far she and Matt had come since they'd first moved to Heaton House. Whatever they were now, she liked it much better.

Thanksgiving dinner was one to remember. The table needed an extra leaf with the boarders and Mrs. Heaton's family celebrating with them all.

And she'd gone all out with the meal. It started with oyster soup and crisp crackers, followed by roast turkey and stuffing, cranberry jelly and mashed potatoes and gravy. Dessert was English plum pudding, assorted cakes, frozen pudding and bonbons.

"I'm so glad we only had that cup of soup for lunch," Matt whispered to Millicent.

"So am I. I'd never be able to eat all of this, if not. But isn't it delicious?"

"It is that." Millicent looked extra lovely tonight in a deep blue velvet gown trimmed in cream-colored lace. She'd done up her hair in a flattering manner and tucked a blue flower into it. And she'd added a becoming new scent behind her ears, he was sure of it.

Everyone took their time and enjoyed the meal immensely. Jenny was quite the little lady sitting between her mother and stepfather. And baby Marcus was growing very fast.

During dinner they discussed the progressive dinner they'd talked about at the album party and Mrs. Heaton was all for it.

"I hope we do get some snow soon—enough to go sledding anyway," Millicent said. "I enjoyed that so much last year."

"Surely we will," Matt said. "We might not have a white Christmas, but we'll have snow at some point."

"We're so excited about taking Jenny to see the windows you've been working on, Emily," Rebecca said. "It must take a lot of imagination to make them turn out so beautiful."

Emily laughed. "It takes many *imaginations* to do it. I'm the new kid in the group, but I'm enjoying every minute of it. I think you'll like those windows, Jenny."

The little girls eyes shined as she said, "I can't wait!"

Jenny's excitement carried over to Matt and he found himself looking forward to going with the group. It'd be fun. He was beginning to feel himself

once more after the tragedy with O'Riley and he knew
the woman sitting beside him had much to do with
that. Everyone here had helped and he was more than
a little thankful to have them in his life.

After dinner they all adjourned to the parlor to
sing songs along with Julia's accompaniment. Jenny
joined Julia at the piano, as she'd loved to do when
she lived there and everyone sang along.

Matt watched as Millicent sat down beside Violet and baby Marcus reached out to her. She put her
hands out to take him and he almost jumped into her
lap as he grabbed her sleeve.

She laughed and cuddled him, and Matt thought
he'd never seen anything so lovely as Millicent holding a child. Her expression as she looked at the baby
sent an intense longing he'd never felt before rushing through him, and he could no longer deny that he
dreamed of having a wife and children of his own.
And without a doubt, the only woman he could see
in that dream was Millicent.

After a few minutes, Millicent handed the baby
back to his mother and Matt moved his gaze away
from the two and forced his thoughts in another direction as Maida and Gretchen came in with after-
dinner tea and coffee.

But his attention strayed once more to Millicent
as she sipped her tea. This Thanksgiving was one
he'd never forget. It'd been a wonderful day from
start to finish and he knew much of it was due to
her. His gaze lowered to Millicent's lips and he believed the only thing that would make this day better would be to have the right to kiss those sweet lips

good-night. She glanced at him and his gaze locked on hers. He smiled as he watched color creep up her cheeks. Could she be remembering…and thinking the same thing?

Chapter Nineteen

Millicent tried to call about the buildings on Friday, the day after Thanksgiving, but there was no answer at two of the numbers and she assumed their offices were closed for the whole weekend.

She took a deep breath and asked the operator to connect her with the last number, the one she was most interested in, and was surprised when she was connected. But the receptionist was the only one in the office and she told Millicent that the broker she was trying to contact would be out until the middle of December.

Disappointment engulfed Millicent. "Oh, well, could you take my name and number and ask him to telephone me when he gets back? I'm very interested in the property on Twenty-first Street near the Ladies' Mile."

"I'd be glad to."

Millicent gave her information to the woman and they said goodbye. She couldn't help but feel disappointed that she and Matt wouldn't be able to look at anything that weekend.

But when he got home from work and she told him, he looked relieved. "I have to work tomorrow, too, and wouldn't be able to go anyway. We're hoping to get another floor framed and floored so that work can continue on good days through the next few months, and we'll have some protection against rain or snow. By the time the broker gets back into the country, I should have more free time."

Millicent smiled at him. "There's no real hurry. It's not like the building will be bought out from under me if there's no one to show it."

"That's true."

So perhaps it was best she couldn't see the space yet. If they did go and she loved it, she'd have to make a decision and she wasn't totally sure she was ready to. She did want a shop, but the thought of leaving everyone at Heaton House, even knowing they'd all remain close, wasn't something she believed she was quite prepared for.

The next day, she, Julia and Georgia made a trip to the Ladies' Mile to get ideas for their Christmas shopping.

Sunday turned out to be too cold to do any looking, so after church and Sunday dinner, the boarders spent the afternoon in the parlor. Mrs. Heaton went to visit Rebecca and her family and while she was gone they took the opportunity of working on the albums. Millicent telephoned Rebecca and asked her to let them know when Mrs. Heaton started home, but there wasn't much left to do and they finished half an hour before their landlady got back.

All that was really left would be to include any photos taken before Christmas.

Monday was a nice day and Millicent was restless. Everyone else was at work and even Mrs. Heaton was out, so she went in search of Georgia and found her reading in the small study.

"Want to go for a walk and to lunch?" Millicent asked.

Georgia slapped the book shut. "Oh, I'd love to! I am so tired of not having enough to do."

After letting Maida and Gretchen know they'd be out all afternoon, they were on their way. Millicent took Georgia to see the buildings she liked, ending with lunch at her new favorite café where she and Matt had shared tea and soup on Thanksgiving Day.

"Oh, this is nice, Millicent," Georgia said after the waiter took their order.

"It is, isn't it? Matt and I found it when we went for our walk the other day."

"You and Matt seem to be spending more time together... Are you sweet on him?"

Millicent felt color flood her face. "We're friends. We both came into Heaton House about the same time and—"

"Millicent, you aren't answering my question," Georgia said. "But I think I have my answer from the way you're blushing."

Millicent didn't want to say yes right out, for she'd been fighting her rapidly growing feelings for Matt for weeks now. But she didn't want Georgia getting any ideas about him, either. So she smiled and shrugged as her new friend chuckled.

"He's a nice man and I've seen the way he looks at you—and the way you look at him, for that matter. I think you two would make a very good couple."

Millicent's heart flipped at the mere suggestion and she didn't know what to say. She'd totally failed at doing what she'd told Matt they should do—forgetting about that kiss and putting it behind them. It came to mind each time he smiled at her, looked into her eyes, came into a room.

"I don't know…"

"I'm sorry, Millicent. I shouldn't have asked. But I do think you both care a great deal about one another."

The waiter brought their lunch just then and Millicent was more than relieved when Georgia changed the subject after he left the table. "Where do you want to go from here?"

"What would you like to see?"

"Everything! Mostly I've only been to the Ladies' Mile and ridden through Central Park a few times."

"Oh, well, maybe we should take the El and go farther downtown. I'll show you where Battery Park and City Hall are. You'll be able to see the Park Row Building, too."

"I'd like that!"

They finished lunch and then hurried to the nearest El stop. After buying their tokens and giving them to the conductor, Millicent played travel guide to Georgia. As they neared Battery Park, Millicent pointed out the Statue of Liberty as the El took a turn and they headed in the other direction.

"Would you like to get off here and walk down to City Hall? We'll go past the Park Row. See there it is." Millicent pointed to the building that already stood much taller than the others around it.

"I'd like that. Oh, it is quite tall. I can't imagine

being up that high on an unfinished building. And you've taken photographs from up there?"

"Yes. It's quite something, isn't it?" They got off at the next El stop and headed toward City Hall. But when they heard the bells of an ambulance, Millicent's heart seemed to stop beating before it began to hammer so hard she could feel it in her ears. Ever since Matt's coworker had fallen, fear gripped her at the sound. She had to find out where it was going.

She picked up her skirts and began to run and Georgia kept up with her. Panic engulfed her as she saw the ambulance at the base of the Park Row. *Oh, dear Lord, please don't let it be Matt or any of his men! And please don't let it be fatal.*

A stretcher was being carried to the ambulance by the time they reached the building and Millicent's heart seemed to shatter as she realized the man they were carrying looked like Matt.

"No!" She ran forward and was caught by Burl, who was there with the rest of Matt's men.

"He'll be all right, Miss Faircloud. A cable broke and the beam it was carrying fell. Matt got hit in the arm and he'll need to be sewn up, but it could have been much worse."

"I have to go with him. I—" She had to see for herself that he was okay. She pulled away from Burl and ran up to the stretcher.

"Matt!"

His eyes were filled with pain, but he gave her a small smile. "Millicent, what are you doing here?"

"I'm going to the hospital with you!"

"Miss, you can't go—" the attendant said.

"Yes, she can." Matt tried to turn and Millicent

knew she'd never forget the moan that escaped through his closed mouth before he said, "Let her come with me."

The man shook his head but helped Millicent into the ambulance once they had Matt in.

Millicent looked out at a pale Georgia. "Can you get home by yourself?"

"I can. I'll let everyone know."

The doors shut and Millicent turned to Matt. His left arm was bandaged but bloody and his eyes were closed, but when she grabbed his right hand he squeezed it.

"I'll be all right, Millie. Don't worry."

Only then did she begin to breathe naturally again. She bowed her head and silently prayed, *Dear Lord, please let Matt be right. Please let his arm heal completely and quickly. He means so very much to me.*

Tears began to flow down her cheeks at her admission. She did care deeply for Matt—whether he felt the same about her or not. All that mattered at that moment was that he be all right.

Matt still felt a bit dazed—or what the doctor called "in shock"—when he was given leave to go home. Millicent hadn't left his side until they took him in to set his dislocated shoulder and sew up the long gash on his arm. They'd given him a shot and he felt a bit groggy, but not so much that he didn't remember the expression in Millicent's eyes when she looked at him while they loaded him into the ambulance.

It'd been obvious she'd been deeply concerned for his welfare, even after he'd told her he'd be fine. It was only later, when the doctor informed her of the same thing, that he could see the relief in her eyes.

His boss was there when Matt was released, and arranged for a hack to take them back to Heaton House. As he saw them in, he said to Matt, "You know we'll take care of this. Just rest and let yourself heal so you can get back to work. I've put Burl in charge until you do."

"Good," Matt replied. "He'll see things get done right until I get back."

"You take care of him, miss. He's a good man," Mr. Johnson said as he closed the door to the hack.

"We'll make sure he takes it easy," Millicent responded.

But as the hack took off, she became quiet and Matt had a feeling she was reining in whatever feelings she had for him. Whatever it was he'd seen in her gaze. She must have been horribly frightened when she realized he was the one on that stretcher—especially after Tom's accident.

He closed his eyes and leaned his head back. He couldn't let fear of what might happen to him make her pull back—not when he'd just realized he was falling in love with her and that she was the one he wanted to spend the rest of his life with. It didn't matter that she could be independent and headstrong at times; he didn't even want to contemplate a day without her in it. And he had to make her see they were right for each other—somehow, some way.

Millicent glanced over at Matt. His eyelashes were dark against the pallor his accident had brought on. His arm was in a sling to keep him from hitting it against anything and he held it still with his good hand.

The past few hours were some of the longest she'd

ever lived through, wondering how badly he was hurt, how long it would take for him to heal and how thankful she was that he was alive.

His boss or supervisor, a Mr. Johnson, had arrived just as a nurse wheeled Matt out, followed by a doctor who came to tell her that Matt was ready to go home. It appeared it'd be after the first of the year before he could go back to work and Millicent had breathed a sigh of relief as Mr. Johnson assured him not to worry and to just get well. She wanted to cry at the very thought of Matt going back to Park Row.

How could she bear seeing him return to work on that building? How could she accept that he loved being up there as much as she loved taking her photographs? She'd had a lot of time to think while he was being treated at the hospital, and much as she cared about him, she felt she should fight her feelings for him even harder. She—

The hack pulled up in front of Heaton House, jostling Matt awake and Millicent out of her thoughts. The front door opened as Mrs. Heaton, Georgia and Joe spilled out the door to help Matt and her inside.

Millicent gently took hold of his good arm and led him up the steps. "Do you want to go lie down for a while or—"

"I'm not sure…"

"Why don't you take a seat in the parlor and put your feet up, Matt?" Mrs. Heaton asked. "You can nap until dinner if you want. Do you think you'll feel like eating anything? Or Joe can get you to your room and I'll bring you a tray if you'd rather lie down there."

"I—think I'd like to clean up a bit before dinner."

"I'll help him down and back up," Joe said. "He's

probably a bit wobbly from the medicine they gave him."

"All right. But if you don't feel like coming back up, let Joe know and I'll bring a tray down for you."

"Thank you, Mrs. Heaton." He turned to Millicent. "And thank you for being with me. I'm not sure how you happened to be in the area, but I believe the Lord must have sent you. I'll be back up in a bit."

Millicent swallowed around the lump in her throat as she nodded. She believed He had, too.

Matt did make it back up for dinner, with Joe right behind him to make sure he didn't get off balance. Concern filled Millicent's eyes once more when she asked, "You look like you're hurting. Do you need one of the pills the doctor sent home?"

"Not yet. Pain isn't too bad. I don't like those things but I'll take one before I go to bed. Quit worrying, Millie. I'll be fine. And I get a break from work. Who'd be upset about that?" His grin did manage to make her smile.

"But will you get paid?" Joe asked as he pulled out Matt's chair.

"I think so." Matt didn't bother to tell him it didn't matter. He'd not told anyone that he'd come to the city with a nice inheritance from his grandfather. He'd been careful not to dip into it, because if he ever did decide to start his own company, get married, get on with his life in a different way, he'd need it. Maybe now that he couldn't work, he'd figure out exactly what it was he should do. He knew what he wanted, but he wasn't sure he'd ever have it.

Over the past few months, his feelings for Millicent

had grown to the point where he could no longer fight them. But he didn't have any real idea how she felt. Blushing when he looked at her didn't tell him what he needed to know. Did he have a chance to earn her love?

"His supervisor was very nice and said they would take care of everything," Millicent said.

Matt chuckled. "I thought he said that, but I was a bit woozy. I'm glad you were there."

Millicent looked him in the eye. "So am I. Do you need help cutting your meat?"

Matt's first instinct was to say no, but he didn't want to sling meat across the table trying to cut with only one hand. "Would you mind?"

"You know I wouldn't have offered if I did." She took his plate and quickly cut his slice of roast beef into bite-size pieces, then set the plate in front of him once more.

"Thank you."

"You're welcome."

"Next time, I'll have it cut up for you ahead of time, Matt. I should have thought of it before now," Mrs. Heaton said. "I really didn't think you'd make it back up here tonight."

He chuckled. "The thought of being down there by myself helped send me back up. I figured being with all of you would take my mind off any pain I might have." He knew it wouldn't take his mind off Millicent. She seemed to fill his thoughts more each day. But it would be the same in his room or up here. And he'd rather be here, beside her.

"Well, I can tell you that once we heard the bells of the ambulance making its way to your building, Millicent took off in a run I could barely keep up with."

"I could only think of what happened to Mr. O'Riley. And fear that the same thing had happened to you, or one of your men…"

Matt reached out with his free hand and touched her wrist. "I understand. I'm sorry you had to go through that."

"I'm just thankful you'll be all right and no one fell over the side."

He nodded. "So am I."

"Yes, we all are," Mrs. Heaton said. "Can you tell us how the accident happened?"

"I don't remember much, but apparently, I was in the way of a runaway beam."

"Burl said the crane's cable broke and the beam hit you. It could have been—"

"But it didn't," Matt said. "And no one else was hurt that I know of."

Millicent nodded and smiled at him. "Answered prayer. But your shoulder looked odd on the way to the hospital, too."

"I'm sure it did. Besides the gash, I was told my shoulder dislocated when I fell."

"Well, Stephen and I will be around to help you get up and down the stairs until you find your balance," Joe said. "I imagine having that shoulder set hurt more than sewing up the arm."

"I wouldn't know." Matt chuckled. "The doctor told me I passed out when they reset it and he went right to work on the arm while I was out."

"Good thinking."

Matt glanced around the table and saw that the women looked a little pale. "I think we should change the subject. This isn't turning out to be good dinner conversation material. I'm going to be fine and I thank you all for your concern and care. But let's talk about something a little more entertaining."

"How about what you're going to do while you're convalescing?"

"I have a feeling I'm going to be a real pest to the women of Heaton House, being underfoot most of the day."

"No, you won't. You might not be able to work, but with Christmas coming we'll find things for you to do," Millicent said. "I have several family photo shoots lined up later in the week. You can carry my camera bag with your good hand."

"Won't that make him more off balance?" Joe asked.

"Not if I'm holding on to the arm in the sling to keep him steady," Millicent replied.

"Sounds like an idea to me," Matt said. He certainly wasn't going to turn down a chance to spend time with Millicent. Not now. Not ever.

Chapter Twenty

The next morning, when Millicent came down to breakfast, she wondered what she'd been thinking. Exactly how did inviting Matt to go with her to her photo shoots fit into her distancing herself from him? She'd tossed and turned all night waking from a nightmare of Matt getting hurt even worse than he had, and then drifting back off to dream sweet, sweet dreams about him...then suddenly the nightmare again.

It was a relief when she saw slivers of sunlight coming in through her window so that she could get up and put them both behind her.

Matt was in the dining room when she got there and his smile shot straight to her heart. *Thank you, Lord, for keeping him from being hurt worse.* She smiled back. "Good morning. You made it up!"

"I did. Joe came up behind me in case I lost balance and fell backward, but the handrail saw me through."

"He did fine," Joe added. "A little wobbly at first but he got the hang of it before we reached the top."

"Want me to get you anything else?" Millicent asked as she filled her plate.

"I'm good, thanks."

"How'd you sleep?"

"Like a log after I took that pill the doc sent with me. Don't think I'll take one again, though. I had weird dreams all night."

Millicent laughed. "I did, too, so don't be too quick to blame your medicine. Are you in pain now?"

"A little. But nothing I can't handle."

He wouldn't admit it if he couldn't. She knew that. "That's good. But we're here to help if you need something."

"I think you're in good hands, Matt," Joe said. "I'll be off to work. Try not to get too rambunctious."

"Oh, we'll make sure he doesn't," Millicent said.

"I've got to be going, too," Emily said. "Hope you feel better soon, Matt."

There was a sudden flurry of activity while the boarders who had to go to work said their goodbyes and hurried out. Then Maida came in to freshen everyone's coffee or tea.

"I believe I'll start addressing my Christmas cards today," Mrs. Heaton said. "Millicent, Georgia, would you like to join me this afternoon? I have so many, I need to get an early start."

"I'd love to join you," Millicent said. "I need to go pick up some cards first, though. I don't have many to address, mostly family and friends back home and here. A box or two should be plenty."

"I don't think I'll need any more than that, either," Georgia said. "But I'd love to join you. We could go pick up some cards after breakfast."

"I've never sent out Christmas cards," Matt said. "But I'll join you all and help if I can. My right hand works and I could help address some for you, Mrs. Heaton."

"Why, Matt, that's very nice of you. I'll take you up on your offer, if you're sure you don't mind. I know so many people now—it's a bit of a task to get them all done. Your help will be greatly appreciated."

"I need something to do. I'm not used to twiddling my thumbs."

"It's settled, then," Millicent said. "Georgia and I can go pick up our cards—do you need us to get anything for you, Mrs. Heaton?"

"Perhaps a couple of boxes more, just in case."

"We'll be glad to. Matt, do you want to come along with us, or—"

"I thought you'd never ask. I would like to come. And why don't you telephone about the other two buildings you wanted to look at. Perhaps we could check them out? Then you could get my and Georgia's opinions on them."

"Are you sure you're up to that?"

"I think so. I can manage stairs as long as there's a handrail and you two will be there with me."

"All right. I'll go make those calls now." Millicent began to slide out her chair, hoping to keep Matt from jostling his bad arm in any way, but he was faster than her and pulled hers out easily with his right hand.

"I'll let you know what I find out."

"I'm not going anywhere," Matt said as he sat back down.

Millicent hurried to the phone alcove and had the operator ring through to the first number. It only took a few minutes to get appointments to see both of the other buildings that morning. She hurried back to the dining room with the news.

"We'd better get ready, then," Georgia said. "Meet you back down here." She pushed back her own chair and rushed out of the room.

"We won't be long." Millicent smiled at Matt and Mrs. Heaton. She was glad they'd be doing something Matt could help with that wouldn't put a strain on his bad arm. Keeping busy would help pass the day for him. And she was happy he wanted to come along and look at the buildings with her.

When she came back down a few minutes later, it was to find Matt in the foyer struggling to get on his coat. With his arm in that sling, he was trying to get that side over his shoulder.

Millicent quickly went to help. "Here, let me do that." She pulled the coat over his shoulder and arm, and began to button it up for him, looking up at his face as she reached the one at the top.

He smiled down at her. "I feel sort of like a half mummy or something similar. At least one arm is free."

"And it's your right arm. That should help a bit."

"It does. Thank you for inviting me to tag along with you and Georgia. I didn't know what I was going to do today."

"I'm glad you suggested looking at those two buildings. Although I must say, I really am hoping the broker for the first one gets back in touch before long. I really want to see it."

"I know you do. But it never hurts to see everything that's available. Then you'll know better if it's what you want when you get to see it."

"True."

Georgia came back down just then and they headed outside. It was quite cool, but the sun was shining and there was no wind. They took off down the walk with Millicent on one side of Matt and Georgia on the other.

Millicent slipped her hand through Matt's arm and he looked down at her. "Going to keep me upright if I bobble?"

"I'm going to try." Millicent smiled back. It promised to be a great day.

Matt was very aware of Millicent by his side. Something about this woman had turned his world upside down and he needed to find a way to get it right side up again. He knew what he wanted. Knew he was falling in love with her more each day and he believed she cared about him, too, but what if she didn't?

Anguish seared his heart at the very thought. It was possible that Millicent didn't feel about him the same way he felt about her. He knew that. But should it stop him from pursuing her, from convincing her that he loved her as she was?

Yes, she was independent—more so than any other woman he'd known. But not so much so that she didn't look to someone else when she needed advice. She seemed to count on his opinion in looking for a building. And as for the business she wanted to build— she'd said point-blank that her family would come first if she did ever marry.

From what she'd said, Matt thought that Baxter

person had made her believe that no man would accept her as she was and he now knew, without a doubt, that the man was wrong. Millicent was a woman worth pursuing. She'd been there for him more than once, and to win her love, well, that was worth taking a chance on—even if he came away with a broken heart, he'd trust the Lord to get him through it. He had to try. But where did he start?

Millicent suddenly came to a stop and Matt looked up to see that they'd arrived at the first building they would look at. The owner was there and opened the door so that they could come inside. But it didn't take long to realize a lot of work would be needed to turn it into a shop and home for Millicent. Not to mention money. It'd only been used as an office building and not taken care of. No wonder it was empty now.

They thanked the gentleman and made their way to the next. Matt couldn't bring himself to be disappointed about it and Millicent didn't seem upset that the building wouldn't work, either. She and Georgia chattered about all the reasons it would not be a good choice until they reached the next structure. But it was in worse condition than the first one and they didn't even go upstairs. Millicent quickly told the owner it wasn't what she was looking for.

They stopped for a bite to eat at Macy's lunch counter before shopping for Christmas cards, and as they waited for their meals, Matt turned to Millicent. "I don't think you're upset about either of these buildings being wrong—you've got your heart set on the first one we saw on Thanksgiving, don't you?"

"I have to admit I want to see it. It sounds perfect. On the other hand, I'm not sure I'm ready to…" she stopped and shook her head. "Being on my own in the city, living at Heaton House and having all the boarders around is one thing. But living by myself—as independent as I like to think I am—I'm not sure I'm ready for it yet. And I do doubt the owner would only let me rent or lease the first floor. But I don't think I can afford to buy a building and live at Heaton House, too."

It appeared Millicent had done more thinking about her future then he'd thought. "You could ask when we do get to look. Or if the owner won't do that, then maybe just start looking for a space to rent for a shop. That would be one way to know for sure what you want to do."

"I don't know why I'm so unsettled about it! I've dreamed of this most of my life. But now—" Millicent broke off and sighed deeply. "I just don't know."

"Dreams can change," Georgia offered. "And the Lord has plans for us that we don't always see when we're planning out our lives. I'm beginning to think I'm not meant to get a position as a teacher. If I don't find something soon, I'm going to have to find something else."

"Hey, don't feel bad, ladies. We all have to rethink things at times. And I believe Georgia has something there about letting the Lord guide us."

He'd certainly been guilty of going out ahead of the Lord—not asking for guidance—but lately he seemed to be turning to Him more and more. And now Matt believed that the Lord had shown him what he should do. And it was time he began to act on it.

They arrived back at Heaton House in time to freshen up and come back to the dining room just as

Mrs. Heaton was setting out her cards and list. She'd also set pens out for them.

Millicent handed her landlady the boxes of cards she'd picked out. "I hope these will work, Mrs. Heaton."

"Oh, they're lovely, Millicent. I do love Louis Prang's cards."

Millicent had chosen card scenes of people gathering around the hearth or decorating their Christmas scenes for herself, but for Mrs. Heaton, she'd picked ones with beautiful children on the front. Matt had decided to send a few cards himself and bought a box of a people sledding in Central Park, and Georgia had selected country scenes.

They began at the same time, but before teatime, they were all helping Mrs. Heaton. They addressed her cards while she wrote personal notes in each one.

When Gretchen came in with iced cakes and tea for the ladies, coffee for Matt, they all sat back in their chairs with a big sigh, ready for a break.

"I can't thank you all enough. It usually takes me several days to get that done and now it's all finished!" She fairly beamed with happiness. "Tomorrow I can turn my attention to decorating the house. I'll start putting up greenery this week."

"When do you put up your tree, Mrs. Heaton?" Georgia asked.

"On Christmas Eve. Michael and Rebecca and their families will be here for dinner that night. I'm sure they'll want to get home to decorate their own, too. But they've insisted they want to be here that night and I'm certainly not going to try to talk them out of it. Actually, the Pattersons and Talbots have asked if they might drop by on Christmas Eve, too, so I invited them to dinner that night. It will be great to have everyone together again. I know it won't be possible every Christmas, but I'll enjoy it when it is."

Millicent knew the others wanted to be there to see her open the gift they'd all worked on together and she was glad Mrs. Heaton was excited about having everyone over.

She looked forward to this Christmas more than she had any in a long time. She'd miss her family, but Heaton House had become home to her, and she thought of the boarders, present and past, as family, too. And Matt would be here. This would be the first Christmas they'd shared and for some reason the thought of spending it with him made her feel all fluttery inside.

She took a sip of tea and glanced at Matt. He smiled at her and then winked, and Millicent nearly choked on the warm liquid she'd just swallowed. He immediately began patting her on the back, but tears were streaming down her eyes before she got things under control.

"I'm sorry, Millicent. I didn't know I had that kind of effect on you," Matt whispered as Mrs. Heaton brought a glass of water for her. He grinned as she took a sip, sending her pulse into overdrive. Oh, that man!

Chapter Twenty-One

When Millicent came downstairs the next morning, she was still thinking about Matt's wink, which led to thoughts of the kiss they'd shared weeks ago—although it seemed like yesterday.

Matt had been quite observant the night before and she'd caught him looking at her each time she glanced his way, which was much too often.

Millicent entered the dining room and in spite of her determination to quit thinking about the wink and the kiss, her glance strayed straight toward Matt.

"Good morning," he greeted her.

"Morning." She filled her plate with fluffy scrambled eggs, crisp bacon and toast before joining him at the table.

"You ready for that photo shoot?" he asked.

He'd remembered. And no matter why she'd offered, or how crazy she might have been to do so, she wasn't going to take back the invitation—no matter what effect being around him all day had on her. If her pulse weren't racing, her heart was hammering, and all because he'd become very attentive—almost…

flirty lately, and she didn't know how to react to him. "Are you certain you feel like going with me, Matt? I have another in a few days. You can go then if you aren't up to it."

"I'll have some pain no matter where I am and won't think about it as much if I'm out and about."

"But your shoulder—"

"I don't have any pain in my shoulder now, and while I'll need to be careful with my arm for a while, not to hit it and to keep it in the sling until the doctor says I can take it off, the pain is manageable. Are you trying to say you don't want me to come along?"

"No! Of course not. I just don't want you to feel you have to go, if you don't want to."

"Millie, you should realize by now that I don't do many things I don't want to."

His gaze was so direct, so sincere, it gave her heart a jolt.

"You're right. We'll need to leave by nine-thirty."

Matt looked at the clock on the mantel. "I'll be ready when you are. Your clients won't mind my being with you, will they?"

"I don't see why they would. I'm sure it'll be fine."

And it was. The Williamses, friends of the Evanses who'd recommended her to them, were quite welcoming to them both. They asked Matt about his arm and he told them about his accident as he tried to help Millicent set up her tripod and camera, and then stood out of the way while she conversed with the couple and found out what it was they wanted.

"We just want photographs like you took of our

friends—we loved the ones of them all smiling. It was so heartwarming and that's the feeling we want our photographs to depict."

"I'm so glad you liked them. I feel many of our formal photographs are much too serious."

The couple wanted one in front of their fireplace and she took several shots of them there, making them laugh together so that she could catch them in a happy pose. But she didn't stop there. She took several more photos of them on the settee, asking them to sit like they normally did.

By the time she'd finished and began packing up her camera, Matt could see why she was becoming much in demand. She worked hard at what she did and he had no doubt the final photographs would be keepsakes handed down for many generations. Millicent had a one-of-a-kind talent that would eventually be emulated by others for years to come.

When he said as much to her on the way home, she looked surprised.

"What? You don't think I know how talented you are? Or that I appreciate it?"

She shrugged. "I just thought you disapproved and—"

"I'm not sure disapproval is what I felt at first, but I can assure you, it's admiration I have for you and your talent, Millie. You're going to be famous one day."

He could tell she was at a loss for words and it was probably a good thing the trolley came to a stop, for the disbelief in her expression had him wanting to pull her into his arms and convince her he meant what he said.

* * *

The next week was one of the best Millicent could remember. Mrs. Heaton had all kinds of greenery delivered on Monday, and she and Millicent and Georgia stayed busy over the next few days, draping it over mantels, the staircases and doorways. The house smelled of the outside and Christmas.

That, added to the aromas coming from the kitchen, made Millicent's mouth water. Gretchen and Maida were making all kinds of Christmas treats—cookies, cakes and candies—to have at Heaton House and give to friends and neighbors.

Millicent and Georgia wrapped their presents, and Matt's, to send home and he accompanied them to the post office. They stopped for hot chocolate at the café near the building Millicent was still waiting to hear about.

When they came out, they paused in front of it to peek in the window again, and Millicent liked it as much as she had the first time she and Matt had looked at it.

When they arrived home, it was to find that the broker for the building she wanted to see had telephoned. She excitedly returned his call and in minutes she and Matt and Georgia were on their way back out to see it.

"I'm sure it's going to be too expensive. I probably shouldn't even be looking at it."

"Even if you decide against it, you'll know if you like the floor plan and the style. It might not even be to your taste," Matt said, moving his arm a bit so that Millicent had no choice but to walk closer to him. "And if it needs a little work, I'll be glad to help."

Her heart seemed to melt at his words as she suddenly realized Matt was letting her know he would be there for her whether he liked the idea of her having her own business or not. "I... Thank you, Matt."

The broker, Richard Green, was there to greet them, apologizing for being out of town when she called.

"But that might be for the best," he said. "The other person interested in the property, who was trying to get his financing together, had to pull his offer and right now, there are none on this building. I know the owner wants it sold as quickly as possible."

Millicent's excitement at his words was tempered with the knowledge that she wasn't sure she was ready to make a quick decision. He led them inside and she knew immediately that she loved the building. The bottom floor was just right for a photography shop, with several other rooms leading off the hallway, one much larger than the others. It would work well as a studio.

"You could rent out one of these rooms for someone's office, Millicent," Georgia said.

"It does look as if there were offices in here at one time."

"Oh, there were," Mr. Green said. He opened the door to a smaller room. "This was used as a supply closet, but could easily be turned into a darkroom for your developing, I would think."

Millicent looked at Matt for his opinion.

"He's right. It'd be no problem at all. Let's see what's upstairs."

"A beautiful living area is on the next two floors," Mr. Green said. "I think you'll love it."

There was a frosted glass door at the top of the stairs and Mr. Green opened it to a nice-size foyer that led to a parlor on one side, a dining room on the other, with the kitchen at the back. It needed a bit of work, but was quite usable as it was.

Then he led them to a room across from the kitchen that had been used as an office, but could be a second parlor or study. They went back into the hall and up the staircase to the third floor that opened up to three bedrooms and a nicely fitted bathroom. It was everything Millicent had dreamed it might be and more. Or at least it seemed to be.

They were shown the attic and Matt poked around while Millicent looked out the window onto the street below. Unless Matt found something horribly wrong, it was perfect to her.

This was truly a home and shop all together. And what work was needed wouldn't be that hard to do. But because it seemed to be in such great shape, she was almost certain she wouldn't be able to afford it.

The broker asked if they wanted to see the basement and Matt immediately said yes. Millicent knew that meant he was checking out everything as well as he could in this short visit. She looked around, but then she and Georgia went back up to look at the living quarters once more, telling Matt to let her know when he was through.

Matt couldn't find much of anything wrong with the building—nothing he couldn't take care of anyway, and he knew Millicent loved it. It would be perfect for her.

Although he was feeling steadier as the day went

on, Matt appreciated that Mr. Green followed him back up the stairs, where they met up with Millicent and Georgia.

"Well, what do you think? Would it fit your needs, Miss Faircloud?" Mr. Green asked.

"Yes, it would. Can you tell me what the owner wants for it?"

Mr. Green named a number that raised Millicent's eyebrows and told Matt that it was out of her price range. His heart fell with disappointment for her as she shook her head.

"I'm afraid that's more than I can afford. The owner would have to come down several thousand dollars."

"He might. He wants to sell it. He's out of state until after Christmas, so you have some time. I'll get in touch with you once he gets back."

"But what if someone else—"

"I'll contact you right away and give you first dibs."

"That's all I can ask. Thank you for your time."

"Yes, thank you, Mr. Green. It's a nice property."

"It's been my pleasure. If you have any other questions, feel free to contact me," Mr. Green said.

"We will." Matt held out his hand and shook the other man's hand. Green seemed sympathetic to Millicent. Maybe he could get that price down for her.

Millicent sighed as they started back to Heaton House. "I knew I shouldn't look at it. It was perfect, wasn't it?"

"It was very nice." Matt patted Millicent's hand that rested on his forearm. "Don't give up. Maybe the owner will come down on his price or rent out the bottom for you."

"I'm not going to count on it. Perhaps now isn't the time. If I'm meant to open my shop, the Lord will show me the right place at the right time."

"That's a good way to look at it," Georgia said.

"Well, I'd miss everyone if I did move out. I'm not sure I'd be happy by myself. It's a big place for just one person."

Matt couldn't argue with her there. "That it is."

That evening Mrs. Heaton's family joined them for dinner, and afterward, the whole group went to see Macy's windows. Emily was even able to go along with them as she was now only in charge of the subtle changes they'd make each day to keep the windows looking fresh up until Christmas.

There was quite a crowd gathered and once they drew nearer one could see why. The displays were quite spectacular.

"Oh, my," Georgia said when they got close enough to look in one of the windows. "I've never seen anything like this. It's beautiful!"

"It's better even than last year, Emily," Millicent said. "I'm sure your touch helped very much."

"Oh, I can't say that. But I think all the displays are wonderful. I did have some input on this one." Emily pointed to the next window along Fourteenth Street.

Once Jenny saw it, she ran forward and plastered her face to the window. "Oh, Granma, look! Isn't it wonderful?"

"It truly is, Jenny, dear," Mrs. Heaton said from behind her grandchild, her eyes sparkling as much as Jenny's.

Millicent felt like a child again looking at the collection of dolls set in all kinds of different Christmas venues. One showed a family gathered around a small Christmas tree to decorate it. And another had a family sitting at a table set with tiny dishes, their heads bowed as if they were praying. She loved it.

There were so many different scenes that when it was time to leave they still hadn't seen all the windows. Millicent's hand was resting on the forearm of Matt's good arm and he leaned over to say, "I've never really done this—come to see Macy's windows during the Christmas season. I won't miss it again."

"Nor will I." Millicent smiled up at him.

"We'll come again," Rebecca promised her daughter as they turned to go. "It will give you something to look forward to until Christmas Day gets here."

"Want to come with me again before Christmas?" Matt whispered to Millicent.

"I'd love to." She could think of nothing she'd rather do than spend time with Matt. Did his invitation mean that he had the same kind of feelings for her that she had for him, or was he just trying to fill the hours of the day? And even if he did feel the way she did—could she endure the worry of something happening to him every time he went to work? If not—could she bear not having him in her life? *Please, dear Lord, help me to know.*

Chapter Twenty-Two

Everyone was very happy to have perfect weather for the progressive dinner the next evening. The houses really weren't all that far apart, and the air more crisp than cold, so they could walk to each one.

Everything would start and end at Heaton House, since Maida and Gretchen would be watching Mrs. Heaton's grandchildren while they were gone.

After they admired Mrs. Heaton's decorations, they headed to Violet and Michael's, where she served canapés to get them started. At Rebecca and Ben's they enjoyed seeing the decorations they'd put up, many of them handmade with Jenny. Then Rebecca served clear soup with breadsticks to warm them up for the next walk.

At Kathleen's they were served baked fish with coleslaw. Her dining table had a beautiful centerpiece spanning the length of it made with fresh greenery and red candles.

The next stop was Elizabeth and John's, which was a little longer walk than the last ones and turned out to be a good thing.

"I think I'm going to be quite full by the time this evening is over, but it's quite fun, isn't it?" Matt asked.

"It is. I hope everyone wants to do it again next year." Would she and Matt be walking together then? What did the next year hold for them?

Millicent shook off her thoughts as they arrived at the Talbots', where greenery was draped and tied with red ribbon on the staircase and over the windows. Elizabeth served filet of beef and duchess potatoes, and by the time they all headed back to Heaton House, Millicent seriously wondered if she'd be able to hold another bite.

When she said as much to Matt as they walked behind the others, he pulled her a little closer and whispered, "Me, either. I don't know when I've eaten so much food for one meal—or four meals in one night. But it's all been delicious and a lot of fun. Now I'm wondering what Mrs. Heaton has for dessert."

Millicent chuckled. "I'm hoping it's something light."

Mrs. Heaton must have realized how full they'd be when they arrived back home, so she'd decided on a frozen pudding and bonbons served afterward.

It'd been a fun evening, getting to see how the married couples had decorated their homes and the laughter and conversation they'd all shared. Everyone declared the progressive dinner a success and decided to do it again the following year.

As Millicent joined the others in seeing the married couples off, she wondered if she would be here or in her own place by then. Her glance strayed to Matt. He turned to her and smiled—he would have to catch her staring at him!

The other women headed upstairs and Millicent turned to join them, but Matt stopped her by putting a hand on her arm.

"You need help getting down, Matt?" Joe asked with a smile on his face.

"No, thank you. I can make it fine."

"I'm sure you can." Joe chuckled as he headed down. "By the way, I saw what you snagged at John's."

"Yep, so did I," Stephen said. He and Joe laughed together as they made their way to the ground floor.

"What did you snag, Matt? And what do you want to speak to me about?"

Matt smiled at her and Millicent's heart did a flip as he lowered his head. "I—"

"Millicent, where are you? Are you still downstairs?" Julia's voice from upstairs jerked them apart, although Matt's arm remained around her. "Would you see if I left my purse in the parlor?"

Millicent heard the deep sigh Matt released as her gaze locked with his. "I'm still down here. I'll see if I can find it."

"Good night, Millie." Matt's voice was husky and thick and she was certain she'd never forget the sound of it. "We need to talk soon. See you in the morning."

With that he turned to go downstairs and Millicent hurried to the parlor, her fingers covering her lips. Had he been about to kiss her? And what did they need to talk about?

It'd turned colder over the weekend, but with no wind, it wasn't too bad. They'd walked to church on Sunday, and the sermon, along with the quiet peacefulness of the walk home, did much to make Millicent realize the Lord was in control and would give her guidance when He thought the time was right, and she did pray it was soon.

On Monday morning, Millicent was surprised when Matt announced he had an errand to run and refused her offer to go with him.

"It's cold out and, well, I want to stop by work and see my crew. Wish them a Merry Christmas and all. I'm not sure how long I'll be gone."

"That's understandable." Still, she was a bit disappointed. Not that she really wanted to go to Park Row, but she was getting very used to spending most of her days with Matt and she knew she'd miss him when he went back to work. The very thought of him working back up so high made her queasy and sent shivers down her spine. She didn't want him on that building any longer, but it was his livelihood and she had no right to ask him to quit it—no matter how much she worried about him.

She wouldn't want him asking her to give up her dream, even if she still wasn't sure she was ready to leave Heaton House and live by herself.

After he left, Millicent went upstairs and put the finishing touches to Mrs. Heaton's albums. They truly were a work of love from all the boarders, past and present. She wrapped them both in tissue and then placed them in a box Emily had brought from work. She added the card everyone had signed and wrapped the package with care, tying a big red bow around it.

Then she went to work on the gifts for the boarders and the couples. She'd kept back photos she'd taken of them and bought frames for each. She'd caught the couples in sweet poses with each other and the boarders together at differing times. They'd each have a photograph of everyone, but the setting would be different in each one.

And she had an extra photo to give to Matt. It was a copy of the photograph he'd asked for of the two of them and she hoped he really did want it. She'd framed a copy for herself, too, and even though she didn't have it out all the time, she pulled it out of the drawer of her writing desk each night, asking the Lord for guidance where her feelings for him were concerned.

Only now, because he hadn't wanted her to go with him, she couldn't help but wonder if Matt was trying to avoid her for the same reason she felt the need to distance herself from him—even though she didn't want to. She was falling in love with that man and there didn't seem to be anything she could do to stop her feelings from growing—no matter how wrong he was for her.

Millicent finished wrapping her gifts and looked at the clock. It was nearing lunchtime and she needed some company. Her thoughts weren't helping her mood at all.

But once she got downstairs and entered the parlor, inhaled the scent of Christmas greenery, she felt better. Christmas was only days away and she felt almost like a child again, looking forward to Christmas Eve when they'd decorate the tree and give Mrs. Heaton her gift.

Georgia came down just then and Mrs. Heaton came out of her study to join them in the parlor. "I do believe it's lunchtime and I'm glad you both will be joining me today. I'll just let Gretchen know we're ready."

Millicent had hoped Matt would be back in time for lunch, but apparently he'd decided to eat with his crew or out somewhere. She told herself that it was for the best, but her heart told her something entirely different.

Matt went to the doctor to have his stitches checked out and was told he was healing well and could do without the sling, but he couldn't go back to work until after the first of the year. Still, it was good news over all. Best of all—the next time he tried to hold Millicent in his arms, he'd be able to use both of them. That thought had him grinning as he headed out of the hospital.

He made it to the top of the Park Row Building just around lunchtime, when he knew his men would be taking a break. They all greeted him as if he'd been gone much longer than a few weeks, and it made him feel good. But he mainly wanted to talk to Burl and he wasn't sure how he'd take what he had to say.

"Hey, boss, you going to eat with us?" Burl asked.

Matt lifted the paper bag of lunch he'd asked Gretchen to make for him. "I thought I might. Looks like you're making great progress here."

"We've been trying. We don't want to get behind while you're gone," Henry said.

"You've trained us well," Burl said.

All the men settled down to lunch asking Matt how he was doing and told him they'd be glad when he got back. Then conversation went on as it always had, about how the job was going, the weather and their families. When the bell rang signaling lunch break was over, they shook Matt's hand and went back to work.

But Burl walked him back to the elevator.

"You've done a great job in my absence, Burl. Think you could keep it up if I don't come back?"

"You mean for a while longer, right? Of course I can."

"I'm not sure how long or even if I'll be back, Burl. This is just between us, but I'm thinking of starting my own company."

"You going to build these skyscrapers on your own?"

Matt laughed and shook his head. "No, I'm thinking homes, smaller buildings. Something a little safer."

"I can sure understand that, especially after all the accidents we've had this year. My wife is after me to find other work every day. Miss Faircloud wouldn't have anything to do with you making a change, would she? She was awfully upset when she saw you on that stretcher."

"She might," Matt admitted, his heart expanding with hope at Burl's words. "If she'll have me. And if I decide for sure to start up my own, I'll need workmen."

"Well, you just keep me posted. Until I hear different, I'll expect you back here after the first of the year."

"I should definitely know by then. I haven't said anything to the supervisor yet."

"I won't, either."

"Thank you, Burl. I'll let you know what I decide."

The two men shook hands and Matt stepped onto the elevator, sending it back to the ground.

He felt better just saying what it was he wanted to do—at least the work part of it. Everything else depended on Millicent. But he'd handed it all over to the Lord and knew he couldn't do wrong as long as he left things in His hands. He felt as if a load had been lifted off his shoulders and that he was on the right path as he took off toward the Ladies' Mile.

Chapter Twenty-Three

Heaton House was a flurry of activity that week and by dinnertime, two days before Christmas, Matt was beginning to believe he was going to have to solicit help in getting Millicent to himself for even a minute.

A few weeks earlier, he might have believed it was for the best, but that was when he was still trying to distance himself from her. It was the last thing he wanted to do now. He was almost certain she felt the same way about him—but what if he were wrong? His Christmas could be ruined—and so could hers.

Oh please, dear Lord, help me to know what to do to find out how Millicent feels about me soon. And please let her love me as much as I love her. I can't imagine…going ahead with the plans I think You've given me without her.

"What do you think, Matt?" Millicent asked from beside him, bringing him out of his prayer.

"I'm sorry. I didn't—"

"I was suggesting we go caroling in Gramercy Park for a while this evening," Julia said. "Want to go?"

Matt groaned inwardly. Another evening spent with the group. "I—"

"I think it'll be fun, don't you?" Millicent asked.

As long as she was with him, it would be. "Of course. I'm in."

Millicent smiled at him and he wasn't sure he could wait much longer to pull her into his arms and declare his love for her. But he wasn't about to do it in front of everyone. He had no choice but to wait.

"I can't remember when I went caroling last," Mrs. Heaton said. "But I believe I'll join you all. I'm sure the Crawfords would be happy for us to stop by."

Everyone seemed quite excited about the outing and Matt told himself he couldn't put a damper on the evening. At least Millicent would be there and he'd get to listen to her sweet alto.

But he must not have been as good about hiding his feelings as he thought, for when dinner was over and everyone began to disperse to get ready, Mrs. Heaton stopped him, a worried look in her eyes.

"Matt, may I speak to you in my study?"

"Why, yes, of course." He followed his landlady to the cozy room one could nearly always find her in.

She sat down in one of the two chairs flanking the fireplace and motioned for him to take the other one.

"What can I do for you, Mrs. Heaton?"

"I was thinking of asking you the same thing, Mathew. You seem a little…discombobulated lately."

Matt chuckled. "You could say that. I'm sorry. I haven't meant to be so obvious."

"Oh, I don't think everyone has picked up on it. But it's not like you and I wondered if I could help you in any way."

"Oh, Mrs. Heaton, thank you. I believe you are just the one who might be able to."

"Well, now, tell me what I can do?"

He proceeded to do just that and by the time Matt left her study, he was in a much better mood. He should have known Mrs. Heaton would have an answer to his dilemma—or at least try to come up with an idea for him. Now he'd be able to enjoy the evening. He'd have the time he longed for with Millicent soon.

Matt joined the others in the parlor and met Millicent's gaze across the room. She gave him a hesitant smile and he wondered if she'd sensed his mood as Mrs. Heaton had. He couldn't let her think he was anything but looking forward to their night out.

It appeared everyone was ready to go and he helped Millicent on with her coat, glad he could finally use both arms to do so—although he did miss looking into her face when she assisted him with buttoning his up.

As they headed outside, Matt made sure he was the one walking beside her as they started out.

"Are you feeling all right? Is your arm bothering you?" Millicent asked.

"I'm fine and so is my arm." He took hold of her elbow to prove it.

"You didn't seem too excited about going out tonight."

"I wasn't too eager about going with the group again," he whispered into her ear, figuring he might as well be honest.

"Oh. We have been doing a lot of that lately, haven't we?"

"A little too much, to my way of thinking." They

passed a streetlight and he saw the glimpse of a smile, sending hope soaring through him.

Their first stop was to their neighbors, the Crawfords. Mrs. Heaton knocked on the door as they began their first carol. The couple came to the door, their family gathering behind them, and asked the carolers in when they finished, but Mrs. Heaton refused for them. "We have more houses to get to before we go home. We just wanted to wish you a Merry Christmas."

"Merry Christmas to you all, too," Mrs. Crawford said. "Thank you for coming by."

"You're welcome!" They chorused as the group headed to the next home singing.

It took longer than Matt had thought it would to make their way around Gramercy Park, but the neighbors all seemed to enjoy them, opening their doors to listen or just looking out their windows as they sang. And he enjoyed having Millicent next to him.

Snowflakes began to fall as they neared Heaton House and although it was light and probably wouldn't last very long, the soft flakes made it feel even more like Christmas. Once they arrived back at Heaton House, everyone was ready for cocoa, and Mrs. Heaton went to the kitchen and returned quickly to let them know Gretchen and Maida had been watching out for them, and the hot chocolate was on its way.

Matt settled down beside Millicent on one of the settees and told himself he could enjoy the rest of the evening. His time with Millicent was coming.

Millicent came downstairs on Christmas Eve morning, excited about giving Mrs. Heaton her present that night.

"Have you finished your shopping, Matt?" Joe asked as he helped himself at the sideboard. "I need to go out for a few things. Want to come with me?"

"Sure, I'll go. There's so much going on here, I think we might be in the way if we stay."

Millicent's heart sank. She'd hoped they might go out and about like they had on Thanksgiving Day. And last night he'd seemed upset that he hadn't had any time with her. But evidently, it didn't matter quite so much today.

"It will be busy around here, for sure," Mrs. Heaton said. "The tree I ordered will be delivered any-time now, and Maida and Gretchen will be bringing the decorations down before they get started on to-night's meal. We'll be serving lunch for those who stay here, but it will be light."

"Oh, don't worry about any of us for lunch, Mrs. Heaton. We can grab something out. I need to go to Siegel-Cooper," Julia said. "Want to make it an out-ing, Millicent and Georgia?"

"Yes, I would. I've got a few more things I want to pick up, too," Millicent said. Mrs. Heaton's mention of Maida and Gretchen reminded her she wanted to frame a photo she'd taken of each of them, too, and she needed to buy the frames.

"I'd love to go," Georgia said.

"And if you need us to run any errands for you, Mrs. Heaton, we'll be glad to," Millicent added.

"Thank you, dear. If I think of anything, I'll be sure to let you know before you leave."

"Sounds like a flurry of activity for everyone today," Matt said to her.

He smiled and it was hard to be upset with him because he'd accepted Joe's invitation.

"It does."

"Why don't we all meet up for lunch?" Matt asked. "We could meet at that little café Millicent and I told you all about."

Millicent's heart warmed to melting at his suggestion. "Oh, what a great idea, Matt."

"Yes, it is. And none of us will be in the way," Julia added.

They all knew Mrs. Heaton wouldn't ask for their help. Part of holding celebrations like this was her gift to them and she loved preparing for them.

"We'll meet you there around noon, then, if that's all right with you ladies," Joe said.

"We'll be there," Millicent said.

As he and Joe set out to do their shopping, Matt couldn't get Millicent off his mind. She'd looked so disappointed when he'd said he'd tag along with Joe that Matt wished he could kidnap her and spend the whole day with her as they had on Thanksgiving.

But he had much to do before that evening and he hoped she'd soon realize how very much he wanted to spend all his time with her.

Mrs. Heaton had told him of what she'd come up with after Millicent had gone upstairs the night before, and he prayed it all worked. He was sure Millicent loved him, he just wasn't sure she'd want to marry him. But he'd do all he could to allay her fears for him and put it all in the Lord's hands. If she rejected him, he'd decide what to do next, but he wasn't going let himself think about that possibility today.

He and Joe went to Macy's and the massive Siegel-Cooper, where there was no end to gift ideas. They went in together on several board games they thought the group would enjoy and picked up some candy for the maids who took such good care of them.

"So, how are things with you and Millicent going?" Joe asked as they were on their way to meet the women for lunch.

"What do you mean?"

"Matt, everyone at Heaton House has known for months that you two are sweet on each other. Even Julia, who's been there since you both moved in, said it was obvious from the beginning that you were attracted to each other. And since your accident—"

"Yes, well, I think that accident might make it even more difficult for me to convince her of how I feel."

"Then you do love her! I knew it!"

"Yes, I love her, but—"

"But what? She loves you, too. I've seen the way you two look at each other. Why do you think Stephen and I haven't competed for her affections with you?"

"I don't know. Why?" He had been worried about them at first, but come to think of it, they hadn't flirted with Millicent in a while now.

"We knew we didn't have a chance, that's why. No need wasting our time when she was only interested in you and it was obvious you felt the same way."

Matt burst into laughter. "You've made my day, Joe. We'll find out soon if you're right. I pray you are."

He filled Joe in on his plans on the way to the café,

and by the time they met up with the women, Matt was ready to find out if what everyone at Heaton House seemed to believe was right. He prayed it was.

Chapter Twenty-Four

Wanting to look her best, Millicent took longer than normal to dress for the Christmas Eve dinner. She chose a green-and-red-plaid gown made of satin—she'd worn it at home the year before, but no one here had seen it and she did love it. After she slipped it on, she finished by adding a red bow to her upswept hair.

She wasn't sure why she felt so nervous about how she looked tonight, but ever since Matt and Joe had joined them for lunch, and Matt sat down beside her, she'd felt all fluttery inside, as if she were anticipating something she couldn't put a name to.

She entered the parlor and her gaze searched out Matt to find him on his way over to her. He reached her side before she made it to the center of the room. "You look lovely tonight, Millie. Christmas colors look wonderful on you."

"Thank you. You look quite dapper yourself. In fact, everyone looks wonderful and ready for the festivities to begin, don't they?"

Mrs. Heaton's family was there, along with the

married couples. It was obvious they were all enjoying each other.

"They do. I believe we're just waiting to be called to dinner."

Matt turned out to be right as Gretchen came in just then and announced that dinner was ready.

After they were all seated, Michael stood and said the blessing. Then Gretchen and Maida brought them a cup of cream of celery soup. After that came roast beef and Franconia potatoes, with macaroni and cheese—a favorite of Jenny's and baby Marcus's, too. Finally, they ended with a dessert of chocolate cream.

Anticipation ran high as they finished their meal and went back to the parlor, where the tree was waiting to be decorated. Jenny's eyes sparkled like stars as she helped put her grandmother's beautiful glass ornaments on, along with cornucopias filled with candies.

Candles were added last, and Maida and Gretchen joined them as Michael lit the tree. Millicent was sure she'd never seen a more beautiful one.

Then it was time to give Mrs. Heaton her gift. Millicent excused herself to pull it out from the telephone alcove, where she'd hidden it earlier. She brought the present in and handed it to their landlady.

"Mrs. Heaton, this is for you, from all of us." The sweet woman's eyes were full of surprise as Millicent handed her the gift.

"Why, I don't know what to say!" Mrs. Heaton put a hand to her chest and looked around the room at everyone. "I— Thank you all!"

"Open it, Granma!" Jenny hurried to her side.

"You help me." Within only a few seconds she

was drawing the first album out of the wrapping and began turning the pages. "Oh, look, there's Michael and Violet before they were married!"

She kept turning pages, oohing and aahing over each one. Tears were in her eyes as she looked up. "Oh! How wonderful this is! I can see this took a while to make and I thank each and every one of you from the bottom of my heart!" She continued to turn the pages, lingering to read the comments.

"That's what we've been doing at our parties, Mama," Rebecca said. "It was Millicent's idea and she graciously let us all have a part in it."

"New albums can be added each year, Mrs. Heaton. We all wanted to do something to let you know how much you and your home mean to all of us." Millicent bent down and gave her a hug and then moved out of the way so everyone else could do the same.

"This means more to me than I have words for." She held the album close to her heart and there was no doubt how touched she was at their gift.

"I don't think there is anything any of us could have given her that she would love like these albums," Matt said from behind Millicent.

"I'm so happy she does."

That would be the only present opened that night; they'd give their gifts to the couples to take home and open the next day. And the boarders would open theirs the next morning.

Even as the married couples put on their wraps and took their leave, Millicent still felt that same anticipation she'd felt earlier. But the boarders seemed in no hurry to go to bed, looking at the lit Christmas tree and enjoying the crackle of the fire in the grate.

"I think it's time we put our gifts to each other under the tree," Julia said.

"Yes, let's do!" Georgia said.

"I brought mine down earlier," Millicent said as the ladies headed upstairs and the men all headed downstairs.

"I have several gifts in my study, but I'm a bit tired. Would you mind going to get them, Millicent dear?"

"Not at all. I'll put them under the tree for you, Mrs. Heaton." She hurried back to the study to find several wrapped boxes on Mrs. Heaton's desk. Millicent stacked them and then, making sure not to drop any, she went back to the parlor to set them under the tree. But the room was empty. Where was everyone?

She put the gifts under the tree as she'd said she would, then stood and turned to find Matt standing in the doorway. He had the sweetest smile on his face as he began to walk toward her, his gaze locked in on her. Millicent's heart began to thud stronger, louder, with each step he took. Soon Matt was standing in front of her.

"I thought everyone would be back down by now," she said, sounding a bit breathless even to her own ears. "Have you seen Mrs. Heaton?"

"Maybe they decided to retire for the night."

"But—" She stopped because Matt looked up over their heads and her gaze followed his, to find a big clump of mistletoe hanging on the chandelier above her. Then her gaze met his as she looked down. He smiled and pulled her close with one arm while he raised her face to his with his other hand.

"Millicent, I hope I never have to use mistletoe

as an excuse to kiss you again, but I cannot wait to find out—"

His lips claimed hers in a kiss she knew she'd never forget. It was firm...and soft...and lingered when she responded.

Then Matt pulled back, but still holding her, he looked deep into her eyes. "Remember I said we needed to talk?"

She nodded.

"It's time. I love you, Millie. Have loved you for even longer than I realized—I think from the day you moved in here. Is it possible you could ever...feel the same way?"

"Oh, Matt. I already do, but I—"

His fingertips gently touched her lips, serving to quiet her. "No buts please. Not until you hear me out. I know you don't want me to work on the Park Row and that you fear something might happen to me. And I'm willing to quit."

"Matt, I can't ask you—"

"You haven't asked me. But you have inspired me to think about starting my own business. I'd been thinking about doing so one day anyway. Do you love me, Millicent?"

"I do."

"Then I think that one day is here. I'm willing to do whatever it is I need to, to show you how much I love you. If you'll marry me, I'll start my own business and work on houses or buildings not so tall. I'll go with you to your suffrage meetings and support you opening your own shop. I love you for the woman you are, Millie. Will you have me? Will you be my wife?"

She couldn't believe all he was willing to give up for her, to accept her just as she was and not ask her to give up anything!

She wrapped both arms around his neck. "Oh, Matt, yes! I'll marry you. But you don't have to give up what you love to do. I can't ask you to do that. What I've realized I *can* do is trust the Lord to keep you safe, and trust Him to guide us in our life together."

She stood on tiptoe as Matt bent his head and they sealed their promise under the mistletoe.

Then Matt raised his head and grinned before yelling, "She said yes!"

Footsteps were heard coming from every direction of the house as Julia, Georgia and Emily came running downstairs, Joe and Stephen running up from downstairs, and Mrs. Heaton, Gretchen and Maida from the kitchen!

"What? You all knew he was going to—"

"Millie, I had to have some help in getting you alone for long enough to ask you."

Millicent began to laugh. "And the mistletoe?"

"He snatched that from Luke and Kathleen's the night of the progressive party," Joe said. "I put it up while you were in the study and then hurried out of here fast as I could."

Matt put his arm around her and looked at everyone over the top of her head. "Thank you all for your help. I should have come to you weeks ago."

"But the Lord had to show me the way," Millicent said. "The timing is perfect and I, too, thank you all!"

The clock struck midnight and they all shouted, "Merry Christmas!"

* * *

On Christmas morning, Millicent still couldn't quite believe Matt had proposed to her. She lay in bed and relived the night before, then flung off the covers. She couldn't wait to see him—to find out if it really had happened.

It was earlier than usual, but she hurried to dress and get downstairs, hoping to be able to see Matt before everyone else came down.

She entered the parlor to see him putting something under the tree and her heart expanded to near bursting with the love she felt for him.

He turned and smiled when he saw her standing there. "I was hoping you'd be down early."

"I was hoping you'd be up early."

They met in the middle of the room and he pulled her into his arms. "Last night *was* real, wasn't it? You accepted my proposal of marriage, didn't you?"

"I did."

His lips captured hers and she wondered how each kiss could be better than the last.

Then he pulled her over to one of the settees and took her hands in his. "You still want that building for your shop, don't you?"

"Well, I'm not sure I can afford it or that—Matt, where *will* we live after we're married?"

"Well, I think we should live there. I can have an office downstairs and we both loved the building. I… uh…" He pulled out the package he'd just put under the tree and handed it to her. "Please, open this now and let me know if I did the right thing."

Millicent carefully unwrapped what appeared to be

a scroll. She unrolled the papers and quickly skimmed the words. "Matt? What is this? I don't understand."

"Well, I knew you wanted the building but didn't think you could afford it. I want you, but was afraid you might turn me down. So I bought the building and put it in your name. It's my Christmas, engagement gift to you."

"But if we're to be married, it should be in your name."

Matt shook his head. "It doesn't matter to me whose name is on the deed. If you'd turned me down, I was going to sell it to you for what you could afford, or rent the bottom floor to you, if you didn't want to leave Heaton House. It is perfect for your shop."

Millicent could barely breathe. The enormity of what he'd done, of how much he loved her...

"Millicent, are you upset with me? Did I take too much—"

"Oh, Matt, how I love you!" She threw her arms around him and kissed him in a way that surely showed him how much. It was only the sound of footsteps on the stairs that pulled them apart just before everyone entered the parlor calling, "Merry Christmas!"

They gathered in the dining room for breakfast before opening gifts, and Mrs. Heaton asked Matt to say the prayer.

He bowed his head and began, "Dear Lord, we thank You for this day, and the food we're about to eat. We thank You for each other and our many blessings. Most of all, we thank You especially for Your Son and our Savior, whom You sent to this earth so that we might have the hope and promise of eternal life with You through Him. It's in His precious name we pray. Amen."

After a joyously happy breakfast, they all went back to the parlor to exchange gifts. The boarders seemed very pleased with their framed photos and Maida and Gretchen seemed especially happy with theirs.

After everyone else had opened their presents and gone up to put them away, Millicent pulled her gift to Matt from under the tree.

"My present to you pales in comparison to yours for me, but I hope you like it." She pulled out the small package and handed it to him.

Matt opened the gift and smiled when he saw the photograph of the two of them he'd asked for. "I love it, Millie. It shows that we've cared about each other, even when we were trying not to. And your gift to me pales in no way. You've agreed to become my wife—an answer to my prayers."

He took her into his arms again and just before his lips touched hers, Millicent sent up a silent prayer thanking the Lord for taking control and answering hers.

* * * * *

Dear Reader,

I knew Matt and Millicent would get together from the day I moved them into Heaton House in *A Place of Refuge*. And while their differences drew me to write more about them, I knew their attraction would eventually draw them together.

Even the other boarders seemed to believe there was something between the two throughout *A Home for Her Heart* and *A Daughter's Return*.

How could they resist once they began spending time together? But it was going to take more for them to ever see that they were meant for each other and that the Lord had plans of His own—even as they fought their growing feelings. It took getting to know each other to find they'd been working on assumptions, to find there might be a way to come together with the Lord's help. I loved watching Matt and Millicent find they loved each other too much to deny it and to finally ask the Lord to guide them and show them the way to each other.

Setting this story at Christmastime and getting to enjoy New York City in 1897 was such a joy! I loved doing more research and it was so much fun to find that Macy's Christmases and those window displays have always been wonderful! I loved getting the old and new boarders together to help make a gift for Mrs. Heaton, and their determination to make traditions of their own. I hope you enjoyed reading this story as much as I loved writing it, and look forward to the next Boardinghouse Betrothals story.

Thanks so much for reading *The Mistletoe Kiss* story.

Please let me know what you thought of it and feel free to connect with me at my website at: janetleebarton. com. I'd love it if you'd sign up for my newsletter there. You can also email me at janetbwrites@cox.net or write me in care of: Love Inspired Books, 233 Broadway, Suite 1001, New York, NY 10279.

Blessings,
Janet Lee Barton

COMING NEXT MONTH FROM
Love Inspired® Historical

Available December 1, 2015

A HOME FOR CHRISTMAS
Christmas in Eden Valley
by Linda Ford

Cowboy Wade Snyder is determined to find his orphaned niece and nephew a loving adoptive home. But soon temporary nanny Missy Porter and the children make him wonder if his wounded heart can find healing with this ready-made family.

THE HOLIDAY COURTSHIP
Texas Grooms
by Winnie Griggs

Bachelor Hank Chandler suddenly finds himself guardian to his sister's two orphaned children. He'll need all the help he can get from sweet schoolteacher Janell Whitman—but could falling in love turn these strangers into a family?

A CONVENIENT CHRISTMAS BRIDE
by Rhonda Gibson

When Josiah Miller rescues Anna Mae Leland from a blizzard, he never expects he'll soon be proposing a marriage of convenience for the sake of his children. But when she's stranded on his farm and later loses her teaching job, honor dictates that Josiah marry her.

HER LONGED-FOR FAMILY
Matchmaking Babies
by Jo Ann Brown

Lady Caroline Trelawney Dowling has always wanted a child of her own and her dreams come true when she becomes caregiver to two abandoned children. What will it take for Lady Caroline to convince her neighbor, Lord Jacob Warrick, that there's a place for him in her life, too?

LIHCNM1115

REQUEST YOUR FREE BOOKS!

2 FREE INSPIRATIONAL NOVELS
PLUS 2 *FREE* MYSTERY GIFTS

Love Inspired® HISTORICAL

YES! Please send me 2 FREE Love Inspired® Historical novels and my 2 FREE mystery gifts (gifts are worth about $10). After receiving them, if I don't wish to receive any more books, I can return the shipping statement marked "cancel." If I don't cancel, I will receive 4 brand-new novels every month and be billed just $4.99 per book in the U.S. or $5.49 per book in Canada. That's a saving of at least 17% off the cover price. It's quite a bargain! Shipping and handling is just 50¢ per book in the U.S. and 75¢ per book in Canada.* I understand that accepting the 2 free books and gifts places me under no obligation to buy anything. I can always return a shipment and cancel at any time. Even if I never buy another book, the two free books and gifts are mine to keep forever.

102/302 IDN GH6Z

Name	(PLEASE PRINT)

Address	Apt. #

City	State/Prov.	Zip/Postal Code

Signature (if under 18, a parent or guardian must sign)

Mail to the **Reader Service:**
IN U.S.A.: P.O. Box 1867, Buffalo, NY 14240-1867
IN CANADA: P.O. Box 609, Fort Erie, Ontario L2A 5X3

Want to try two free books from another series?
Call 1-800-873-8635 or visit www.ReaderService.com.

* Terms and prices subject to change without notice. Prices do not include applicable taxes. Sales tax applicable in N.Y. Canadian residents will be charged applicable taxes. Offer not valid in Quebec. This offer is limited to one order per household. Not valid for current subscribers to Love Inspired Historical books. All orders subject to credit approval. Credit or debit balances in a customer's account(s) may be offset by any other outstanding balance owed by or to the customer. Please allow 4 to 6 weeks for delivery. Offer available while quantities last.

Your Privacy—The Reader Service is committed to protecting your privacy. Our Privacy Policy is available online at www.ReaderService.com or upon request from the Reader Service.

We make a portion of our mailing list available to reputable third parties that offer products we believe may interest you. If you prefer that we not exchange your name with third parties, or if you wish to clarify or modify your communication preferences, please visit us at www.ReaderService.com/consumerschoice or write to us at Reader Service Preference Service, P.O. Box 9062, Buffalo, NY 14240-9062. Include your complete name and address.

*Could Hank Chandler's search for a wife lead to
holiday love with schoolteacher Janell Whitman?*

*Read on for a sneak preview of
THE HOLIDAY COURTSHIP,
the next book in Winnie Griggs's miniseries
TEXAS GROOMS*

"I wonder if you'd mind giving me your opinion on some potential candidates," Mr. Chandler asked.

"You want my opinion on who would make you a good wife?" Apparently he saw nothing odd about asking the woman he'd just proposed to to help him pick a wife.

He frowned. "Not a wife. A mother for the children. I need your opinion on how the lady under consideration and the children would get on."

"I see." The man really didn't have an ounce of romance in him.

He nodded. "You can save me from wasting time talking to someone who's obviously not right."

"Assuming you find the right woman, may I ask how you intend to approach her?"

"If you're wondering if I intend to go a'courtin'—" Hank's tone had a sarcastic bite to it "—the answer is no, at least not in the usual way. I don't want anyone thinking this will be more than a marriage of convenience."

"I understand why you wouldn't want to go through a conventional courtship. But don't you think you and your prospective bride should get to know each other before you propose?"

He drew himself up. "I consider myself a good judge of character. It won't take me long to figure out if she's a good candidate or not."

"I would recruit a third party to act as a go-between," Janell said. "It should be someone whose judgment you trust."

"And what would this go-between do exactly?"

"Go to the candidate on your behalf. He or she would let the lady know the situation and ascertain the lady's interest in such a match."

"So you agree that a businesslike approach is best, just that I should go about it from a distance."

"It could save a great deal of awkwardness and misunderstanding if you did so."

"In other words, you think I need a matchmaker."

"I suppose. But you *do* want to approach this in a very businesslike manner, don't you?"

Hank nodded. "I have to admit, it sounds like a good idea."

Happy that he'd seen the wisdom of her advice, she said, "Is there someone you could trust to take on this job?"

He rubbed his jaw thoughtfully for a moment. Finally he looked up. "How about you?"

Don't miss
THE HOLIDAY COURTSHIP
*by Winnie Griggs, available December 2015 wherever
Love Inspired® Historical books and ebooks are sold.*

*Amelia Klondike promises to help amnesiac
Finn Brannigan get his memory back. But can they
also give themselves a merry Christmas?*

*Read on for a sneak preview of
A RANGER FOR THE HOLIDAYS,
the next book in the Love Inspired continuity*
LONE STAR COWBOY LEAGUE

"Everything has changed, hasn't it?"

Finn heard the same catch in her tone that he felt in his own chest. He knew he was Finn Brannigan, but didn't know if that was good news. The sense that the life he'd forgotten wasn't a happy one still pressed against him.

"So it's just your name? That's all you remember?"

"And my age." *Tell her you're a Ranger*, the honorable side of him scolded the other part that foolishly refused to confess. It felt as though everything would slam back into place once tomorrow dawned, so would it be terrible to just keep this one night as the happy victory it was? She'd be perfectly entitled to refuse his friendship once all the facts came to light.

Amelia laid her hand on his arm and he felt that connection he had each time she touched him. As if she needed him, even though it was the other way around. "I can't imagine what you must be feeling right now."

The return of his memory was a double-edged sword. "There's a lot floating out there—fuzzy impressions I can't quite get a fix on, but…I can't tell you what it means to know my whole name." He hesitated for a moment before admitting, "For a while I was terrified it wouldn't come back. That I'd end up one of those freak stories you read about in supermarket tabloids."

She laughed. "I can't imagine that. You're far too normal."

Normal? Nothing about him felt normal. The scary part was the constant sense that his normal wasn't anywhere near as nice as right now was, sitting out under the stars near a roaring fire hearing…

Christmas carols. A group of high school students began to sing "Away in a Manger." Finn felt his stomach tighten.

He waited for his unnamed aversion to all things Christmas to wash over him. It came, but more softly. More like regret than flat-out hate. Finn closed his eyes and tried to hear it the way Amelia did, reverent and quiet instead of slow and mournful. Why couldn't he grasp the big dark thing lurking just out of his reach? What made him react to Christmas the way he did?

Don't miss
A RANGER FOR THE HOLIDAYS
by Allie Pleiter, available December 2015 wherever
Love Inspired® books and ebooks are sold.